IN THE LONG SHADOWS

BOOK I
The Long
Shadows Series

BEAR MEAWASIGE

Second
Story
Press

Drowned Palace
Long Bridge
Mists and Marshes
Deepwood
N
W
E
S
Great Turtle Island

Broken Waters
Sunset
Bridge
Elderglade
Ember Ruins
Broken Waters
Half-Dead
Harbor

Library and Archives Canada Cataloguing in Publication

Title: In the long shadows / Bear Meawasige.
Names: Meawasige, Bear, author.
Description: Series statement: The long shadows ; book 1
Identifiers: Canadiana (print) 20260157198 | Canadiana (ebook) 20260157201 | ISBN 9781772604733 (softcover) | ISBN 9781772604740 (EPUB)
Subjects: LCGFT: Novels.
Classification: LCC PS8626.E247 I5 2026 | DDC jC813/.6—dc23

Designed by Laura Atherton
Edited by Jordan Ryder

Printed and bound in Canada

Second Story Press gratefully acknowledges the support of the Ontario Arts Council and the Canada Council for the Arts for our publishing program. We acknowledge the financial support of the Government of Canada through the Canada Book Fund.

ONTARIO ARTS COUNCIL
CONSEIL DES ARTS DE L'ONTARIO
an Ontario government agency
un organisme du gouvernement de l'Ontario

Canada Council for the Arts | Conseil des arts du Canada

Funded by the Government of Canada
Financé par le gouvernement du Canada | Canada

Published by
Second Story Press
120 Carlton Street, Suite 412
Toronto, ON M5A 4K2
www.secondstorypress.ca

CERTIFIED CANADIAN PUBLISHER

FSC www.fsc.org
MIX
Paper | Supporting responsible forestry
FSC® C103567

For my grandmother, who survived the residential schools, and my grandfather, who evaded them. For my mom, who taught me to read almost as quickly as I could walk, and my father, who will never hear this story. And to Eli, who has been with me every step of the way.

CONTENTS

1

LEAF

THE BURIED DAWN

From her perch in the tree, the air was warm, wet, and alive, carrying the scents of earth and yesterday's rain.

Leaf had always had a talent for climbing. To hear Koomis tell it, not a day had passed since she'd learned to walk that her grandmother wasn't dragging her down from somewhere.

Ahead, a small opening in the trees let the sunlight spill onto the green clearing below. Between the patches of purple and green and yellow flowers, a small strip of red fur moved.

Leaf held her breath and waited a long second. The hare had yet to notice her. His back was turned, but his head bounced between bites, anxiously watching the forest. She lifted her bow slowly, the thin wood just another branch swaying in the wind. She drew its string tight and the hare's ear twitched.

"I wish you luck, my friend," Leaf whispered the same way she had heard her grandmother do many times before.

The arrow flitted through the air and found purchase deep in the soil where the hare stood only a moment before. In the slow seconds that followed, it seemed to hang suspended, turning to stare at Leaf mid-leap before vanishing into the forest beyond.

Leaf tutted to herself cheerfully. "Root stew tonight." She hadn't set out that morning with the intent to hunt, but her bow was never far from hand, and she was never one to let an opportunity pass. Returning to the Elderglade with fresh meat in hand might have helped to soothe her latest disappearance, but she put the concerns of the clans to the side. She had more important work to do today.

She walked through the trees gracefully, the soft brown of her hands matching the warm bark as she followed its grooves. Ringlets of stained-green hair fell around her shoulders, fading into the foliage as she moved whisper-quiet through the branches. If anyone else were roaming this stretch of the wood, they would have heard only the slow swaying of leaves and whistling wind.

The tightly pressed tree trunks spanned wider than she was tall, but hidden under the shadow of the forest, prying like a great white finger through the span of green, Leaf could just make out the tall spire that was unmistakably the work of the stonefolk.

The land around its edges had been stripped long ago, and the ghosts of old watchmen still kept new growth at bay. At least, that's what the stories said. The tall stone walls jutting from the earth held back a wild wave of green, moss and vine creeping along its edges, threatening to swallow the top, but the lands beyond remained sterile. The forest had always been wary of the old kingdom proper, and the clans and all their peoples followed its lead.

All their people, that is, except for Leaf. She circled along the edge of the great wall, running her fingers over exposed stone until she found her way to a set of ancient, barred gates. They were long rusted shut, the iron now a dull brown. Leaf gripped the greenery and lifted herself up and over the wall.

In the days of the old kingdom, this would have been dangerous. Barbed iron points sat atop it, and back then, there would have been armed patrols of soldiers. The stonefolk had always been ready for war with the clans. The walls had been unmanned since before Leaf's time, however, and mostly forgotten to all but the few aged enough to have lived through those dark days.

The grounds beyond were barren, devoid of life. She had seen the poisoned earth of other ruins, but it still brought a shadow over her heart. Even the light of Grandfather Sun seemed dim, the dust of dead earth rising to swallow more and more of the light. Still, she tread with quiet reverence. The legacy of the stonefolk was terrible, but seeing their ruins, Leaf couldn't deny that their works had also been great. After their arrival from over the salt waters, they had quickly claimed the Great Turtle as their own, raising massive towers and statues, spiderwebs of stone roadways through the mountains and valleys, and carving faces into cliffs. Villages, towns, and entire cities still scarred the forest's floor, marking where the old kingdom once stood.

In the central clearing of the walled yard was a statue, twice as tall as a normal man, with several adult-sized children running at its feet. Leaf had seen the central figure many times before. The First King of the Stonefolk adorned many castles and keeps left behind by his people, depicted with a serene, almost kindly smile, since smoothed from years of rain. The surrounding children stared up at him with faded adoration.

It was a lie. Leaf had heard the stories of this place. She knew that while time had stolen the features of the stone, it was the stonefolk who had stolen the smiles from the children.

The main hall was a dark shadow rising out of the grounds, carved from cold rock and decayed redwood. The wooden walls were half-collapsed, and several sections of the roof were leaning dangerously inward, but the skeleton of the structure remained.

From the broken windows, the place was at least four levels tall, and there was a lean, spindly tower sticking up from the roof.

"Found you," Leaf said, smiling at the lone barred window at its peak.

She pulled an old iron lantern from her pack, carefully wrapped in heavy hide to preserve the unbroken glass. Elaborately woven metal rings ran around the basin for the flame. It had been fixed to the wall of a cliffside keep overlooking the ocean, and the sea salt air had turned the metal to rust. A mix of oils given to Leaf by a Salmon woman had scoured away some of the rust, and since then, she had kept the tool with her. Having been strictly forbidden from entering the ruins, she kept it well out of sight of the clans.

In her other hand, she took a small bundle of berries and squashed them between her fingers. A sharp, sour scent filled the air, and she quickly smeared the juices around the inner glass of the lantern before wiping her hand clean. For a moment, she wondered whether the dead air could even carry the scent, but soon, pinpricks of light rose from the distant forest like so many stars through the trees, drifting hesitantly over the walls before flowing like a river into the basin, feasting at the bounty of berries within. She smiled at the starlight flies.

"Thank you," Leaf said to the hive before sealing the glass shut. "I promise not to take too much of your time."

She raised her hood against the chill set over the place, then her lenses. It had taken careful work to smooth the shattered orange glass and bind them into their leather wrapping, but they were invaluable. Together with the lantern, they brought even the darkest ruins and caves a taste of daylight. That she had crafted and fixed them all herself brought no small amount of pride.

Leaf lifted the lantern and stepped through the aged double doors into the hall. The yellow flies and her orange lenses blended into a somber amber that was something like daylight, only more restricted. Her lantern could only strain so far against the black, touching on the carved wooden bannisters of a stairwell rising into the dark beyond, where the barest glint of a great chandelier gleamed behind the gloom. Her footsteps echoed quietly through the grand entryway, barely audible beneath the meager buzzing in her lantern. Alternating white and black stone was checkered across the floor, covered in places by a soggy, faded red carpet that sank under her approach. There were painted faces on the walls, colors faded to little more than effigies of mud. Other faces were carved from stone and set into the structure itself, and the shadows from her lantern twisted over their features, bringing them to life in a grim memorial as Leaf moved beneath. They seemed to twist as she passed, eyes following her through the hall, keenly aware that she did not belong in this place.

The must was so thick in the air that Leaf almost gagged. She raised a small scarf over her mouth to block the taste, but it was a half-measure at best. The air behind the walls didn't seem to move, and where it wasn't thick and wet, it was filled with floating motes of dust. Much of it had settled to dirt and grime over the years, muffling her steps over the stone and making her feel as if she were sinking into the old ruin.

"Koomis told me about this place," Leaf whispered to the lantern. "Well, she was speaking with the other elders about it. I had to stay low in the bushes so they wouldn't notice me."

The insects droned in quiet response. Leaf crept low through the halls, bringing herself to the height of a child, and tried to imagine what it must have been like. Taken from her clan by the stonefolk, kept prisoner in this strange place by the point of a sword…

"She doesn't like to speak of it with anyone. Especially me."

Leaf was heading to the fourth floor. The stairwell was the clear path forward, but the darkened halls branching off through the ground floor called to mind memories of her grandmother's few stories. She veered into a side hall off the main room, running her free hand over the old wood and stone, tracing over the detailings carved into the stonework, hidden beneath the layers of cold and damp and dust.

There were several rooms with rows of tables and chairs all facing the same way, toward small wooden stands with black stretches of wall behind them.

"This is where they tried to make Koomis more like the stonefolk," Leaf said, gesturing the lantern about the room. She frowned at all the tables and chairs. "They must have brought a lot of kids through here..."

Stepping across the room to the nearby window, Leaf was suddenly overcome with the urge to throw herself back into the forest. The glass was shattered, small, rain-smoothed fragments remaining in the frame, but the rusted iron bars still held tight. Even squeezing and jostling to work her way between them, Leaf only managed to reach a single arm out into the sunlight, flexing her fingers in its warmth. Beyond the stone walls of the courtyard, she could still hear the sounds of distant life in the wood and breathed deep to take it in. It was only a glimpse, but it was enough.

The starlight lantern guided her through many more rooms, all of which were equally strange. Stocked with tools and old equipment and furniture, the rooms must have been used for the "instruction" of the children. Leaf had seen some of it before in other ruins, and their jagged edges, tight restraints, and twisted features called to mind the whispered stories of the last elders to live within these walls. Leaf had glimpsed the hidden scars behind their words and on their flesh, and she left the room with a full-bodied shudder.

Another set of double doors waited for her at the end, made from felled redwood, with old peeling strips along their edges.

Leaf couldn't discern what color the paint might have been, or what it had depicted. The swollen wood wouldn't open, so she braced her hands against the frame, and kicked until, finally, they lurched forward with a screaming creak that called through the depths of the ruin.

In the room beyond was warm sunlight, and Leaf drank it in heartily. She was in a large chamber, and a path ran down the center of the room to a large window, laid with bare carpet and flanked by plain stone benches that raised right out of the floor in one seamless mass. The window, or at least its remnants, were stained glass, shattered and rain-smoothed like the others. Beneath it was a small wooden podium, showered in broken fragments of colored light.

Leaf raced down the center path to claim the glass. The clans didn't make it often, but Leaf couldn't help but admire the way the colors danced in the light.

"This place is for prayer," Leaf said, setting the lantern down and searching through the dust and debris. "See that statue?" She pointed to a large set of stone hands carved into the wall beside the podium, palms pressed together and fingers pointed to the sky. "They're asking for forgiveness. Don't ask me what for. Koomis never told me, even though she still does it herself sometimes. She doesn't like to talk about it."

The people who ran this place had been stern, cruel even, and insisted that within these walls, their word was law. "They stole children from the clans and punished them for breaking rules they'd never learned, set by a king they'd never met. But how can someone be a leader if they don't even know their people?"

The lantern buzzed contentedly with starlight flies.

Looking up at the balconies above her, Leaf saw more hallways extending off into the darkened ruin. She picked up a long, dulled shard of bright green glass and carefully wrapped it in leathers before storing it gently in her bag. Then she fastened the lantern to a loop off its side, and with her hands free, started to climb along a column carved with winged people.

Climbing was faster than walking around old places, and it was easy to find purchase in the grooves of wings and stone feathers reaching out lifelike from the column. Under the roof, where it was harder for the wind and rain to reach, the stonework's fine detailing remained. The winged folk seemed to watch her mournfully as she made her ascent.

The Elders had always taught her that the spirits of old lived on through the trees, and that she would join them when her time came. Leaf sometimes wondered if the stonefolk believed their spirits would carry on in the rock. The statues' sharp eyes were haunting in their own beautiful way, and she would have believed it if someone told her that behind them, spirits watched, jealously coveting her life and freedom. She could leave this place any time she wanted, but they would remain here forever.

When she climbed high enough, Leaf kicked off hard from the column and twisted through the air, latching onto the railing of the stone balcony behind her. The railings were solid iron, and stable enough to hold her weight. Behind the bars, ornate wooden chairs rotted, the stuffing long ago taken for use in nests by what creatures were brave enough to enter the ruin. Leaf pushed on to the hallway beyond, unfastening the lantern from her pack, and taking it in hand once again.

The second floor was even darker than the first. Starlight did its best to press back the gloom, but the hallways here were tighter, like the walls were reaching out to crush her. Leaf pressed her arms against the stone, willing them back. Sometimes, she liked to play a game where her hand was a tiny person, running along the colossal landscapes of walls and cliff faces and tree bark, jumping the chasms of doorways.

A long line of stone busts ran along the walls. More faces, grim and stern and glowering at her as she passed. "Do you think these were the works of the headmaster?" she wondered. The name had been whispered among the Elders and older children as a cursed title, but Leaf wasn't afraid of stories. She didn't really understand the word anyway.

The wing seemed to all be bedrooms. There were two or three bare bed frames in every room, hangings for lanterns, and unbarred windows. The doors were fit with heavy locks that clasped from the inside, although many had been broken inward. The story was told in the walls, where faded scorch marks licked the stone and deep gouges clawed along the wood. There had been fighting here. Leaf followed one of the gouges to a small metal implement embedded in the wood, its rounded end sharpened to a rough point, red with what she could only hope was rust.

The last bedroom at the end of the hall was larger than the others, and contained a single, brilliantly detailed bed. Shreds of light fabric hung in tatters from its upper frame, reaching after Leaf as she passed. In the corner between the bed and wall was a small chest with a large, rusted lock sat atop the rotted wood. Leaf brought her foot crashing down through its top. Her leather shin wrappings kept her from cutting her leg, but the wood was so wet it practically bent anyway.

A large mound of shining yellow metal spilled across the floor. Leaf took one and examined it in the lantern light. There was a small face engraved on its edge, matching the statue outside. Small markings ran along its rim as well, though she had no idea what they might mean.

She took a few pieces of the yellow metal and stuck them in her pack, leaving the rest behind. She couldn't imagine any use for them. The metal was soft and too easily bent.

There were other finds far more interesting. A small stuffed doll in the shape of a bear, well-worn but at least protected from the worst of the elements, was abandoned in a corner. Necklaces of fang and feather, all aged near to withering, hung along the wall like a hunter displaying his trophies. A dulled claw with small engravings hung over the mantle of the fireplace. She recognized the markings of the Bear clan.

Everywhere she looked, there was history. A large portrait on the wall, colors muddied, depicted a cruel-faced man in impractical garb. His hat was too tall, more like to ride off in the wind or catch in a branch than to protect from the sun, and he wore a colorless lens on a chain that seemed ready to fall from his face. Even muted, he retained the pale skin of the stonefolk. There was a heavy coating of hair on his chin and around his lips. Leaf ran her fingers over the portrait and took off a heavy layer of dust as well as several flakes of paint.

The fireplace in thc center wall had been unlit for years, and Leaf almost overlooked it. As she went to leave the room, a spark ignited from under the ash and dust, and she thought it might be a gleam off the old metal weave that held the logs, but the iron there was rusted, and the logs long rotted to a fine carpet of moss and growth. Rain had fallen down through the chimney and into the deep piles of soot. Leaf dug her fingers into the soil, searching for the gleam that had caught her eye. Her fingernails were caked with earth, but her search came up empty.

She was sure she had seen something. There were always secrets hidden in these old buildings, things overlooked by the fleeing stonefolk. Leaf took the lantern and held it high over the fireplace, hoping to catch the gleam again. She swept the piles of soot aside with her foot carefully, turning the faded red carpet an ashy black, and cleaned her fingers on the scraps of fabric still hanging from the bed.

Beneath her was a small pile that had been burned in the last fire of the stonefolk. Long, blackened strings that she was sure once held more baubles and trinkets, carvings of the other clans. Bits of claw had been charred to nothing, as well as many other marks and reminders of identity that the children had carried with them. The man who had lived in this room, with his cruel face and strange garb, had collected only some as curiosities or trophies and had left the others to burn. He had taken their histories, their culture, their family, and weighed over what looked best on his wall before discarding the rest.

Leaf picked up the remnants of an old spiderweb charm, its complicated weave-work still tight despite its age. She lifted it carefully from the soot, untangling it from the metal framing of the fireplace before cleaning it on the hem of her cloak, and admired the way the flaxen string caught the light. Beneath it dangled painted symbols charred and stolen by the fire.

Beneath those, Leaf spotted the light again. Just a glint, breaking through cracks in the wood like the sun through heavy clouds, but it was there. She cracked the charred wood in her hand like an egg, and from beneath the blackened fragments came a burst of light so bright she thought it must have been mirrored silver. Covering it with her hands and moving to a dark corner of the room, she tried to get a better look, but the light burned so fiercely that she was forced to remove her colored lenses and set the lantern behind her.

Whatever she had found, it was cool to the touch, and small enough to be concealed in the palm of her hand. Leaf studied the strange object carefully through her fingers, trying to cut off any source of light, but the stone continued to glow like an ember from the fire. More strangely, its light seemed to shine alone, failing to touch anything else in the room, or even pierce the darkness of her hands. Whatever it was, she had never seen anything like it.

"Hello," Leaf whispered. "What are you?"

The ember kept its secret.

It could be a spirit, she thought suddenly, *or a fallen star*. She had seen her share traveling through the sky, the scattered children of Grandmother Moon trailing in her wake, and even some falling into the seas beyond the Turtle. The ember might have come from the sky.

She admired the strange stone, pondering over its purpose and origin and the nature of its shy, sunlight glow. No matter what she did, she couldn't get it to light anything around her, and this only made her more curious. Still, she packed it very delicately into her bag, checking and rechecking to make sure that it stayed in place, and that she hadn't somehow imagined the whole thing. Then she took her lantern and continued back into the hall. Perhaps one of the Elders might be able to tell her what it was. The trick would be in asking the right questions without revealing what she had or where she had found it.

The stairway to the third floor was smaller than the entry hall's. Rather than a grand wooden walkway, there were simple stone steps snaking around a central pillar. Leaf couldn't help but notice the lack of detailing on this stairway. There were no statues or carvings save for two children at prayer engraved into the door. It was fitted with a broken lock, which had been forced open from the other side. Leaf's breath caught in her throat.

This was where the children had made their escape.

Leaf traced her fingers over the broken lock, imagining their desperation as they fought their way free. She smiled sadly for her grandmother. Most of the children had found their way to freedom that night, but the scars they carried had never truly faded.

She had to brace herself against the walls to keep from slipping as she ascended to the third floor. Something cried out from the darkness overhead and Leaf ducked low, imagining all sorts of creatures from the Deepwood that could be resting here. Giant spiders, skinchangers, blackfooted ghost men, the spirits of vengeful stonefolk—before she pushed them aside, catching her wits again and holding the lantern forward.

Above her, a lone raven was perched on a wall sconce.

Leaf laughed to herself as it cried out again, feathers bristling in the dark. "Sorry," she whispered, inching slowly around the bird. "I didn't think anyone still lived here." The raven huffed as she passed but didn't fret or flee. Leaf bowed her head respectfully.

The walls here were even tighter than those of the second floor and with none of the detailed flourishes that defined stonefolk work. The floor was thick with bird droppings as well, trailing along the wall under sconces and overhead supports. Leaf imagined just how many might call this place home once the sun set.

The rooms up here were all for sleeping as well. They were significantly smaller than those downstairs and more tightly packed. Four, six, sometimes even eight to a single room, all pressed so close together that even Leaf, small as she was, could only walk between the frames by pressing sideways. The floor was bare stone as well, the beds little more than rotted wooden frames with the remnants of ragged blankets. Even before the long years of wear had set in, Leaf couldn't imaginc this was a nice place to be. The windows wouldn't have been large enough to get her head through even if they weren't heavily barred. It was a dismal place, and she was starting to understand why Koomis never liked to speak of it.

There were memories buried in the stone. A deep sadness trapped in the walls that threatened to burn through Leaf like a flame the longer she stayed here. While the caves and cliffs of home were warm and open, the stone dancing warmly orange from the many fires kept by the clans, the stone here was cold. It loomed inwardly, like a warning that it could claim Leaf, too, if she stayed too long.

Still, Leaf couldn't leave yet. She needed to know. It didn't seem to matter which bed she picked, so Leaf settled into the one nearest the window, hoping to catch a glimpse of the sky. Beyond the walls the forest grew too high, only occasional lances of light falling through the canopy, and never toward these windows. Somehow, the sight of the forest only made her feel more like a prisoner. Picking herself back up, she returned to the tower stairway.

She continued up the winding tower to the fourth floor. It was the smallest of them all, with only a sliver of air passing between her shoulders and the walls. She held the lantern directly in front of her, because there was no room to hold it aloft, and imagined it her defender against the crushing darkness. This was what she had come for, after all. She was close.

There were only a few rooms along the hallway, smaller than all the others, and each equipped with only a single squalid bed. A small, barred hole, more to ensure the children didn't suffocate than to provide light, teased a glimpse of the world they had been stolen from.

Leaf moved to the furthest end of the hall and sat down at the foot of the bed. It was much too small, and the walls far too close for her to lay down, but she bunched her legs and tucked into the ancient frame anyway, squeezing herself into a ball and turning her head out the small hole in the wall.

"They used to send my grandmother here," Leaf said to the lantern. The flies were dimming now, resting peacefully behind the glass after their long meal, and she knew their light would fade soon. "This was where they put the 'bad children,' she said, so she was bad every night. Acting up, breaking rules, failing her classes, all just enough to be punished without being beaten." Leaf smiled sadly. Like her grandmother, she too knew how to push boundaries with the right touch, but unlike her grandmother, it had never been done out of necessity, or with the knowledge that if she pressed too far, someone might just decide to end her life.

"This was the only place where she could be alone," Leaf whispered. Through the small hole in the wall, out beyond the gap in the trees, Leaf could see the distant mountains standing in sharp contrast to the brilliant orange sky. From here and nowhere else on the grounds could she see the peaks of the Great Turtle, where the clans still roamed. Leaf finally understood just how valuable this small piece of the world had been to her grandmother. Koomis had been banished here every night so that she could dream of home.

Leaf smiled and stared up at the ceiling.

The light was dimming by the time she ventured back over the wall and into the forest. Her lantern buzzed angrily now, with the berries gone, the starlight flies were getting restless, and so Leaf released them back into the trees with a whisper of thanks. She had new finds to study when she returned to the Elderglade, and a few stolen crafts to return to their clans.

There was also a new question burning inside her. Leaf took the strange glowing ember from her pack and stared at it. She had never heard of such a thing before, but there were many customs among the clans, and many more still among the stonefolk and their long-fallen kingdom. Surely someone out there would recognize the ember for what it was.

Something rustled in the grass ahead. Leaf, by instinct, fell silent in the still brush, drawing her bow. In one of the last fading beams of the falling sun, a red-furred hare ventured into view. Leaf drew an arrow and whispered Koomis's words.

"I wish you luck, my friend."

2

REED

THE DRIFTING NATION

"That's it? Good luck?" Reed asked, his foot tapping on the dock. Beneath him, the boards were rising and falling in steady waves, seawater pushing through the old wood in swells to slosh around his boots. Around him, travelers swayed uneasily.

"And all the fortunes of storm and sail," the captain shouted over the bustling crowd. He was a burly, bald-headed man with too many muscles and even more tattoos. Reed recognized the long painted serpent of the southern Stepstones that wound from wrist to neck, bright inks writ fresh over the faded sunburst that marked him a man of the Sun Eternal. So he had been navy once. "Sorry kid, but you're not cut out for this line of work. Not yet." The captain gripped Reed's upper arm. He probably could have closed his grip completely if Reed hadn't padded the inside of his jacket.

Reed pulled back defensively, drawing a sharp breath of salty air, and flattened his too-short sleeves so that they fell again over his wrists. A large, warm—if somewhat scratchy—woolen shirt, ragged from years of unbroken wear, helped pad his jacket further.

"You're off to the Whispermoss, right?" Reed said, trying a different approach. He'd heard a few sailors grumbling about the length of their journey, and from the captain's desperation to catch the wind, they had to be heading south. Between that and their cargo, guessing their destination had been easy. "I was there just a few months ago," he lied. He'd seen the Whispermoss islands only once, at a distance, years ago when the Flotilla last passed them by. He tried to summon stories of those lands. "I was doing cargo work for one of the Listeners. Father something-or-other. Martin, maybe. Good guy, bad breath. Had hair like a dead spider. I've got connections out that way if you need an introduction. Maybe I need a bit of help moving the heavier cargo around, sure, but I can show you where to sell it if you want the best price."

The captain sighed and reached for a heavy-looking crate, lifting it with the ease that Reed might lift an apple. "You were friends with a holy man?" he asked, suddenly dour. "Sorry to tell you this, but he's probably laying beneath the sea with the rest of his lot. The Whispermoss has new rulers now."

"Damn it," said Reed. This news hadn't reached him, although it wasn't surprising. The islands of the Broken Waters were always changing hands.

"I'm sorry for your loss, my friend," the captain said more quietly, patting him softly on the shoulder, mistaking his failure for mourning. Reed tried to look sad. "If you require passage to pay your respects, we will take your booking. Otherwise, it would be best to try your luck with another crew."

Reed searched his pockets, hoping somehow that the last of his coins might have bred between the morning and now, but all they had done was wear his pocket thinner. Moving swiftly back through the docks and the rush of cargo and heavyset men, he thought that it just wasn't fair. A lifetime at sea had made his footsteps more sure than half the bumbling drunkards around him, and the other half looked like they couldn't even remember their own names, much less the tongues and tales of the many islands he'd passed. And yet, because they looked the part and he didn't, they were the ones hired to work and see distant shores, while Reed sat bitterly back on the Flotilla. He grimaced at the sounds of laughter and camaraderie on another departing ship. Another missed opportunity.

He settled back into the empty market stall he kept as a watch post over the docks. Someone might come along to boot him out, but generally, no one wanted this place. It was too high and too out of the way, terrible for foot traffic but terrific for spying over the many ships of the Flotilla. If nothing else, he could sell the information later. There were always ears eager to learn which ships were moving what cargo to what destinations, and they paid well enough. As for what they might do with that information, well, Reed preferred not to dwell.

He counted ships for a time. The merchants were headed nowhere exciting, and the passenger ships all charged far more than he had. Even if he could sneak his way aboard one, there was no guarantee he ended up anywhere worth being. Aside from that, the tickets of stowaways were usually good for a one-way trip to the bottom of the sea. He'd seen it happen.

"Eating today?" asked a high-pitched voice at his side. A hand tugged the corner of his jacket gently, wrenching him from his thoughts. A young girl, six or seven maybe, with a scraggly nest of pale hair, was standing next to him. She was quiet and dutiful, but her smile was eager. *Too good for this place*, he thought. *Stay here long enough and it'll ruin you.*

"Right," said Reed, forcing an easy smile. His problems weren't hers, and he wouldn't force them on anyone. He pulled two of his last three coins from the purse hidden in his sleeve and handed them to her. "Something sour today, if you can find it. I know there's plenty of fruit in, so they'll be competing for the best price. Get two for me and use what's left to get something for yourself."

The girl beamed a gap-toothed grin and saluted him in the way she had seen the other sailors do. It was the same salute Reed had learned at her age from watching the docks. Ten years on, and he was still stuck in the same stretch of ships, doing the same petty work with nothing to show for it. He was just another ship rat scurrying about for scraps.

The girl hurried off in the direction of the market ships, taking the crisscrossed planks over the many decks at a run. Sails were plentiful against the clear blue sky, their insignias too many to count. There were military vessels, commercial traders, alchemists peddling snake oil brews, and ships from the far west promising more exotic wares. Those last sort were too private and privileged to permit someone like Reed even a glimpse inside their strange, smoking hulls. Silent priests gave wordless prayer on eerily quiet decks. There were the sigils of countless independent crews for hire as well. Some of them were pirates, he knew, dressing themselves up with fancy titles like "privateers" or "mercenary companies." Even those unsavory folk were allowed to dock with the Flotilla, so long as they didn't ply their trade whilst visiting. The only rule when docked was not to rock the boat.

None of the ships out today were of much interest, however. Reed never had the heart for piracy, or any interest in the religious pilgrimages that wound through the sea. Neither did he desire to sign his life away with the naval services of some fledgling nation, or a recklessly formed militia looking to claim some corner of the ocean. Allegiances, be they with deities or nations, were an idea altogether foreign to Reed.

There were others who sailed the sea, however, with dreams besides those of conquest and glory. Some vessels chose to ride the currents, charting new routes on the ever-shifting sea. They explored forgotten lands, crawling over the bones of fallen nations searching for long-abandoned riches, and spent their days traveling wherever wind or whimsy carried them. That was the sort of ship Reed was looking for.

Reed had seen few such ships and met fewer such people. In fact, he only knew one personally, and he was a self-aggrandizing drunk. Old Tarn claimed to be many things during his youth, and young sailors were always crowding him, buying him drinks in return for stories that fueled their dreams of finding riches of their own. Reed was one of them.

A gnawing in his stomach reminded him that he hadn't eaten since the previous day. The markets would be busy this late in the morning, and he worried the girl might have been victim to a pickpocket or run off with his money. He remembered vividly how it felt to be her age, scurrying between the ships' underbellies, the threat of hunger always on your heels. You grew up quick on the Flotilla.

"*Watch it, you hapless oaf!*" whined a pointed voice over the docks in a tongue Reed hadn't heard for years.

"Out of the way, blueblood," was the reply, gruff and frustrated.

Reed turned his head to the commotion. A sharply dressed man, backed by three men in uniform, was admonishing a large and threatening-looking sort. The larger man had a knife concealed in the back of his shirt, his hand already hovering over it. Between the two, several items had fallen to the dock while the uniformed men kept onlookers at bay.

"*Well, don't just stand there. Pick up my things and I might just forgive you,*" said the sharply dressed man. He was half the size of the other fellow, but his expression was withering.

"I don't know what you're saying, blueblood, but it sounds like a threat." The larger man's hand crept closer to the knife at his back. "I don't much care for threats."

The uniformed men, who Reed assumed must be bodyguards, were slowly reaching for their weapons as well. Everyone looked unsure as to who would move first.

"He's just asking you to pick his things up," Reed said, walking over to the man with the knife. "*My father doesn't understand you,*" he said in turn, switching tongues for the sharply dressed fellow. "*Most folk here only speak the trade tongue. You're from Thunder's Basin, aren't you?*"

"*Yes,*" the man said, huffing and straightening his jacket. He looked disdainfully at Reed down the end of his raised nose. "*Why?*"

"*Recognized the dialect,*" Reed said, nodding. *And the make of your boat, the uniforms, and your style of clothing*, he thought. "*You might have noticed folk around here aren't the 'upper society' sort. If I help my father pick up your things, maybe we can all avoid some trouble here.*"

"*I assure you, there will be trouble if you don't,*" the man hissed.

The large man paused in reaching for his knife and grunted down to Reed. "You know what he's saying?"

"More or less. I've got an ear for tongues," said Reed. "I'll pick up his things for you if you just look busy. Does that work for you?"

"What's in it for you?" the large man asked, his eyes narrowing.

"The fool looks rich. Might toss me a coin or two if I solve this amicably."

The large man snorted at that, but motioned for Reed to go ahead.

Reed shuffled uneasily between the both of them, slowly gathering up the scattered luggage. Most of it was clothing already gone damp from seawater. There was a locket that looked to be made from real gold, but everyone was watching too carefully for him to pocket it, so he handed it to one of the uniformed men. None of them took a second glance at the book lying on the ground, however, much too focused on more valuable-looking things, and so no one noticed when Reed slipped the small leatherbound volume up his sleeve, concealed behind a mound of sopping clothes he handed to yet another bodyguard. After all was said and done, the sharply dressed man stomped his foot, and without a word, all four departed.

"Don't go out of your way for folk like that," the large man said, laughing darkly to himself. "No one gets rich giving away their money. You can give 'em your whole damn life and they'll stiff your family on the bill."

"Maybe," said Reed, smiling at the weight of the book in his sleeve, "but sometimes things work out."

He scurried away from the docks before anyone could realize what he had taken. When he remembered that the girl was supposed to be coming back with his food, he left his last coin hidden on the seat where she would come looking for him. The kid had been good to him the past few days, always coming by looking to do any fetching or gathering he needed, and he didn't want her to think she'd been forgotten. The coin was his promise to return, even if he knew it might be an empty one.

As he walked the network of docks and planks crisscrossing the many ships of the Flotilla, Reed watched the waves rippling distantly off into the horizon. Little dots of land sometimes crested briefly in the space between sun and ship, but all the rest of the world was water. Reed's was a life of ships and sails, and he weaved nimbly through the crowded decks and spiderweb docks.

He would need to find another dock to watch today, lest the sharply dressed man realize what had been taken and come back for him.

A strong gust of wind from the east caught in his long, greasy hair. Reed turned, pulling his jacket tight, and spotted a new vessel passing between the masts and sails. Its mainsail crested over the waves like the rising sun, a mix of reds and yellows and oranges, and a few bits of white as well. As it drew closer, he saw it had been torn and repaired many times with different fabrics and colors. Compared to the rest of the ship, however, the sails looked pristine.

The little boat must be a tough one, Reed thought. A grimacing, fanged lizard was carved into the prow, nicely detailed if heavily faded. The construction of the ship looked haphazard, patched together in a dozen places with as many materials. Dark reds and browns and a few spots of bone-white wood were fixed into the hull. The materials looked to be gathered from all over the seas.

Normally, he was able to tell where a crew was from just by the look of the boat and the materials of its make, but this ship seemed to have a little bit of everywhere to it. The slim prow was favored by spice peddlers, and the wide central helm was common to Northern whalers. Detailings carved into the woodwork had the look of nations from far to the south, with armored sidings like the warring naval vessels the Flotilla frequently passed. The strange ship held his gaze as it rounded the edge of the Flotilla before vanishing between taller ships.

Reed had to know its story.

He followed the strange lizard ship all the way to the docks along the far north side, watching as sailors went to help rein it in. Reed made sure to meander nearby, looking busy while not really doing anything at all. He was good at that. Being seen as "the help" was almost the same as not being seen at all. As he wound his way closer through the crowd, his eye caught the bright orange lettering on the ship's side, rippling almost flame-like against the light of the sun: *Dragon's Breath*.

The first crewman to disembark was a tall woman with pale skin and pitch-black hair. She wore a full suit of plated armor that glistened with a dull blue sheen in the sun. When she stepped down the ramp, all the dockworkers made way for her, cautiously eyeing the greatsword at her back. Reed thought she must be crazy to risk wearing full plate on the water, but her stride was sure even as the dock swelled and fell beneath her. The second was different in almost every way. He wore no armor at all, only a rough, golden leather vest and a pair of loose-fitting trousers that looked a sorry state. His skin was ebony, save for a swath along his left side that looked almost like tree bark. Reed realized a moment later that these were burn scars, and that they ran all across his arm, chest, and even onto his face, where a strip of red cloth covered the pit of his ruined eye.

The burned man was smiling an infectious grin, however, which cut deep laugh lines into his face. He looked to be somewhere in his upper thirties, perhaps forties, but moved like a man half his age onto the dock. Thick, braided hair like knotted ropes swayed behind him as he walked.

Reed kept a careful distance from them. The woman was sizing up everyone around her carefully, one at a time, and he didn't want to be noticed by her just yet. The man, meanwhile, was striding proudly over the decks, splitting the crowds before him with effortless smiles and broad gestures.

A young woman followed subtly behind them both. She looked closer to Reed's age than theirs, but she probably had a few years on him at least. She was short and olive-skinned, with close-cropped brown hair. Her heavy-lidded eyes darted about the crowd, and he made sure to seem unremarkable as they passed his way. Her focus seemed to be on anyone who got too close to the group, so he gave them a wide berth.

"Be excusing me, good sir, but are you perhaps knowing the way to the Halfmug?" The burned man spoke with a silk-smooth voice to passing sailors. His accent was thick, Reed's ear placing it from somewhere far to the south, but he spoke the language well, and his voice was loud and commanding in a friendly sort of way. Reed made to look like he was browsing a merchant's stall as he moved closer to listen.

The sailor pointed the man in the right direction. "I am thanking you kindly, sir," said the burned man. He gave a short bow, and a smile cracked along the burned side of his facc. Strangely, Reed had to fight from smiling along with him.

"We shouldn't go around telling everyone where we're headed, Keresh," said the girl with the heavy eyes. She watched the crowd suspiciously. Reed strained to hear her quiet tones over the din.

"No one is caring who I am or where I am going, Finch," said the burned man, drawing out her name in a teasing fashion. Finch rolled her eyes. "And you are calling me captain, please."

"Is that an order, Captain?"

It was Keresh's turn to roll his eyes, laughing as he did.

"Why are we meeting at a tavern?" asked the pale woman. "Couldn't he have come to us? I don't like leaving the ship unattended."

"Old redcoat wants to be in his own territory," said Finch. "I would, too. Gives you the upper hand in negotiations. Hell, he's probably too fat and comfortable to bother with the walk."

"I am hoping you are not speaking this way to the client."

So they were here for a job, Reed thought, but they hadn't managed to work out the terms yet. He couldn't help but wonder what sort of employer might be hiring out of the Halfmug. The girl, Finch, was right about the negotiation, but the place was far from comfortable. The boat was old, for one thing, and at risk of sinking, as Reed had learned from the water pooling at his feet when he spent a night in its bowels. The drink selection was poor, and its clientele poorer still. Reed didn't drink, but he had gotten a fair taste from all the drippings falling from the floor above onto his cot. All the Halfmug had going for it was cheap rates for lodgers. These travelers weren't from around here if they didn't know any of this, and that was good for Reed.

"Did his message say anything about the job?" asked the pale woman. "I know he asked for you by name, but where does he want us to take him?"

"Turtle Rock, I heard," said Finch. Reed's ears pricked at the name. "Not that I was listening in or anything, Captain," she added hastily.

The burned man laughed as he led them slowly through the market stalls, taking his time browsing through the menagerie of gathered goods. "You are knowing more than you are meant to," he said, still chuckling, "but not as much as I am needing. How am I to find a ship in a maze of ships?"

That's my opening, Reed thought. He straightened his coat and collar and slicked his hair back down. Before he could step forward, however, a hand gripped him roughly by the shoulder.

"Hello, friend," sneered a familiar voice.

Reed froze in shock. "Hello Fre…Fox," he said, turning slowly. The bony fingers at his shoulder were those of another ship rat who had, until recently, been known as "Freckles." Lately, Freckles was concerned with building a new reputation for himself and insisted on going by "the Fox." Reed wouldn't have entertained it if it weren't for the set of mean-looking muscle at his back. His hair was a wiry mess of red, brighter than the dull rust of Reed's, and he had a horrible tendency to squint at people when talking to them, not exactly endearing. Reed thought he looked more like some type of rodent than a fox.

"You got something for us?" Fox asked, leaning up to Reed with a horrible grin. Reed turned to look for the crew of the *Dragon's Breath*, who were already vanishing further into the crowds. "Whoa whoa whoa, you don't got somewhere to be, do you?"

Reed turned his attention to the larger youths at Fox's back, who cracked their knuckles. Together, the trio had been making a name for themselves among the other rats. They did grunt work for some of the mercenary vessels among the Flotilla, mostly collecting debts from younger children and having *spirited* exchanges of ideas with those who couldn't pay.

Those like Reed, for instance.

"I was just on my way to see you guys," Reed lied. The smile came to him easily. "Got a gem runner heading out east. Plans to make a sale with one of those new warlords, you know the type, the one making all the fuss out at the Wavebreaks? They're leaving in an hour, and I thought maybe I'd point you in the right direction, you know? Square off that debt of mine, and maybe give you a bit of shine with your boss."

While the story came easily enough, maybe he hadn't said it with enough fear. Fox studied him for a moment before flashing an equally fake grin of his own, tinged with a thin and feral edge. "That's a good offer, Reed. You know, maybe you should run it to the bosses yourself. Get in good with them, you know? It's past time you started making a name for yourself. Come with us, we'll show you the way. Wouldn't want anything bad happening to you before you could give 'em the good news."

The threat was plain as daylight to Reed. "Are you worried I'll get lost? That's sweet, really. I didn't know you cared so much."

"Just don't want you ending up somewhere other than where you're supposed to be. Now get walking."

Fox led Reed by the arm away from the crew of the *Dragon's Breath*, who were now lost somewhere around the bend of ships. This wasn't good. Either Fox and friends would take him to the bosses, who would see right through any lies he could throw at them, or they would take him somewhere out of sight. No matter how he looked at things, his journey ended with a knife in his back.

Reed glanced around, but he knew better than to call out for help. The knife now pressed into his side was subtle enough not to be noticed by anyone else, and most folk wouldn't care to help a squabbling ship rat anyway. If anything, he would be thrown in a cell for causing a commotion, or rolled into the sea so that cargo haulers could continue unimpeded. He was on his own.

"Look," said Reed, amicably, "if this is about my debt, we can settle that right now."

"That right?" asked Fox, sniffling. The promise of coin was too good for him to pass, even when it was likely a lie. That had been true when they were children, and it was even truer now. "What do you got for me?"

Reed raised his arms slowly so as not to spook the muscle, who looked ready to jump him over the slightest movement, and carefully reached into his sleeve for a heavy bag. He made sure to jangle its contents loud enough that everyone could hear. "Let me just count out what I owe you."

Fox snatched at the bag, eyes narrowing, but Reed kept it out of his reach. Fox's mouth curled to a thin sneer. "Where did you get all that?"

"Don't worry about it," Reed said, raising a finger to his lips.

"Let me see it!" Fox jumped up, pulling at Reed's arm. Reed made a show of letting it slip from his fingers, looking as if to catch it while actually drawing open the top, and the contents scattered, gleaming in the sunlight as they clattered along the docks.

Passersby were interested now, their attention caught by the sound. Panic flashed in Fox's eyes as he and his muscle all fell to their hands and knees, chasing the bits of broken glass and twisted metal—the clatter they had mistaken for coin.

Reed smiled and turned to leave, but something caught his eye. An exposed coin purse was showing from Fox's back pocket. He shouldn't push his luck, but unable to resist, he snatched it. Turnabout was fair play, he figured. They were going to rob him, so he robbed them first. Reed walked away quickly and quietly, hoping not to draw any attention as desperate fingers reached between the dock for the fallen "coins." Others in the crowd were still drawing closer, looking for a spare piece.

"You son of a bitch!" Fox yelled, standing suddenly. He wiped a bloody hand on his vest. "Reed! Get back here!"

Reed couldn't help laughing as he started to run.

No one cared much for the squabbling rats save for the travelers whose toes they scurried across. Reed hadn't gotten as much of a lead as he should have, and Fox and his muscle were moving fast. The loss of so much coin must have stung even more than the glass under their nails.

"Sorry!" Reed shouted, jumping through a thick cloud of smoke billowing from a nearby ship. "Must have mixed up our bags!" A circle of women shouted at him, and then started throwing curses at Fox and the others when they followed after him.

It was quickly becoming clear, however, that Reed wasn't going to beat the others in a straight race. Already they were gaining on him, and he wasn't built for this. Navigating the web of bridges and planks and rises on the many decks of the Flotilla, he used the crowd to his advantage, slipping through gaps between dock workers and trying to lose himself in the commotion. When Fox and friends followed, he took a sudden turn, leaping onto a lower deck and tucking into a roll. This deck wasn't open to travelers, and freehands reached for him, protesting as he wove between bushels of berries and stalks of corn that had been carefully grown on their vast, soil-covered decks. Before anyone could stop him, he managed to leap to another ship, and then was making pace over the gangways to the largest ship in the fleet, the *Free Man's Pride*.

No one knew who had named it, just what the ancient markings along the side of the iron hull meant. It had been the core of the Flotilla for so long that no one even remembered who had first owned it, or what nation could construct such a monster of a ship. It was a titan of iron, impregnable compared to the many wooden ships and dinghies, and its many rooms and corridors and great open market spaces had been leased and subdivided between so many hands that no one could truly claim ownership of the whole. It rode in the middle of the fleet as the biggest marketplace on the seas. A perfect place to hide.

By the time Fox emerged from between rows of corn, Reed was already at the doors to the *Pride*. A couple of freehands grabbed Fox's friends as they tried to follow, and Fox himself barely had enough time to jump over the side of the ship and into the sea, pulling himself back up onto the lower docks. Reed couldn't help but give a teasing wave as he disappeared into the *Pride*.

Inside the great ship, the crowds were pressed so tightly that there was scarcely room to breathe, and they moved like a slow river over the many stalls and booths of the inner market. The merchants, attempting some semblance of order, had erected large tents over their stores, turning the inner hull into a confusing plumage of mixed colors and signage. Hundreds of voices yelled in dozens of languages about their wares and goods, calling to the travelers. A lifetime on the Flotilla and a gift for tongues meant Reed could understand most of them.

He stepped into the first large tent the crowd brought him to and ducked low, worming his way between displays of brightly colored cloths and silks.

"*Welcome, welcome!*" a round-faced man bellowed. He was covered in layers of fine silk, each a different color, making him look like a walking rainbow. Reed supposed the sweat on his brow was the rain. "*And how might I be helping the discerning young gentleman this afternoon?*"

"*Change of clothes,*" Reed gasped. He hadn't realized how out of breath he was until the words wheezed from his lips. Polished silver on the wall reflected his boney face, red and running slick with sweat. When had his hair gotten so long? It fell down near his shoulders like damp ribbons of dried blood.

"*We have many fine fabrics to peruse, brought from every corner of the sea. Name me a material and I promise we have it in stock or will have it soon! Tell me a style of garb and if we don't have it, we can tailor it!*" The round man was beaming as he gave his spiel, but his eyes narrowed. "*Given you have coin, of course.*"

Reed was ready to decline the man's offer. Everything here was far out of his price range. He'd found his newest shirt lying sodden and forgotten on the docks, and he hadn't changed jackets in years, even though the sleeves now only fell halfway down his forearm. He'd rarely had the money for a steady diet, let alone a new wardrobe.

But Fox's coin purse was jangling in his pocket, the boy and his goons must have been busy collecting today. With a wide smile and growing giddiness, Reed realized that a change of look might be exactly what he needed.

"*Lead the way, my good man,*" Reed said with a smile, hefting the heavy bag from his pocket. The round man's smile returned in full force. "*I'll need a haircut as well,*" he added.

"Of course, of course! I know just the person to help you in that regard. My daughter, you see, is excellent with hair. She's seen every style there is on the seas, and you have much hair to work with, my friend..."

As the round man went on, asking about preferences and taking measurements, Reed's mind was already starting to drift. The crew of the *Dragon's Breath* was meeting their new client at the Halfmug. The "old redcoat," they'd called him. The Flotilla was a big place, and they were having trouble finding their way around. Even with his unexpected detour, he could still reach the Halfmug before them. They had mentioned Turtle Rock as well. An idea was forming in his mind. A promise of work, perhaps even escape.

Old redcoat. The Halfmug. Turtle Rock. Reed repeated the words in his mind. *Old redcoat. The Halfmug. Turtle Rock.* It was all starting to come together.

Old redcoat.

The Halfmug.

Turtle Rock.

3

ASH

THE EYES OF THE FOREST

Ash watched from her nestled place high in the trees as the sun rose over the Turtle. Bleary-eyed men and women woke below, donning the bearskins and antlers of the Elderglade, and wind wafted the charred smoke of yesterday's hunt from low cookfires. In the distance, there was a howling. She sat up sharp at the hint of danger, eyes scanning the tree line, and relaxed just as quickly seeing the lone coyote wandering away from the clans.

Ash stifled a yawn and rose from her nook in the bark. The trees were ancient, their wide branches like roads, and she wove through the upper canopy, her footsteps careful and measured. Whisper-quiet, cloaked beneath her white wolf's pelt, she was a ghost in the trees above the men and women and children walking below.

While she made her rounds through the canopy, the many folk of the clans all walked the trails through the darker stretches of forest. They followed the lingering glow of starlight flies returning to their many hives, and continued on to the tables and benches where everyone gathered for their communal meal. The adults were calm and patient as they stalked the trails and formed long lines waiting to be served, while the children piled together in a clangor of empty bowls and plates, screaming to be heard over the older children attempting to instill some calm.

By the time everyone was served, the sun had risen, its long rays reaching like thin fingers through the gaps in the trees. A few straggling families had stayed by their cookfires, eating leisurely before finally setting out. Only when everyone was gone did Ash finally descend from the canopy. The cooking men and women always made sure there was food left for the Watchers. She took a handful of apples and a few hard pieces of bread, tucked them into the pouches sewn within her furs, and vanished back into the trees. No one had seen, which was just the way she preferred things.

Moving through the upper trees, Ash followed a small group of fishers traveling down to the nearby lake. Their footsteps wore even deeper into the thick growth of the mountain forest. In some places, the forest grew so dark it remained a dim twilight even at full noon, and the few pathways wound around mottled hives of starlight flies, their patchwork homes giving off a soft glow. Children chased motes of light as they followed behind their parents.

"My cousin said there were strangers on the road again," one of the women below said. She was small and round with a broad but worried smile. Ash didn't recognize her, but from her beeswaxed pale leathers and the braided net woven into her long brown hair, she placed the woman as a Whitehead. "He says they're poking around more and more lately."

Another woman nodded beside her. She was older, with long strands of white hair streaking the fading brown. "Stonefolk," she said grimly. "Probably venturing out from their ruin on the coast."

"No," the round woman said. "Not these ones. They were carrying weapons, my cousin said, and their clothes were different. They didn't look like stonefolk to him. He said a few of them even had skin like ours."

"Diggers, then," the old woman spat. "Probably looking to see what they can find out in the graves. Fools, the lot of them. Might as well dig a grave for themselves while they're out there. They'll be lucky if even half make it back..."

Ash repressed a shudder. The women's talk of diggers and travelers brought to mind her journeys with the Old Wolf along the borders of the old kingdom, and those haunted ruins still ran a chill through her bones. The scars left from the stonefolk showed through the gaps in the forest, where trees refused to grow. Their slowly crumbling ruins reminded her of an exposed skeleton rotting long after the kill.

"Don't you get any closer now," the Old Wolf had warned her. "Watch from here for what might come out, and keep those we can from going in, but don't step on those cursed grounds yourself. Don't even look at them too long. The stonefolk used to steal away the clan children, and their ghosts still roam the ruins, waiting to claim unwary pups." The children would gasp and squeal around the fire, and play and laugh bravely in front of each other before bed, but in the dark as they lay awake, all of them held those warnings tight to their hearts. And as the years went on, many of them, Ash included, still carried shadows of those fears born by the light of the flames.

The mystery of the old kingdom haunted Ash. The idea of an entire people turning to stone overnight filled her with an unspeakable dread. Whatever had happened to them, whatever had brought about their sudden end, kept her awake through many nights. It was too clean an ending for such a bitter story.

Ash lowered her hood to wipe the sweat from her brow. The wolf's head was heavy and too warm, but she lowered it only as long as she needed. Its bright white fur would have been a beacon for anyone else traveling the forest, but she had learned to conceal herself in the trees a long time ago. The heavy white cloak stayed with her at all times.

The women below continued to talk about rumors they'd heard from all over the island, and Ash listened intently. The Salmon had begun their yearly migration downriver, and the Bear were pushing their patrols further downhill, which was how the Whitehead woman had heard the news of strangers in the first place. Intermarriages between the clans were common and helped to deepen the ties between communities, so it wasn't uncommon to get your news of the Bears from a Whitehead, or to learn the activities of the Beavers from a Salmon. Fighting wasn't unheard of between the clans, either, and so marriages were encouraged to build friendly ties.

When the women began to speak of the Wolf clan and their latest wanderings over the Turtle, Ash strained to listen, a sudden dread falling over her. *Would they come this way?* she wondered, but the women changed their talk to Beaver traders too quickly. Ash was left to continue wondering where the Wolves might be now, and what they might be doing. None had ventured into the Elderglade since the passing of the Old Wolf.

Wolf clan liked to venture along the vast stretches of ruined towns that lay between the wrecks of the old castles. They were still vigilant even two generations on, prowling the edges of crumbling relics while the rest of the clans gave them all a wide berth. Ash wondered sometimes which fear gripped her more tightly. Could some forgotten horror truly come crawling out from the old ruins even now? And what would the Wolves do when they found it?

The fishers finally reached the lake and Ash settled into a tall tree at the edge of the water, enjoying the cool air drifting off the waves. Men and women below waded through the shallows and climbed into small boats, casting their nets. The lake was nestled into the valley between five high mountains and was fed by several rivers from their icy peaks. Out here, one was free of the thick-shrouded forest, and so they could enjoy the sun in full. Children spread along the shorefront, even out of sight of their keepers, free to run and play when not learning the crafts of their clans.

Ash's attention drifted out to the center of the lake, and lingered. The water ran clear across the surface, and Ash could see schools of fish traveling through the shallows when the waves weren't too bad, but toward the center, it grew dark where the water fell too deep. It was in those depths that she'd first noticed the silhouette months ago. Only two great fingers breached the surface, two small rocky islands that a flock of gulls sat and swam and fished from. The rest of the mass, which looked to her like a hand, faded deep into the black. Some of the Elders of the clans liked to tell stories of how the stone giant had drowned when the lake was first created. A great storm had raged so long and so fiercely, it was said, that people could no longer count the days because the sky was too dark.

While the Elders told their stories, others said the rocks were simply a natural formation. On slow days, Ash sometimes wondered which story might be true. Sometimes, she even daydreamed of great stone titans sleeping in the mountains beneath her, the rocky surface of the hills little more than the shells of their eggs. She imagined mountains that rose to rival the stars, who strode through the sky with steps that shook the entire world.

Excited laughter shook her from her daydreams. Children were running along the far shoreline, away from the waters where they might disturb the fishers at work. Some splashed with nets of their own, but rarely did they manage to tangle anything besides each other. The lake poured through the mountains in the distance, curving around cliffs and forest bends until it fell out of sight completely, but Ash only needed to watch this one small stretch of shoreline. The world beyond was not her concern.

A small flock of red feathered birds from the two finger islands were lazily drifting over the water and sprawled along the shoreline. They drew the attention of the children, who crept low between the tall grass at the sand's edge to get a closer look. One carried a small bow and blunted arrow, a toy meant for training, and Ash stood to follow through the trees in case he started any trouble.

Up close, the birds were fairly large, their long beaks like sharpened knifepoints. Occasionally one would spear the water, rising with an impaled fish, while others settled into the warm sands in a large, protective flock, drying their feathers as they baked under the sun. A few of the more intrepid knifebeaks ventured further out into the grass where the children were smart enough to withdraw, and dug through the earth for roots and small game.

Ash came to rest just above the flock. She took one of the loaves she had saved from the morning meal and began to rain down crumbs onto the sand. Some knifebeaks walked over cautiously, pecking curiously with one eye on the surrounding forest. A few others wandered slowly closer, and then a few more, until the whole flock had joined, and Ash realized the entirety of her bread was gone. She shrugged. The birds had probably enjoyed it more than she would have anyway.

Hunger was starting to scrape at her insides, though, so she felt around her bag for an apple as the knifebeaks honked and pecked each other over the remaining scraps. She felt some guilt, she hadn't meant for the birds to get so worked up, but was relieved they never resorted to fighting. While they puffed up their feathers and hissed and honked, one of the other knifebeaks, less imposing but clever, used the distraction to take as much bread as he could for himself, then waddled off to the water at a breakneck pace while the others cried out. Ash laughed quietly enough that no one could hear.

Ash sat in the trees contentedly, enjoying her late meal, when she noticed a subtle movement in the woods beyond. She knew well the sounds and silences of the forest.

She tracked it through the brush and tall grass, catching glimpses of shadow through the swaying branches. It was too large to be a person but too low to the ground to be a moose or bear. And whatever it was, it was moving very quietly. The telltale mark of a predator.

She sniffed the air but found nothing.

The shadowed creature moved along the edge of the tree line, stalking the shore of the lake closer to the gathered clan fishers. The knifebeaks had yet to catch wind of it either, whatever it was stayed downwind. *Smart*, Ash thought, a hunter's instincts, and she realized only a second before it emerged from the woods what it had to be.

The serpent slithered into the reeds along the water's edge, poking a head the size of Ash's torso up just long enough to take stock of its prey. Its scales were midnight black and flecked with stars of red, roughly stacked one over another like thickly armored plates. It reminded her of the metal suits the stonefolk wore in the old stories. At the head of the serpent were two protruding nubs of horns just beginning to grow, and beneath were a pair of terrible red eyes. None of the birds took notice, nor did the children, who were thankfully on the other side of the flock from the serpent.

One of the knifebeaks wandered closer to the reeds, unaware. It was probably looking for a warm rock to sun itself on. "Come on," Ash whispered, hoping it would notice the predator. The knifebeak continued forward as it looked this way and that, giving a small, confused honk at some instinct that came too late. The serpent struck. At full length, it rose taller than a man. Its fangs pierced the side of the knifebeak as the poor bird panicked and squawked in confused terror, pecking helplessly at scales too thick for bone to pierce. The rest of the flock was rising now, puffing up their chests and racing forward, but it was too late. The serpent pulled the bird back through the reeds into the tall grass, vanishing into the depths of the forest.

The children started to scream, pointing at where the serpent had been. Fishers wading the shoreline dropped their nets and baskets to run to their side. People grouped together, moving further down the shore from where the snake had struck, and keeping far from the forest's edge. Some had taken up weapons while others sounded the shrill, trilling horns that warned a predator from the Deepwood had been spotted. Someone else called for the Watchers, not knowing that Ash was already here.

This was the nature of the forest, she reminded herself. Predator hunted prey. Taking a life wasn't done for cruelty but hunger. The serpent had probably slept through much of the winter and was only hunting now that the snows had left. She told herself that there were fish in the lake who would live another day because the knifebeak wasn't there to eat them, but no matter how she tried to justify it, the violence weighed on her. She took the last bite of her apple, tossed the core to the remaining flock below, and took off after the serpent.

With the fishers already aware of the threat, Ash's duty was to follow the serpent's trail and make sure it didn't linger in the mountains, or worse, take nest in one of the many caves that wormed through the rock.

She was glad she was already here. Ash was quieter in the woods than the other Watchers. Wolves always made the best hunters. Watchers were trained to move silently, but for Ash, it was her nature.

The Old Wolf had trained her to hunt and track, but Ash still found the serpent difficult to follow. Scattered red feathers marked only as far as the forest's edge, after which the knifebeak must have been swallowed whole. The flattened grass and flowers were already straightening, but she followed their bent stalks further into the wood. In a few places, where they grew too thickly for the serpent to squeeze between them, bark had been stripped right off the trees.

Thankfully, the surrounding trails were devoid of travelers. Ash fought to keep her pace even, training flattening her fear for others into the steady march of duty.

She followed the trail into the hills until she heard something moving in the distance. Clumsy footsteps trampled through the woods, snapping branches underfoot. It wasn't the serpent, but something else. Something small. Ash picked up her pace through the branches. If the serpent was still nearby, it would hear the sounds as well, and Ash needed to make it there first.

She was horrified to find a lone child with dark soot under his eyes—a Magpie—chasing a very large frog along the edge of a small stream. The frog was fat and frantic, leaping ahead as the child splashed through the shallows behind it. The young Magpie caught the bulbous creature in his hands and lifted it to his face, laughing.

Then the grass rustled, and Ash knew the danger had already come.

The Magpie noticed as well. Silence fell on the forest like a sudden rain, the stillness at the eye of the storm. Either the boy had been taught well by his elders, or it was primal instinct. He released the frog back into the stream silently before grasping a large stick at his feet, slowly swiveling to the many shadows of the forest.

Good instincts, Ash thought, reaching for the axe at her side. She should use a bow, but she'd always been a poor shot. The axe was more familiar in her hand anyway, the Old Wolf had made sure of that, its leather handle long molded to the shape of her palm.

Eyes wide, the boy crept slowly and quietly to the base of a tall tree, never taking his eyes from the grass, but he didn't have the chance to climb.

The serpent rose from the green, its tongue flickering, tasting the air, and then it leapt forward. Ash dropped from the trees in silent fury, landing just behind the boy. He screamed and swung his heavy branch as Ash's axe matched its arc, catching the underside of the serpent's chin and deflecting its fangs into a nearby tree.

"Stay behind me," Ash said to the Magpie. "Don't run." The young boy didn't move, stick drawn, a determined scowl masking his fear. She pushed him by the shoulder and forced him back, keeping her eyes on the serpent as it unburied its fangs from the bark. Slowly, its eyes set on her, it rose to over twice her height with a long, rattling hiss.

Her own green gaze reflected back in its twin pools of blood. Briefly, her mind went back to stories of the stonefolk, and the tales of serpents who could turn men to stone with their gaze.

"I don't want to hurt you," she whispered. The serpent's tongue flashed again, perhaps searching for others like her. Unfortunately for Ash, she was alone. The serpent half-lunged, pulling back just as fast, trying to gauge how well Ash reacted. She held firm, as the Old Wolf had taught her. The serpent hissed again, and she answered with a howl.

Scraping bark behind her told Ash that the Magpie was climbing the tree, and her eyes flicked to check on him. The serpent noticed, lunging forward with two great fangs the size of her forearm. Ash rolled to the side, and they sank deep into the dirt. A raven cried out overhead as a great coiled whip cracked into her back, the serpent's tail spinning around, and she rolled into the grass, the ground tilting away beneath her.

Ash leaned into the fall, tumbling over rocks and thorns and the whip-sharp grass, hissing pain and spitting dirt as the serpent bit the earth behind her. The wind knocked from her as she tumbled over a heavy tree root, pain blooming in her chest. In her frenzied spin, she caught sight of the Magpie again, watching from the trees high above. *Safe.*

The serpent's eyes were twin red lanterns swimming down through the tall grass, following Ash into the clearing where the hills finally leveled. She rolled to her feet and caught herself on a tree, swinging the axe as the serpent struck again. There was a resounding crack as it split into scales that felt more like ancient bark than flesh, and the snake gave a loud hiss of surprise, or perhaps even fear, as warm blood gushed from the wound. Ash felt sick at the sight of her axe coated red.

She struck again, but the serpent bent low, retreating into the grass. It knew now that she wouldn't be easy prey, so it slunk back into the forest, away from the lake and the Elderglade.

Ash trembled in the silence that followed, shoulders heaving as she watched every shadow through the trees and every twitch of the foliage. Beneath the sounds of her own ragged breathing, she heard creatures slowly returning to the grass. There was a timid chorus of birdsong in the trees at first, then the soft drone of insects resuming their work, and finally, further away, the call of a bullfrog. Only then did she let herself fall to her knees, half in relief, half in exhaustion. Her whole body was sore from the tumble down the hills, and a long thin gash ran from elbow to hand where a fang must have caught her. It began to sting in the cool spring air.

"Are you okay?" asked the young Magpie. His voice echoed across the forest as he scampered down the tree.

Another labored breath stitched in her sides. "I'm fine," said Ash, finally loosening her grip on the axe. Her fingers were bone white. "Are you hurt?"

"No," said the boy, checking over his arms and legs after he'd run down to her side. "You're bleeding, though. A lot." He walked over and pulled at her cloak. There was a rip in the wrappings on her forearm, and her free hand was slick.

"I can help," said the Magpie, tugging at her cloak and urging her to sit. He looked seven, maybe eight, but his face was stern and studious. "My mom taught me. Let me see."

"I'll be fine," Ash insisted, although she was unsure of how true that actually was. She flexed her arm, hoping the serpent wasn't venomous, and winced at the sting. At least it could move.

"No, you're hurt. Let me help," the Magpie said. He started to undo her wrappings carefully, and although Ash winced as he peeled the leather off her skin, she didn't stop him.

He gasped when he wiped away the blood.

"What's wrong?" Ash asked, already knowing the answer.

The Magpie looked up at her in confusion that slowly turned to fear, and he took a large step backward. His eyes were wide, locked with hers, not daring to turn away. "Are you a spirit?"

Showing under her thick furs and leather wrappings, beneath the pooling blood, Ash's pale skin was clear. She had the skin of the stonefolk, likely nothing like the boy had ever seen.

"No," said Ash sharply, wincing as she wrapped her arm tightly under her cloak. She'd heard enough of those questions as a child. "Now come with me. We need to get you back to the Elderglade."

The Magpie hesitated before taking her hand in his. His eyes stayed fixed on her, while Ash kept hers on the forest. She couldn't walk the boy back through the treetops, but it was far more difficult to see through the green from so low on the ground.

They were only walking a short while before the Magpie's fear subsided. "Why is your hair like that?" he asked, pointing to the free strands of red that fell from between the wolf's head hood. "Did you always look like that? Where did you come from?" Ash sighed quietly. The Old Wolf had once told her these questions came from a place of innocence. Ash had even wondered them herself, but they still wore at her patience.

Magpie poked his fingers at all the freckles on her hand. "A Salmon girl told me once that birthmarks show how you died in your last life," he said curiously.

"Maybe I ventured too far alone into the tall grass and got lost in the brambles," muttered Ash. Magpie mistook her bitter bite for humor, and laughed.

When they reached the edge of the clangrounds, Ash spotted a young Magpie woman looking nervously into the forest. The young Magpie boy noticed too and ran to her excitedly. They hugged, the Magpie woman holding him tight and asking where he'd been.

Ash disappeared into the trees before he could look back. Her arm stung as she pulled herself into the canopy, but it would heal in time. She would see the medicine women in the morning if it looked worse.

When the Magpie boy went to point her out, Ash was already gone. A ghost in the forest. The young boy's mother looked to the upper trees instead and began to wave. Although she couldn't see exactly where Ash might be, Ash could see them, and she watched as Mother Magpie nudged her son, who finally remembered to call out "Thank you!" Mother did the same.

This was Ash's role. Her purpose. The children of the forest would always be safe, knowing that there was always someone watching over them.

Ash rarely slept for long, so it was late in the night when she descended to the forest floor again. Tufts of smoke were rising from the many tents and longhouses and the burrows dug into the earth. Living beneath the ground was warm enough, but the clans were always bringing the elders more wood to keep their fires strong. The clan families all worked hard to keep their elders comfortable, and the Watchers worked in turn to keep the families safe. Even at the height of their power, the boldest of the stonefolk's warriors had never made it this far into clan lands, and there were few Elders living today who could even remember those times. Word had spread about the serpent as the boy dramatically reenacted the tale of his rescue. Ash shook her head, suppressing a smile. She could almost believe that he had bound her wounds and carried her back to the glade himself. But while his tale of heroism grew to fable, what remained true was that he had saved her from having to recount the story herself. For that, she was grateful. As the story spread wide, the other Watchers would send other patrols further into the woods to make sure things were safe.

In the dark away from the fires, between the quiet of night, Ash dropped from the trees before a tiny sapling growing from a collapsed burrow. Guided only by the sparse light of

Grandmother Moon and the many children that trailed in her wake, Ash knelt. The tiny sapling barely rose to her chest, but the first leaf of the season had sprouted.

"Hello, Ingan," she whispered. "I fought a serpent today." She looked at her hands, and for a moment, they still seemed stained in red. "I…I'd like to think you would have been proud. I didn't want to fight, but I did. It was going to hurt one of the children. I didn't kill it, though," she said, her voice a conflicted chorus of guilt and relief. "I just…drove it off."

The Old Wolf had taught Ash everything she knew about hunting and fighting, but she had never managed to convince Ash she should want to kill. Even now, Ash ate fruits and vegetables and bread over meat. "What sort of Wolf dines on apples?" the Old Wolf would tease, but she had never insisted. Ingan had been the only one to stand for her against the rest of the pack.

"I still don't know if I made the right decision."

The sapling listened in silence.

Somewhere overhead, a raven cawed. Ash straightened, berated herself for her lapsed guard, and caught sight of something moving through the trees. The presence crept with practiced quiet, but without the deadly silence of a predator. Ash followed it through the trees until moonlight fell on the shoulders of a small-framed, green-haired girl.

"Hey, Ash. How you doing?"

Ash let the tension fall from her shoulders and smiled even as a pang of annoyance shook through her.

"You snuck off into the ruins again, didn't you?"

Leaf held a finger to her lips over a wide smile as she stepped into the open glade. "Just got back. No one has to know, right?" This was their secret. Leaf had been going to the ruins for months, no matter how many times Ash told her not to.

"You wouldn't ask if you didn't know it was wrong," Ash said quietly. "Why are you always sneaking around like that?"

"Wasn't sneaking," said Leaf, looking curiously at her feet. "Everyone else is just too loud."

Ash didn't want to argue. "Where were you off to this time?"

"You sure you want to know?" Leaf teased, and Ash had to fight to keep a smile from her face. She was a Watcher. She was supposed to be stern about these sorts of things. She shouldn't tolerate this kind of behavior, especially in front of the Old Wolf, but Leaf had a way about her that set Ash at ease, which wasn't an easy thing to do. "I've got something really great to show you, if you promise to keep it secret."

"You can't bring things back here," Ash said, searching the trees overhead for shadows. A howling sparked a twitch in her fingers. "I'm already taking a risk not informing the Watchers *right now*. There's dangerous things out in the woods, do you realize that? I can't let you keep doing this."

Leaf waved off her concern and started digging through her pack. "You're not *letting* me, you're just not *stopping* me."

Ash buried her face in her hands. "Those are the same thing."

Leaf thought for a moment, then shrugged. "Fine. I won't show you, then," she said, cupping something tightly in her hands. Ash took a step back. "Too bad, too," Leaf continued. "It's really neat. I'm gonna ask Koomis about it in the morning." With that, the girl bounced off into the woods, almost silent, though the wind seemed to follow her through the trees. "I'll look for you tomorrow!" she called, her voice barely a whisper.

Ash sighed. Leaf was one of the few people who didn't look at her strangely, and it was for that reason alone that she had kept quiet about her ventures off into the ruins. But the thought of what she might have seen at the ruins ran a chill through Ash's spine. For a moment, she wondered if she should follow Leaf, even raising a hand after her, but the sudden sting that shot through her arm told her that this was a worry for another day.

She'd have preferred not to show herself at all, but Ash forced herself into the tent of the medicine women further on in the glade. Hidden under her cloak, with only her bloodied arm showing, they applied crushed flowers and herbs to the wound before rebinding it, then Ash wordlessly returned to her place in the trees. Grandmother Moon was out in full tonight, and from her place high in the canopy, Ash lifted her wolf's head for the first time that day, her mane of bright red hair drifting in the wind. She fought off the urge to howl.

Tracing along her arm where the serpent had left its mark, she was sure now that it would scar. The Old Wolf had collected many over her years, and Ash only saw it as an honor. She had traded wound for wound with the horned serpent, and if that was the price of keeping the children of the clan safe, she would pay it every time.

4

FINCH

THE SEEKER OF LOST THINGS

"I'm not paying that," said Finch, scoffing indignantly as she pushed past the fisherman in her path. His speech was a slur of tongues, salted with tall tales to drive up the price of the day's catch. The sea's bounty surrounded them to the edge of every horizon, and still he somehow thought she needed his help to eat.

The walkways were packed with every sort of parasite one could find on the water; robed preachers and charlatans boasting prayers and snake oil, burly sailors' booming laughter shaking over the docks, disciplined navy men marching in strict formation, and rough-looking sorts in ragged clothes who seemed all too eager for a fight. She kept her distance from all of them as best she could, although she felt a brief pang of kinship for the ragged men.

There were far too many children underfoot to count. Finch was reasonably sure that only half would rob her if given the chance, but the other half would be quick to look away when they did. She eyed a wiry pickpocket making his rounds amongst the hurried crowds and danced a small knife between her fingers when he looked her way. The child took the hint, venturing off elsewhere on the docks.

Finch did not care for the Flotilla. It was the largest gathering of ships anywhere on the Broken Waters, they said, practically an island nation itself. The rough motley of boats weathered all the dangers of storm and sea while remaining bound by the rules of the land, making it the worst of both. To Finch, the inhabitants were nothing more than frightened ducklings, pressing together for safety against a sea they weren't ready for and too fool to realize that the greatest dangers always came from other people. The Flotilla was an oil stain on the water, living above but never with the sea, and ever at odds with its own nature. There was no freedom to be found here.

"Am I the only one feeling hunger?" the captain asked, scratching the pit of his ruined eye. The pain always burned in him, he'd once told her, but he had gotten used to it long ago. Now it was just his itching wounds that bothered him.

Finch had to suppress a shudder. "I could eat," she said, eyeing the nearby market stalls. They clustered like barnacles over the decks, but the smell of their cookfires mingling with the sea salt breeze set her mouth to water. Aside from the typical fish and dried meats, hints of various spices and fruits and other rare things hung in the air.

"We should be careful with our coin, Keresh," said Tamn. Her voice was cool and quiet in stark contrast to the boisterous Captain Beldrick. Sometimes, Finch thought his shouting could be heard halfway across the sea.

The captain was already on his way to a small fruit stand, where rows of bright lemons and peaches and plums stood on display. Tamn sighed and followed after him. *Sidetracked again.* They were sure to be late for their meeting with the new client at this point, although Finch didn't mind making rich old men wait their due.

"And what is it we are having here?" the captain asked, clapping his hands excitedly. The young girl behind the stall looked half asleep, but she jumped awake at his booming voice. Her eyes wandered to the captain's burned side, which he insisted on leaving open to the air, before snapping pointedly away, back to the others. Finch bemoaned the lost opportunity to nick something.

"We sell fruit," the girl managed to stutter.

The captain knelt low enough to match her height and turned the good side of his face to her, smiling broadly. His voice fell to something warmer and even more friendly. "I am seeing this, and it is all looking very delicious. Impressive, to be running a business at such a young age."

That was nonsense, of course. Her family would have put her up to this. Finch doubted she had any choice in the matter. Her father, if she had one, was probably sleeping off a drink somewhere while she kept the business afloat.

The compliment worked its charm, however, and the little girl raised her eyes back to the captain's, smiling. She spoke so quietly that Finch could barely hear her, but the captain just leaned forward and nodded, taking a coin purse from his vest.

"Two for the fruit," he said, walking the coins over his fingers and into her palm, "and one in secret for the girl who is selling it, yes?" They smiled together at that, and then he helped himself to four peaches. The excitement in the young girl's eyes made Finch wonder if she had ever been given coin of her own before. If she was smart, Finch thought, she would hide it away before her family returned. If she was even smarter, then everything she had told the captain, including her name, would have been a lie.

"Keresh," Tamn grunted dutifully, "we don't have a lot of money to throw around." She looked down at the peach he handed her as if it were some rodent. "We have food back on the ship."

"Probably even more at the Halfmug, if we ever get there," Finch reminded them both.

"Salted meats, dried meats, hard biscuits, and biscuit soup, yes," the captain sighed, "but not in a long time are we having a peach so sweet as these." The captain took a deep bite, the juice running out the side of his cracked lips, and wiped his face with the back of his hand. "We are to be enjoying what we can, while we can. There is never telling what tomorrow is bringing."

Nonsense. Finch was reasonably certain that tomorrow only ever held another swift kick in the teeth, and she preferred to brace herself. The captain wasn't as keen on planning for the future, however, and while he called the shots, their money went wherever he whimmed it. That was probably why, Finch reasoned, they were so desperate to take this job in the first place. Still, the captain's approach had carried him through twenty odd years of war and mercenary work, so she supposed there was something to his madness. That, or he was simply very, *very* lucky.

When the captain almost finished with his peach, he threw the rest into the sea. Finch was halfway through her own, carefully guarding it from the tightly pressed crowd and taking furtive bites. Tamn, ever the practical sort, seemed determined not to enjoy it out of principle, taking stoic, almost pained-looking bites.

"You shouldn't waste food," Finch chided the captain, watching the remains of his peach sink below the waves. "I would have eaten the rest."

"A kindness to the waters below, so they might be kind in turn," said the captain, nodding as if it was some kind of wisdom.

"Superstition," she said, shoving the rest of the peach into her mouth. She nearly choked on the pit. "And a waste of good food."

"Superstition is another way of saying old truths, I am once being told. It is advice that carries well."

Finch shook her head, but she knew better than to continue arguing. While Keresh Beldrick might be a pleasant person, he was also as stubborn as they came. Once his mind was set on something, there was little anyone could do. That must have been how he managed to bring Tamn to his side, because the woman seemed to dislike everyone and everything. Even Ridae, who was back watching their ship, had only a little more charm than the spiders one might find between stacks of firewood. The captain's easy but commanding presence was how he'd recruited Finch, although service was the furthest thing from her mind when she'd first spotted his sail.

"You will be leaving the talking to me, yes?" the captain asked her in a way that made it clear it really wasn't a question at all.

"I already apologized for last time," Finch groaned.

Captain Beldrick laughed long and loudly. "Yes, I am remembering this apology," he said. "I am also remembering the many sweet things I am not eating even now. On the day that I pass from this world, the rare delights of the fruit gone uneaten shall be among my many regrets. Perhaps there will be sweeter things waiting for me in the next life, yes?"

Finch turned away from his concerns and stared with disdain into the sea. Their last escort, a fat-faced fruit merchant with more cents than sense, had wanted them to serve as glorified bodyguards. He hadn't made his fortune by being generous with wages, and so the crew's stipend was just enough to prevent revolt. He also ate so much of his own wares that Finch thought it a miracle he had anything left to sell. She wasn't sure if she had said that part out loud, but she had definitely done something to rattle his delicate shell. Maybe many somethings. The last time she'd seen him was when his boat left them behind, spitting in rage, his face near as purple as his plums.

Finch followed behind the captain for a long while as he asked around for directions. Finally, after far more walking than she thought should be allowed on the sea, they found it. The place was a run-down tavern ship with tattered sails, a ruddy coat of paint and grime, and air thick with the smell of cheap ale. A small iron sign bent into the shape of a half-empty mug hung over the doorway, and thick black smoke drifted through cracks in the dirty windows.

It was exactly her kind of place.

"Don't cause any trouble," said a well-muscled man with complicated tattoos that ran the breadth of his arms and under his short shirt. He nodded at them as they walked through the entryway, giving Finch a second glance before noticing the knife at her side. It was one of many. She gave him her meanest look and sidled up close to the captain, and the man shrugged before stepping aside.

The inside of the Halfmug was even worse than out. The porthole windows were so stained with soot and smoke that the sun was a distant dream in this dreary place. Candles sat at every table, and although most were unlit, the few that were threw up enough acrid fumes that black smoke gathered in clouds along the ceiling.

The few patrons turned to eye the newcomers. A withered man with a stern face and the memory of strong arms watched from the bar, giving the captain and crew a curt nod. A row of bottles of various shapes and colors lined the shelves behind him, but Finch guessed that a good half of them were filled with the same washed-down blend of ale and seawater. Stained glass was good for hiding whatever terrible things you wanted behind the right colors.

"What was our guy's name again, Captain?" Finch asked, looking around at the sad collection of derelicts.

"He is calling himself Wright, I am being told. You are calling him 'Yes, sir.' Are we in understanding?"

"Yes, sir," Finch muttered, rolling her eyes. The captain laughed to himself.

Looking over the clientele of the tavern ship, Finch didn't notice anything particularly impressive. There were a few men huddled in a corner playing dice, but they were all fairly young. She glanced suspiciously at another young man who was dressed in what must be his least ragged outfit, speaking with a comely young woman over a shared pie that Finch recognized as eel. He seemed far more interested in the conversation than she did.

There were sad old men sitting around drinking their remaining days away, and sad not-quite-as-old men doing their damndest to catch up. A younger fellow with rust red hair was nursing a bowl of brown-looking sludge that she could only suppose was stew. In the corner booth behind him, however, she spotted the old man in the red coat.

He's already watching us, Finch realized. Both the old man's hair and beard were snow white and neatly cropped. He was scarred, with knicks on his ears and face, and probably many more under his neatly tucked sleeves. His coat was pristine despite its long years of wear and seemed to be of a naval make, although any patches or emblems looked to have been lost long ago. Dark rings ran circles around his eyes, which seemed almost yellow in the light of the low tallow candle. It pushed deep shadows into the crags of his skin as well, giving him a gaunt, hungry look.

"Found him," said Finch, directing the group over to Wright's booth.

The captain led their approach. "Greetings to you, my friend," he said, vigorously shaking the old man's hand as they sat down. "The *Dragon's Breath* is hearing your call, and here we are to answer."

Wright returned the handshake firmly and nodded curtly to Finch and Tamn. "Bartender," he called, waving to the corner. His voice was harsh and torn, as if he were speaking through a throat full of broken glass. "A round of drinks for my company and I." He finished off the last of a tall mug. "Captain Beldrick, it is a pleasure to make your acquaintance at last. I must say, it's good to finally put a face to the stories."

"A good face for good stories, I am hoping?" Keresh laughed.

"Depends on which side of the battles you were on. Hero or monster, your character changes with who's telling." The old man looked at him skeptically, sizing the captain up. Tamn, always on guard, was looking over her shoulder to see if they had walked into some sort of trap, and Finch followed her lead. "The one thing all the tales have in common, however, is that you are an exceedingly competent man."

"And on which side of the battles are you falling?" the captain asked, one hand dropping to his side. "I am coming a long way to speak with you. I hope it is not only to inflame old wounds."

"No. We've never fought," the old man said, waving his concerns aside. "My homeland was gone long before you came sailing along." With his lack of emblems and patches, Finch didn't find this to be entirely a surprise. Nations didn't last long in the Broken Waters. There was simply too much territory spread too thinly for anyone to hold it all. Rarely did anything grow larger than the free cities of the islands, and even those were unruly.

"But you are a navy man," the captain said.

"Once," Wright agreed, somewhat wistfully. "When I was young."

The captain nodded to the old man's coat. "And your uniform. It is not causing us trouble in the journey ahead, I am hoping."

"I doubt anyone alive even remembers these colors." Wright laughed bitterly at that.

The bartender came by with their drinks. It was a poorly brewed ale for poorer company, but Finch found it chased off her thirst well enough. She carefully watched which glass the old redcoat reached for and drank from it before he could, just in case he was up to something.

"Well, to being young again," the captain said, raising his glass. He wasn't near as old as Wright, but he had hit his forties some years prior. He often liked to complain about how his reflexes had slowed, and how the aching in his leg always got worse before heavy rains. Having seen him in action herself, Finch was sure he was playing it up.

Wright lowered his glass quickly. "I'll cut right to the heart of the matter. I would hate to waste your time," he said, with the air of a man who very much felt his time was being wasted. Finch didn't care for him already. "I'm looking to charter transportation on your vessel and further overland escort and protection to my final destination."

The captain leaned back and downed his drink. "This destination being?" He opened his hands in a gesture of friendly confusion. Finch doubted he hadn't already learned everything there was to know about their prospective new client. The captain might like to play dumb at times, but his coy ease only reminded her of the swamp lizards that liked laying down in the water, looking for all the world like harmless driftwood.

"Turtle Rock."

The captain raised a brow at the name, but his face remained flat. He stared the old man down impassively. "A difficult place to reach, it is said."

"Not so difficult for one as well traveled as you," Wright countered, nodding at the captain. "Your reputation precedes you, both in deed and capability. There's a reason I asked for you by name."

Yeah, because no one else was crazy enough to take the job, Finch thought. She hated flattery and doublespeak. It was a delicate waltz, and she wanted nothing more than to put a hammer to its knees.

The captain smiled again. His was brash and boisterous without a trace of false modesty. "It is true. I am walking half the hundred isles of these Broken Waters," he said, flagging down the bartender for another drink. "And still I seek to see the rest, but Turtle Rock is not a place I am visiting before. I can be taking you there, I am sure, but as guide in these lands, I fear I am ill-equipped. You might be better asking one of the natives."

"Neither hill savage nor ruin dweller are keen to welcome outsiders in their lands," the old redcoat said sternly. "And I'm afraid they would all lack the traits I seek regardless. Traits that you have in abundance. Besides, it's the waters that trouble me the most. Even experienced sailors know to avoid the shifting currents surrounding the island. You, however, are an accomplished navigator."

"This is true," the captain said, nodding again. "I can be bringing you to the island, yes, but it is a harder thing to guide the...be pardoning my words, the *inexperienced*, across lands of which I am knowing almost nothing."

A new voice spoke behind them. "I might be able to help with that." Finch turned to the rust-haired man, barely past a boy, who was rising to his feet. Despite his forced stagger, and the hollow ease with which he leaned up against their table, Finch noticed his trembling knees. "The name's Reed," he said, extending a hand.

Wright refused to take it, eyeing his hand as if it might bite him, but the captain turned with a mix of surprise and interest. When no one shook his hand, the outsider continued. "Sorry, I didn't mean to listen in, but when I heard you say Turtle Rock, my ears perked up, you know? You're talking about my home. It's a beautiful place, but not the most friendly, as you might well know. Not if you're a stranger to it, anyway."

You wear that smile too easily, Finch thought. She distrusted smiles with intent behind them, especially when they suggested someone knew something you didn't.

Wright shifted in his seat, tucking his coat in at his chest. *Hidden weapon in the pocket?* Finch wondered. Wright's unease with the outsider's sudden appearance gave her an idea. She had found her hammer.

Finch nudged a chair gently with her foot, just enough so the stranger took notice. He sat at the end of their booth, waving for the bartender to bring him a drink. The captain chuckled and nodded his acquiescence to the bar rat's intrusion.

"So, what's the story, then?" Reed asked, lowering his voice to a dramatic whisper. "Exploration? Cartography? Forgive me for saying, Captain Beldrick, but you never struck me as the map-making sort. I'm thinking treasure hunting is the name of the day, yeah?"

Only after a swig from his refilled glass did the captain respond. "You are knowing of me?"

"Stories pass through here," Reed said, weaving his fingers together, "and I like to collect. You can hear all sorts of fascinating things on the Flotilla if you listen well enough."

"We're not interested in story time," Wright barked, waving the young man away.

"I bet you do," Finch said, ignoring the old man and looking directly at Reed. She held back a self-satisfied smirk. The captain watched her carefully, probably considering the very close runaround shc had done on his orders. Sure, she wasn't allowed to speak with the client, but nothing had been said about friendly conversation with barflies. And if that barfly and the old redcoat didn't happen to get along, well, the blame for that certainly couldn't be placed on her.

The captain watched her, laughing to himself before nodding to Reed. "Go on."

"Well, every sailor on the Broken Waters has heard stories of Turtle Rock," Reed said, leaning into the table. The candlelight caught his features in their soft glow, igniting an excited shine in his eyes. "Cursed lands guarded by savage clans and feral beasts. It's a dangerous venture, and not for the light of heart. They say only fools brave the storms and shifting currents around the island, but those who do are left to pick over the bones of their fallen kingdom. The stoneshaper's treasures are still plentiful in the wild, if only you're able to reach them. You've heard of the stoneshaper kings, yeah?"

"Stories and tall tales, all of it," Wright scoffed. "I'm looking to lead a serious expedition here, son, not some child's tale of a treasure hunt."

"The tales are what drew you out though, am I right?" Reed asked, not missing a beat. *He glides from point to point like he's soaked in snake oil.* "I can't imagine why someone would be so interested in such an out-of-the-way island if it weren't for what they'd heard about it."

"You are right," the captain said. He broke a wide grin that showed too many teeth and cracked the burned side of his face. "We are all hearing the stories. And if half of them are being true, I would be seeing many and more rich men on the seas. But here we are," he said, gesturing at the dingy tavern.

If Reed was put off by the captain's cracked lips, he didn't show it. He looked ready to say something further, but Wright barked impatiently.

"You weren't invited to this discussion, son." His heavy boot tapped slowly under the table, and Finch caught sight of his ground-down sole. "If I wanted stories, I would have sat with the drunks. I'm here to discuss business."

"Yes, exactly," said Reed, nodding in agreement. "You need transportation over the seas, and further escort along the land." Finch's eyes narrowed. *He was listening longer than he said he was.* "Unfortunately," Reed continued, "it seems Captain Beldrick, and I mean this with much respect, lacks the knowledge to fully plan your journey. While I wouldn't doubt his prowess in providing protection, it would be far easier if he had knowledge of someone native to the island." He spread his hands, as if to mean himself.

"You don't even know what the job is," growled Wright.

"But I know *where* it is," Reed countered, "and it sounds like I know the island better than anyone here. Again, respectfully speaking." He raised his hands in contrition and backed his chair from the table slowly. "My apologies for intruding. Like I said, when I heard you mention home, I couldn't help but overhear. If you don't need my help, I won't push the matter."

Either the captain was amused with the young man's pitch, or he had taken the bait. Finch couldn't guess which. He gestured for Reed to stay and sit. "Please then, tell us what you are offering."

Finch could see that the old redcoat was fuming beneath his forced decorum. The bold young man was working under his skin in a way she wasn't allowed, and she couldn't help but twist the knife a little. "Got any unique skills?" she asked.

Reed spoke some words in a tongue she didn't know. They all looked at each other, confused. All save for Wright, that is, whose expression only darkened.

"I just introduced myself as Reed of the Salmon, child of the Great Turtle Rock. If you're going to be heading that way, it's probably good to bring someone who speaks the language."

It was impressive if true, but of course they had no way of confirming he was being honest or if he'd simply spouted a bunch of gibberish.

Tamn, dour as ever, ruined things for her by pointing this out. "How do we know what you just said was true?"

"If, between the four of you, you need to ask, then you definitely need a translator," Reed said, smiling. "Besides that, why would I want to venture somewhere I know nothing about and offer myself as the go-between with people who have a reputation for killing outsiders?"

"Even if what you say is true, I don't recall inviting you to this negotiation," said the old redcoat.

"So, it is a negotiation then."

"My intention was to hire the crew of the *Dragon's Breath*," Wright seethed. "Not some half-washed vagabond with a penchant for wordplay."

"I know more than just wordplay," said Reed. "I know the Turtle as well as anyone else on the Flotilla. Half the roads on the island have been swallowed up by the forest, and the other half are half as bad. What's left is a realm of beasts and brigands and things that go bump in the night. The first two you can handle, surely, but you'll be wanting someone who can tell you what's waiting out there in the dark. You want someone who knows what I know."

Wright had heard enough. "Superstitious nonsense shared by broken men," he spat. "Do you believe those stories are of use to anyone?"

"Superstition is the ghost of old truths," Reed countered, and Finch knew then that he had sealed the deal.

"My friend is being right," the captain said, gesturing to him and the old redcoat. "He did not come here to hire you. He came to hire the crew of the *Dragon's Breath*."

Wright nodded, letting loose a slow sigh of relief. He was about to shoo Reed aside, but the captain continued.

"My young friend, welcome to the crew."

The rest of the conversation was more negotiation of payment, timetables, and travel between Wright and the captain, which was the sort of talk that threatened to put Finch to sleep. Wright would be accompanying them back to the ship tonight, while Reed planned to meet them in the morning. Apparently, he had things to gather.

The trip back to the ship was uneventful. The captain wanted to browse the various wares, of course, and they passed foods and cooks and ships with more strange, thick smoke billowing from their hulls. A man dressed in long, flame-colored robes bowed to Finch and gestured for her to enter, but she continued in the direction of the ship. Another man, shifty-eyed and with a knife poorly hidden at the small of his back, offered to find some good work for her; she refused him with a fist to the stomach.

The captain seemed right at home with the other captains and merchants who were all too eager to trade stories and news of the Broken Waters. He descended into the bowels of some dark-hulled ship, laughing alongside cloaked men who wore colored lenses over their eyes. Tamn was left to lead Wright back to the ship alone while Finch, not wanting to bother with the old redcoat, waited for them to disappear before she went to find her own way back.

Only when she returned through the maze of walkways and ships and obnoxious peddlers was she finally able to drop her guard. It had been only a year, but already the creaking hull of the *Dragon's Breath* called to her almost like a home, and she rested over the side of the deck, facing the water.

Silently, Ridae appeared at her side.

"You set out for one and came back with two. So, which red is ours, then. The coat? The hair? Or are they the same?" The robed figure bowed, their bug-eyed mask staring at her intently before leaning over the deck beside her. A lantern swayed gently at the end of a long staff held in their hand, sending shadows dancing across the ship.

"How do you do that?" Finch asked, irritated. They'd left Reed back at the Halfmug, but the lantern keeper had a way of knowing things. It made Ridae a great sentry for the ship, but it also unnerved Finch in a way she couldn't, or wouldn't, put to words.

"Do what?" Ridae asked with too-sweet concern. "I look, I see, I listen."

Finch sighed. "I'm not playing at riddles."

"And I'm not offering any. I'm telling you that a red-haired stranger has been the shadow to your flame ever since we arrived in this patchwork dream. I thought he might be the client getting a look at us in disguise. Was I right?"

Finch gritted her teeth. "You saying that little rat was following us right from the beginning?"

"By your surprise, I would guess that he was not, in fact, our client in disguise, and that you had a run-in with him anyhow. Tell me, how did that go?"

"He's our new crewmate," said Finch. "Said he had some things to pack, but he'll be joining us in the morning. The captain can tell you more."

"Oh dear," Ridae said, the sound of their *tsk tsk tsk* echoing hollowly inside their mask. "Well, he knows where to find us, at least. I don't suppose he had to ask for directions before departing?"

He hadn't. Finch realized she hadn't caught that, either, and stabbed a knife into the railing out of frustration.

"I'll take that as a no, then," said Ridae. "Strange. Normally you're so sharp about these things. But then, I guess we all only see what we want to see."

And like that, the lantern keeper disappeared back into the depths of the ship.

So, Reed had been following them right from the beginning. It burned her to even think about it. Finch wouldn't be mentioning that to the captain, of course, not wanting him to learn she had lapsed in attention. The lantern keeper, oddity that they were, probably wouldn't mention it either unless she brought it up first. They were too clever in their own strange way, but their attention was always shifting to something new. No, pretty soon, it would just be Finch who knew how Reed had played them. She didn't begrudge it, especially considering the way she had been recruited by the captain herself, but she resolved not to be played a fool again.

Finch danced her knife between her fingers, finding herself somewhere between gritted teeth and a grin. The next time Reed tried to get one over on her, she would gut him like the day's catch.

5

LEAF

THE ROOTED ELDERS

Leaf was woken with the sun slowly rising through her cupped fingers and a sharp cane jabbing her side.

"Up now, lazy child, unless you mean to be buried with me." Koomis was scowling down at Leaf, bracing against the dirt wall, and balancing precariously on her leg.

"Sorry," Leaf murmured. Her dream fell away like water through her fingers, cold stone walls melting into their earthen burrow. An early morning chill seeped in through the entryway, and Leaf rolled toward the wall, out of her grandmother's way. The space wasn't very large, but it was comfortable enough for a single person.

"You could sleep anywhere and still you choose the dirt," Koomis said, tutting as she hobbled over to their small chair. The burrow was a round room with a central fire and a few mounds of shaped earth. Draped with blankets, they became chairs, table, and a bed, and shelves dug into the walls displayed the few crafts that Leaf's grandmother had kept over the years. Between the shawls, charms, and art crafted by the clans, there was a poorly woven basket that Leaf had made when she was young; a crude doll that had been her childhood companion sat beside it.

Her father's old hunting bow was on display as well, repaired and still waiting for him.

Leaf helped Koomis into her chair by the fire before going to find something to stoke the flame. She almost tripped over her bag in the entryway and nearly stopped to show Koomis what she had found in the ruins, but she didn't know what Koomis would think as it wasn't supposed to be in the Elderglade at all.

Only once the fire was at a gentle roar, with Koomis comfortable under several blankets, did Leaf finally sit on the floor beside her grandmother.

"Need anything?"

"No, I'm all right. Thank you, child. The only thing I'm lacking these days is quiet…" Her grandmother's voice had a sharpness to it like the hidden thorns beneath the brush. When Leaf was young, her grandmother's hair had already been going gray, and time had turned the last of it to white. Koomis was shrunken in her seat, her hands spotted and fingers curled like gnarled roots, and deep wrinkles folded her cheeks like draped curtains. Her eyes were still sharp, however, and missed nothing. She glanced at Leaf's pack. "You've been busy, haven't you?" Koomis wheezed, a wry smile creeping over her lips.

"Yup," Leaf answered, warming her hands by the fire. She hadn't realized just how much of a chill had fallen during the night. Usually, she woke up when it got this bad.

"Still haven't learned to rise with the sun, though." Koomis tutted again, and Leaf bowed her head, embarrassed. "Been running around all night again, have you?"

"No."

"Don't lie."

"I wasn't. I didn't run," Leaf said. She played with the embers of the fire using a small branch, making the flames dance. Koomis *harumph*ed sternly. "I walked very quietly and politely through the Elderglade so that I wouldn't wake anyone up," she said, enunciating carefully.

Koomis scoffed and drew the blankets tighter. "You know what I meant."

"I know what you *said*," Leaf argued. "People don't always say what they *mean*. It's very confusing."

If Koomis had a fault, it was not explaining her feelings clearly. This was common to just about everyone Leaf had ever met. People were always saying one thing when they meant another. Once, when she was very young, she'd let a good portion of their meal burn to cinders after Koomis had told her to "watch the fire." Leaf insisted, even as Koomis beat down the flames, that she had been watching the entire time.

"I suppose I should be thankful you were only gone a day instead of weeks. Anything you want to share with me?" Koomis asked, gesturing with her cane to Leaf's pack.

"Maybe," Leaf said. She knew her grandmother wouldn't approve of her trip into the ruins. "I'm not sure it's a good idea, though."

"Well, you've got the day to think about it then," Koomis said sharply. "I don't have much time this morning, and I need you to leave. Now."

Leaf was taken aback. "You're kicking me out?"

"Believe it or not, child, I do speak with others from time to time. Most of them are kind enough not to lay about on my floor."

Leaf brushed the dirt from her knees and stood. "I thought you didn't like visitors."

"I don't, and yet they come anyway. Hurry up now and take your things with you. I don't need anyone tripping over them." She waved a hand to the bag still at the entryway, its seams threatening to burst, and frowned. "I taught you to pack better than that, you know."

Leaf shrugged. "Takes too long." Hefting the bag over her shoulder, she remembered. Careful not to spill anything, she reached through to the bottom for a small bundle of meat and fur. "Almost forgot. This is for you." Hare had always been Koomis's favorite. "When can I come back?"

Koomis's eyes narrowed, however, on the iron lantern peeking out of the pack. "I thought I told you not to carry that thing around here."

Leaf kept her eyes to the floor, looking at anything that wasn't her grandmother's stern gaze. "You did."

"Then why do you still have it?"

"You never said I had to get rid of it."

Koomis sighed. A voice called down from the top of the burrow, asking if she was awake. Leaf quickly shoved her lantern further into her pack.

"Wait up there, I'm with my granddaughter," Koomis shouted. Then she turned to Leaf. "I'll have visitors most of the day. More and more are coming with the spring thaw. I don't expect I'll get much peace until sundown."

"But what if I want to ask you—"

"Come back at sundown," her grandmother insisted. "I suppose I won't be having any peace tonight then, either," she muttered, smiling gently. "That you have yet more questions is never a surprise, child, but you need to learn to wait for answers. With community comes responsibilities, and mine are at the door now." She sighed again, then called to the visitor.

The guest leaned his head down, careful not to catch his horned headdress on the ceiling as he entered. He was thin with the beaded braids and painted vest of a Deer craftsman. "I didn't mean to intrude," he said softly, studying the craftwork along the walls. Spiderweb charms hung everywhere, each finely made save for one at the center, its tightly pulled strings lopsided and uneven. That one belonged to Leaf, her very first. She couldn't understand why her grandmother kept it. "I'm here for the lesson?"

"Then why do you sound so unsure?" Koomis shook her head, waving her hand impatiently at a chair. "Don't mind my granddaughter, she was just leaving."

Leaf had been studying the detailing of the headdress, the curved and rounded ends of the young velvet antler, before she caught the hint. Then she waved a quick goodbye and scampered up the tunnel entrance. It was only once she was outside that she remembered the polite thing to do would have been to introduce herself to the young man before leaving.

The small village around the Elderglade was slowly waking, voices rising from burrows and tents and longhouses. Leaf hurried through drifts of charred smoke, ignoring the crackling fat of yesterday's hunts sizzling over the flames, but stopped a moment as a family laughed together behind the walls. The last remnants of the morning peace broke as children ran outside in packs and began to chase one another. They pushed past Leaf in feigned terror, one yelling that he was a beast from the Deepwood come to devour them, screaming and gnashing his teeth.

Leaf tried to ignore the noise, folding herself back into her thoughts, but was pulled from them just as quickly when a child ran right into her stomach. Leaf steadied herself as the child staggered backward, almost tripping over a root. She screamed when Leaf reached out to steady her. "Skinchanger!" the young girl shouted, running away.

Curious heads turned, their wariness fading when they realized it was just a children's game, but a few continued to watch Leaf when they thought she wasn't looking. She did her best to ignore the heat of their eyes on her back, her breaths picking up in lockstep with her pace.

Leaf knew the children were afraid of her, but sometimes she wondered if the adults were as well. She was practically a stranger to the clans, having just arrived with Koomis almost a year ago, and whispers circled the two of them. Bullhead and Bear, Lynx and Crane and Loon, all of them wondered about the outsiders who, while clearly of the people, did not belong to a clan. This had never been a source of shame for Leaf before, not when it was just her and Koomis traveling the Great Turtle, but now that she was among others…well, there was a reason she was always sneaking off.

From overhead, she could hear rustling leaves and rough footsteps in the high branches matching her pace. The Watchers had probably been drawn in by the children's screaming. Whoever was up there was far too loud to be Ash, so Leaf pretended not to notice them as well, and their rustling faded after a few minutes.

She wandered past the burrows of other elders and more empty tents, as the hunters departed early. The longhouses confused her most of all. Leaf was never one for staying in one place, and seeing trees felled and made into permanent homes felt strange to her. With a tent and trees for shelter, you could wander anywhere, but with one's home fixed so firmly in place, how were you ever supposed to see the world beyond it? Koomis was stuck now, too, because of her lost leg, and that made Leaf deeply uncomfortable. While she didn't like the thought of straying too far from her grandmother, she liked being confined to such a small span of the Turtle even less.

Crowds milled about where covered tables stood in a clearing, and Leaf joined to wait for food. It was a strange thing to have so much at hand, fruits and berries and warmed meat with bread, whatever you wanted whenever you wanted it. It was a far cry from the food-sparse nights of her childhood, when the day's hunt had turned up nothing, and they scraped through the last of their preserves while Koomis insisted she wasn't hungry. Leaf had to admit the abundance was one of the few upsides of clan life, even if she had to brave the crowds to share it.

Their chatter cut through the morning peace, the chorus of cluttered voices tangling together in her head. She startled when a bowl clattered suddenly on the table, dropped by a child, but besides her mother mopping up the mess, no one else even seemed to notice. The clamor of too loud conversations, children laughing and screaming and crying amongst themselves, drove the animals far off into the forest. Occasionally, someone gave Leaf a strange, questioning look, but most pretended not to see her at all.

A young girl with the stained red hair of Salmon carried a double portion of everything, carefully balancing it all as she walked. The cook checked and checked again to make sure she could hold it all before the girl went bounding off into the woods, probably running food to an elder or relative.

This was maybe the perfect excuse to return to Koomis early. Her brief walk among the clans was already wearing at her, the stares and whispers almost too much to bear. She couldn't waste the day lingering like this. When her turn came, she grabbed two of everything. The cook joked that Leaf was too big to be a food runner, which she thought strange, because she really wasn't that much taller than the children. Several of the younger boys were near her head, and a few were even taller. Balancing the meals in her hands, Leaf took back off toward Koomis's burrow, wondering how children did this so quickly without dropping anything. She managed to make it back with everything mostly intact, tripping only once.

"She already ate," said a voice from overhead as Leaf approached the burrow. Ash was like a whisper in the wind. "And she made it very clear she was to have no unexpected visitors."

Leaf leaned back and huffed, her feet wandering impatiently in place, then laughed at how well her grandmother knew her. Defeated, she held a handful of food over her head. "How about you, then? You eat yet?"

They had their morning meal in the low branches. Leaf found it difficult to climb with her pack so loaded down while carrying a meal in both arms, but she made it work. Ash picked at the fruit offered to her, and they watched together from the trees as others set off about their morning routines.

"How do you do this all day?" Leaf asked. She tore a large bite from a flank of deer, which Ash had traded for a second loaf of bread. "Nothing ever happens here."

"Not usually," Ash agreed. She stretched her fingers slowly, frowning more than usual under her wolf's head.

"I'd go crazy if I were you."

Ash's gaze fell to the ground, where a chipmunk scavenged quietly below. "I prefer when things are quiet."

Leaf nodded, the quiet holding between them for a moment. "I heard one of the kids saw a serpent yesterday."

"Yeah?"

"Yep. Overheard it by the cooks."

Ash nodded. A long strand of hair fell from the wolf's head, and she tucked it quickly back inside. "The others are on the lookout now in case it comes back."

"Well, I guess that's kind of exciting." Leaf bit her lip to keep her face straight and gave Ash a knowing look. "They should just send that Magpie boy out. The way I hear it, he's quite a fighter."

The two of them laughed as the Deer left Koomis's burrow and was quickly replaced by a gruff-looking Bear.

"I hate waiting around," Leaf said.

Ash hummed sympathetically through a bite of apple. "You should find something to do."

"Like what?" Leaf asked, gesturing emptily at the glade. "What are you doing today?"

Ash stared Leaf down for a long moment, then sighed. "Waiting."

Leaf huffed and dropped from the branch. "You're no fun sometimes, you know that?" she yelled up to the trees. "I'll see you later." She waited a moment for an answer, but the trees were silent. She caught a brief glimpse of white fur moving through the green, and then Ash was gone. From somewhere overhead, a raven cawed.

Her heavy pack reminded her of the herbs she'd gathered for the medicine women, so Leaf decided to pay them a visit. They thanked her kindly in their longhouse and treated the scrapes and cuts she'd gathered in the wood. The women *tsk*ed and tutted, lecturing her about how to do things properly. When Leaf offered to help, she was ushered out the door.

The rest of the clans were hard at work around the glade.

A Whitefish woman was teaching children how to make shakers from turtle shells. Leaf saw no use for noisemakers in the forest, and she gave them a wide berth.

A group of Bears stood under a small grove of trees. As she passed, Leaf heard them whispering something about the Wolves. There was rivalry there, she knew. Both clans served as eyes against trespassers, and they didn't always agree on how to deal with threats. Leaf moved on to the cookfires, where many were still hard at work stripping meat from bone and turning it into preserves. At first, they accepted Leaf's offer of help, but their methods quickly proved too different from hers. The cooks insisted things had to be done their way or not at all. Leaf chose not at all, grumbling to herself that her way was just as good.

The sun had not yet reached center sky, and Leaf was restless. She grasped the light between her fingers and imagined forcing the sun down over the distant mountains. The sky did not bow to her.

A garishly dressed Crane woman in a large feathered headdress passed by with a small escort, clucking amongst themselves. One looked down her nose at Leaf before moving on. Their eldest, Leaf knew, was almost as old as Koomis and had lived through the horrors of the stonefolk. While, unlike Koomis, he had family to retreat to, the experience still left him cautious of outsiders. For years, the Cranes had lived higher up in the mountains than almost anyone, and Leaf thought they felt they were better than the other clans for it, even though they'd dwelt in the lowlands and marshes before the stonefolk had come.

Wherever she went, Leaf found people were busy and either didn't need her help or wanted her to do things in ways she'd never learned. The hunters had already left for the morning, the fishers were already on the water, and the children were all collecting herbs and berries with their parents as they learned the forest.

For a moment, a young Marten warrior mistook Leaf for one of his own, seeing her cloak. He must have been eager to meet one of his clan because their numbers had dwindled significantly upon the arrival of the stonefolk and had only fallen lower since. When told who she really was, he quickly retreated and walked off into the forest without her.

Leaf decided it was best to just stay out of sight. She hid in the trees like Ash and the other Watchers but was careful to avoid them as well. Being amidst the growth and brush was the only time she ever felt at home, even though the illusion was broken by snippets of conversation from the people passing below. Life in the glade moved on without her. She wished Koomis could still walk, and that the two of them could wander somewhere far away from here.

Finally, the trees' shadows fell over the forest floor like long fingers. Children returned, eager to play, but many flocked toward a small cave in the side of the mountains where Mother Loon would soon be telling stories. Curious, Leaf followed them.

The cave didn't run very deep but had enough turns that the light quickly disappeared. The clans had spent years painting the carved walls with murals in their many voices and styles. The carvings seemed to bend and move under the flickering torchlight, catching her imagination and reenacting tales, from the Wolves' defeat by the stonefolk at the Howling Plains, to Crane's flight to the mountaintops, and many, many more, from long before the stonefolk's arrival. While some of the children stopped to study these with her, most continued to the end of the cave, where Mother Loon had already begun to tell how Raven stole the sun.

"…the crafty bird was too curious to let this chance pass her by." Mother Loon's voice carried along the walls as Leaf rounded the corner to see her twisting her hands above a fire, forming the shadow of a bird on the wall. Leaf took a seat behind all the other children. "So, clever Raven hatched a plan. She would disguise herself as one of the Chief's daughters, for he had a great many, and would live in his longhouse alongside them."

The shadow on the wall changed shape to a large, angry-looking man. "This was a dangerous plan, she knew, but the Chief's house was brightly lit and warm, far beyond the meager camps of the endless dark beyond. There was something he kept in his secret chest that allowed his fire to burn brightly. Raven became a pale young woman, who grew and lived and played beside the Chieftain's many sons and daughters. When asked for her name, she told them all she was Raven, and so never told a lie.

"It was a long time before the Chieftain let his guard down enough for Raven to get close to the chest, but the night finally came. He never left the lock off, but Raven was a clever girl, and knew how to fake a key just as well as she could fake being a child. She worked all night while the Chieftain and his children slept, but finally, in the hours when his snoring was loudest, she cracked the lock."

The children sitting all squealed in delight, knowing what was coming. One loudly asked what was in the chest while the others shushed him. Leaf sat forward as well. This had always been one of her favorite stories as a child, although Koomis rarely wanted to tell it.

"Light and life like nothing Raven had ever seen filled the room when she opened the chest," said Mother Loon, "and the love and warmth of endless stars danced through the longhouse. But the Chief felt it as well and woke from his slumber, knowing that his secret treasure had been seen." Mother Loon turned the shadows again, this time to both bird and man, which danced gracefully along the walls.

"Raven knew her time was fleeting. She gathered the sun and stars beneath her wing and made her escape. The Chieftain stood before her, swinging his arms and grasping at the empty air, calling for all his sons and daughters to stop the thief, but Raven was craftier than all of them. She turned from the front of the longhouse to the windows, and when she saw that they were already guarded by the children, turned again to the fireplace. Even as the flames roared and spat beneath her, she was unafraid for she knew no flame could burn as hot as the sun she held beneath her wing. She ascended through the chimney, through soot and smoke and into the sky, where she released the sun and stars over the Great Turtle."

Mother Loon let loose a plume of powder from her long sleeves into the fire, and the flames leapt and crackled. The children cheered, and Leaf smiled.

"And so, the time of the long dark was finally brought to an end," Mother Loon proclaimed. "The Chieftain could no longer hide the light for himself, and the other clans could see the world in all its beauty. Raven flew through the skies, surveying the world and all its wonders below her, but it was only when she finally landed and made her way to the water for a drink that she realized what had been done. Her journey through the fire had turned her white feathers black, marking her for all time as both a thief and a hero. This is why we still pay respect to her now. Remember that, children, the next time you walk through the woods and spot a raven. It is only because of them that we can see the world for what it is."

The children began to clap and cheer, and Leaf clapped alongside them. As the children began to leave, only a few stayed to ask Mother Loon further questions.

"Does this mean I can steal my brother's toys when he hogs them?"

Mother Loon smiled patiently. "No, child, that is the sort of thing you go to your parents for."

A young girl clutched a cloth raven doll tightly against her chest, looking worried. "How come the world used to be so dark?"

"I don't know, exactly," Mother Loon said, exaggerating her face into deep thought. "There are stories about that as well, but with so many different ones saying so many different things, it's hard to know exactly what the truth really is."

A petulant boy with dark hair that fell to his shoulders looked incensed. “Does that mean the story was a lie?”

“All stories are true, and all stories are lies,” said Mother Loon. “The important thing to remember is what we can learn from each of them.”

Another child yelled over the others. “A raven stole my apple once!”

The others were running out of the cave and back into the woods, spreading their arms like wings or pretending to be the blustering Chieftain and his children. One grabbed a burning torch from the wall.

“I’ve got it! I’ve got the sun!” he yelled triumphantly.

Leaf stood to go after him, but Mother Loon’s hand caught his wrist first. “Stop!” she yelled sharply, guiding his hand back to the wall. “Fire is a wondrous thing,” she said quieter but sternly. “It can give us light and warmth, and through its shadows, we tell the stories of old. But it is dangerous, too. You could have burned someone, or yourself, or even set the forest alight. What would you have done then?”

The boy began to stammer he was only playing, that he wanted to be like Raven. Leaf sat in the back, hidden in the shadows of the cave, until his lecture was finished and the crowd was almost entirely faded. The last child to leave wondered aloud why Raven didn’t just wash her feathers white again, and Mother Loon gently explained to him that some things ran deeper than feather and skin.

“And how about you?” Mother Loon said, once they were alone in the cave. She watched Leaf in the shadows as clearly as if she were in daylight. “Did you have any questions, or are you waiting for the next story?” Her smile was soft, and her eyes were kind. She was an older woman, only beginning to form crow’s feet at her eyes.

"You tell the story differently than my grandmother," said Leaf.

"Do I?" Mother Loon asked, inviting Leaf to sit beside her at the fire. Its light was warm and inviting and set the painted pictures dancing along the wall. "Stories often change in the telling. It's no surprise they grow in different ways, told by different people. Tell me though, to your knowledge, did I get most of it right?"

"I think so," said Leaf. "All the important stuff happened the same way."

"That is good."

"Do you know any other stories?" Leaf asked, then grimaced, realizing what a silly question it was.

"I do," Mother Loon answered kindly. "Many and many more. Were you asking just to ask, or because there was one in particular you wanted to hear?"

It wasn't exactly a story, and she wasn't sure exactly how to ask for it, but her thoughts had turned to the strange glowing stone sitting in her pack. Mother Loon, who carried all the stories of the clans, would likely know what it was. "Sort of," said Leaf, struggling to collect her thoughts. "I was wondering about something, but I don't know if..." She bit her lip. "It might be a stonefolk story."

"I know those as well," Mother Loon said a little more sadly, her eyes turning to Leaf, nodding for her to continue.

"Well..." Leaf tried to find her words. "Do you know anything about what they left behind? Their ruins, and their relics, and stuff like that."

Mother Loon looked at her quizzically. "I do," she said, "but I'm afraid I'm far from a witness to that history myself. Most of my knowledge is from the retelling of secondhand stories. I couldn't speak to the truth of them."

"That's true of any story."

Mother Loon smiled again at Leaf. "I'm getting the feeling that you have something in particular you want to ask me."

Leaf took a deep breath, trying to decide if this was wise. She didn't have to show Mother Loon the strange relic she'd found at the children's home, she just needed to ask about it. "What do you know about glowing stones?"

Mother Loon raised an eyebrow.

"Like, sort of a rock, but with a light to them. Not like the old lanterns though, with fire behind the glass, but like…if the stone itself was made of fire. Have you ever heard a story like that?"

Mother Loon sat quietly, looking somewhat puzzled as she pondered for an uncomfortably long moment. Leaf knew her thoughts came spilling out too fast sometimes, that she often said too much, but she had to know if there were stories about the relic she'd found. And there were fewer better to ask. Mother Loon's shoulders dropped as she sighed, looking concerned at Leaf. "We haven't gotten to know each other very well," she started. "I understand you like to keep to yourself. You weren't raised alongside the others, and that must make things hard for you. The same was said for many of the elders after they returned from their time in the stonefolk's…custody. I do hear things, however. Whispers and stories. Like, for example, that a young, green-haired girl is often wandering near the stonefolk ruins. Are those tales true?"

Leaf bit her lip. "Sort of," she said. "I used to pass by a lot of them with my grandmother. We even walked along the old roads. Just a little, I mean." Mother Loon was still smiling, but she looked more and more sad. "Anyway, I was just curious if you'd ever heard of something like that. In a story, I mean."

"Might be that I have," Mother Loon said. "Might not. Could be that I heard the tale without understanding that I did. Do you understand what I mean by that?"

"I think so," Leaf said, unsure.

"You're opening the doorway to a dark time when you ask those sorts of questions," Mother Loon cautioned. "The elders that remain to us, those who lived through those times, would not wish to see the matter revisited, but as a chronicler of our history, neither can I let them be forgotten. As to the ruins that remain, well, I shudder to imagine what sorts of spirits still haunt those places."

"I'm always careful."

Mother Loon sighed. "You're not of my clan. I can caution but not forbid, and I fear my warnings will pass right through your ears regardless, so let me just say this: The elders do not avoid the ruins out of spite or malice. There is fear in their actions, yes, but there is more as well. The stonefolk left a great many scars on this land that run far deeper than we understand, and the clans are kept at a distance so that the Turtle might heal to what it once was. Whatever you've found," she glanced toward Leaf's pack, "I would suspect it is very, *very* dangerous." Leaf shifted in her seat nervously. "You would be wise to carry your discovery far from these grounds, or better still, return it to where it came from."

"I'm sorry," Leaf said, sitting up in a hurry, the strange ember in her bag suddenly heavy on her mind. "I shouldn't have bothered you." Mother Loon rested a hand on her shoulder, ready to say something, but Leaf tore free and walked quickly out of the cave. Mother Loon called after her gently but didn't pursue, and soon Leaf was gone.

The sky was turning purple when she finally returned to the burrows. The sun was just beginning to fall behind the distant peaks, barely visible through the forests growing like moss on their backs. She wasn't sure if that counted as sunset, exactly, but it was close enough.

The forest was silent; she was truly alone. The Watchers must be off somewhere. Leaf ran into Koomis's burrow with no one to stop her or tell her no, and to her that was as good as an invitation. Descending into the earthen pit, she was relieved to find her grandmother without a guest.

"I can still see light outside, child," Koomis chided gently, but gestured toward the fire.

"Sorry," Leaf said, shifting restlessly on her feet. "What do you know about spiderweb charms? I know you know how to make them, but what else? Are they ever used to…hide things? Do you know anyone who did that?"

"Slow down," Koomis said, gesturing for Leaf to come beside her. "Sit. Breathe. Take a moment to gather your thoughts and speak only once you're ready."

Leaf sat anxiously, she hadn't even realized she was out of breath, and took a moment to take in the smells of the burrow and the warm air near the fire. It was hard to settle her thoughts, and harder still to force herself to relax, but Koomis insisted on silence, and on giving Leaf her time. Finally, once her breathing had settled and her chest had stopped thumping so fast, Koomis nodded for Leaf to continue.

"I found something in the ruins yesterday," she said quietly, turning her eyes from Koomis. "They were the same ones you grew up in."

Her grandmother drew a sharp breath.

"I know I'm not supposed to go there," Leaf said, "but you never talk about what happened. Neither do the other elders. I don't mean to be so bad all the time, I just…I wanted to understand you better."

Leaf dug her fingernails into her palm when she noticed that Koomis's lip was trembling and started to sway softly as she sat. The old woman collected herself, nodding slowly, her closed eyes growing wet.

"You were too busy this morning," Leaf continued softly. "I wasn't sure what to tell you, but when you kicked me out and I lost my chance, I realized all I wanted was to talk to you about it. I ended up going to Mother Loon. I didn't mean to ask, at least, not directly, but she found out that I'd brought something back from the ruins." Leaf's stomach pinched. "I know I shouldn't have done it, but I was hoping you might be able to tell me what it is. I don't think anyone else in the glade knows."

Heart racing, Leaf reached into her pack carefully, digging through her things to the stone tucked safely at the very bottom. Koomis watched her in stoic silence, but she gasped when Leaf unwrapped the glowing ember from its wrappings.

"What is that?" she asked in a horrified whisper. She didn't take her eyes off the stone. "Child, I'm sorry, but I have no idea what you've found. And if it's from the home, I don't want any part of it."

Leaf understood then that this had been a mistake. Who was she to take the worst time of her grandmother's life and bring one of its ghosts into her own home? She buried the ember back into her bag as if she could shove her shame down alongside it. "I'm sorry. I'm sorry."

"Why?" Koomis asked. Leaf was waiting to be met with surprise or shock, even anger, but there was deep sadness in her grandmother's voice. "Why would you go there?"

"I just wanted to understand you better," Leaf said quietly. She cleared her throat, forcing herself to speak up when Koomis leaned closer. "Why did we have to live alone? How come everyone else grew up together while we hid away? I wanted to know what happened to make you distrust people so much. I wanted to know our history."

"That stone is not our history," Koomis said, looking to the bag. She rubbed her wrists under her heavy shawl. "These scars are not our history. That home is not our history. The mountains, the trees, the forest around us, *that* is our history. That is what I tried to teach you on all our journeys over the Turtle. Did you not understand?"

"The stonefolk are part of our history, too," Leaf argued. "Even if it's a bad part, it's a part of our story now. Everywhere we went, I saw those scars, and every time we ran into people, I couldn't understand why we had to be afraid." The last words barely choked out of her, and it took a long time for her breath to steady again, the slow crackling fire filling the silence. "We can't just pretend that all of this never happened. It's still happening now." She kept her eyes on the dirt, letting the water well in her vision.

"I never wanted that for you," Koomis said finally. Her grandmother's voice was small, with none of the edge Leaf had expected. "I wanted you to have what I didn't. To give you what I couldn't give your father. I wanted to give you a life free of the pain my generation felt, free from the burdens we carry."

Leaf wiped her eyes. She'd heard this before, but she didn't understand it. "Remember how you taught me that fire was dangerous? You let me play with it until I burned myself, and after that I was more careful. I think hiding from things means you never learn how dangerous they really are."

Koomis nodded slowly. "I tried to teach you enough to sate your curiosity," she said. "But, like your father, it seems I've only stoked it further..."

Something in Leaf burned at the thought of the father she'd never known, a feeling she couldn't put into words. What did it mean to be like him in all the ways that led to his leaving her life?

"I can't confine you any longer," Koomis continued wearily. "Nor should I. I know too well how it feels to see a forbidden horizon." Koomis's hand was trembling on her cane, and Leaf reached over to steady her. The folds of her grandmother's cheeks fell with quiet fear, her shoulders weighed down by unspoken burdens. "The thought of you exploring those places scares me, do you know that?" Her eyes shot to Leaf's, and she grabbed her granddaughter's wrist, her soft, frail fingers holding tight. "I'd sooner lead you to the heart of the Deepwood than see you in those ruins, but I'm afraid that's not up to me anymore." Releasing her, she gestured to her leg and the earthen walls around her, laden with crafts and mementos of a life wracked with pain, but a life well-lived regardless. "This is my place now, and it will be my place until I pass from this world."

"I wish we could walk the Turtle again," Leaf said, her voice shaking with frustration. There was nothing she could do to heal a missing leg.

Feelings battled inside of her, and she had trouble knowing exactly what they were even as the hair on her arms rose and her fingers trembled, but she knew enough to reach out and hold her grandmother.

"So do I," Koomis said softly. "But even if I'm confined here, you are not. My place is here, but yours is out there. You're young and free to make your own path, regardless of what anyone tells you."

"But what if what I want upsets the other clans?" she said, thinking about the ruins and the glowing ember in her bag. *What if I upset you?*

Koomis raised an eyebrow, a sly sharpness returning to her face with a growing smile. "You think the other clans were happy I raised you alone? Bah! 'She won't know our teachings,' they told me, but I taught you stories from every clan while the Wolves only heard their own howling. 'She won't know our ways,' they said, but you learned them all. You fish like the Salmon and fight like the Bear. You pass through the woods without trace like the Muskrat and you climb better than anyone I've ever seen. You might not weave so well," she said, laughing to herself and gesturing to Leaf's spiderweb charm, "but that was my skill to pass to you, and I'm a damn good teacher. If you didn't learn weaving, it's because you didn't want to."

Leaf started to laugh with her grandmother. It was true that she was always too restless to sit and wind flaxen string around hoops. She always pulled too tight, eager to be done, and half her charms snapped before she finished.

Still smiling, Koomis continued. "I might be here by custom, and because it's more comfort than I could know alone." She gestured again to her missing leg. "But I will never fit here the way the others do. My childhood was taken from me. The stonefolk tried to take my culture, too, and in many ways, they succeeded. It is something I will never fully reclaim." Koomis looked like she might start crying but something in her refused. "I've held on to my own fears of that time all my life. I shouldn't have tried to instill that same fear in you. How fortunate I am to have a granddaughter too stubborn to learn that lesson."

Through the tears and tension, a grin started to break over Leaf. "I can't be afraid of something I know nothing about. Like the fire."

"No, you can't, can you?" Koomis was smiling, too. "I admire that about you. I hope you know that." Leaf blushed. "But your actions scare the others. Already, the children come to me asking about you, whispering their fears. They say you're the Woods Witch in disguise, or else one of her spies." Koomis outright cackled at that. There had always been whispers and rumors about the two of them. But Leaf was relieved that any hint of tears was gone from her eyes. "I'm afraid I might have helped them along with a few of those worries."

"I'm not a witch," Leaf said defensively, but it gave her an idea. "Do you think she might know more about the ember?"

"It's possible," Koomis conceded, but Leaf sensed her hesitation. "You're not the only person to go crawling through the ruins, after all. I'm sure there must be others who've found similar things. The Woods Witch might be the person to ask." Leaf could see her grandmother's thoughts leading her down into the Deepwood, her hand moved toward Leaf but pulled back before she touched her. Their eyes locked. "That is, if you can find her."

"Maybe I will," said Leaf. She sat up, going through things in the burrow, unpacking what she wouldn't need from her pack and shoving in others that she might. Tearing a large knit blanket from the wall, she turned to Koomis, who was watching her strangely.

"You never were any good at packing your things," she said. "Give it here. You're a strange child, Leaf. Too eager to go running over mountains with no care for where your feet might land."

"It's the only way to learn," said Leaf.

Koomis nodded, then turned her face away, suddenly very interested in the patterned blankets on the wall.

Leaf took some of the spare preserved foods that Koomis kept for herself. The hare was already boiling over the fire for a late-night stew, and the clans would ensure that her grandmother ate. It was with a heavy heart that Leaf realized, with the spring thaw finally here, she would finally be leaving, but her grandmother was here to stay. The hope that something could happen between now and a nebulous future, some miracle that restored things to how they were—Leaf and Koomis traveling over the Great Turtle—would never come. It was just her now.

She could be gone for weeks. Maybe even months. Going by the tales gathered from travelers over the Turtle, the strange woman known as the Woods Witch dwelled far below the valleys at the base of the mountain, somewhere in the wild forest called the Deepwood. The Deepwood was uncharted, and Leaf felt a crawl up her spine at the thought of going inside, but she couldn't help her excitement, too.

Then a shadow appeared at the entryway of the burrow.

"Leaf? Are you here?" It was Ash's voice, but the words were too loud.

Leaf narrowed her eyes. Something was off. "Yeah," she said, moving cautiously to the entry of the burrow.

"I need to speak with you." Ash sounded hesitant. Worried, maybe. *Something is wrong*, Leaf thought. *Ash never shouts.*

"Come in, then, and stop yelling through my door," Koomis called from her place by the fire.

Ash looked more pale than usual as she stepped into the burrow. When Koomis flinched back from the fangs of the wolf's head, she lowered it, hesitant, and met Leaf's eye.

"What's wrong?"

"I've been told you brought forbidden items into the Elderglade," Ash said carefully. She was trying to say something with her eyes, but Leaf had trouble reading her gaze. *And why is she still talking so loudly?* This wasn't like the Ash she knew.

"Told by who?"

"The Watchers are coming to confiscate your bag, and anything you might have taken from the ruins," Ash said. "You can't be allowed to threaten the safety of the clans."

The words hit her hard. "I'm not a threat," Leaf whispered, surprised that it sounded almost like a question. "I would never hurt anyone."

"Ridiculous," Koomis said. Her voice was edged with thorns. "Bring me someone to speak with and we'll sort this out right now."

"I'm sorry, Elder, but the decision has already been made." Ash swallowed, and then she spoke more quietly. "I thought I should tell you myself. That it might…I don't know, make things easier somehow."

Leaf paced anxiously. Mother Loon must have brought her concerns to the Watchers. Who else could it have been? But to send someone to take her belongings? To declare her a threat to the clans? This was all wrong. She couldn't let them tell her how to live, or where she could go and what she could do.

"No," said Leaf.

Ash frowned. "No, what?"

"No, that doesn't make it easier," she said unsteadily. "No, I'm not giving you my things. And no, I won't go with you. Just tell them no, you understand?"

Ash's shoulders fell, and she looked to the floor with a sigh. "I thought you might say something like that."

"I'm going to take my things and leave," said Leaf. "I was already going anyway."

Ash looked back up with a cautious, curious look. "Where are you off to this time?"

"I'm going to see the Woods Witch." There was no turning back now. "There's a question I need answered, and I think maybe she's the only one who can. I'll leave the glade behind, and I don't know how long it'll be before I'm back, so the Watchers don't have to worry about me anymore."

Ash looked shocked. "The Woods Witch? Seriously? Leaf, please tell me this a joke."

Leaf looked to her grandmother, the way she always did when she needed guidance, then realized this might be the last time she could ask for it. Koomis was smiling proudly. "It's decided, then. Up now, lazy child, unless you mean to be buried here with me."

The sight of her grandmother, small and shriveled in her warm blanket, alone beside the fire, was almost enough to change Leaf's mind. Leaf may not have cared for the Elderglade, but she cared for her grandmother. They had always traveled together, and even Leaf's secret journeys into the ruins always ended with a return to her grandmother's side. But she knew that by the time she returned, the burrow might be collapsed, and the sprout of a new tree could be waiting for her. The clans might even forbid her from the Elderglade for running. But Koomis was right. If she stayed here, she would be here forever.

"I love you, Grandma," Leaf said, grabbing another blanket and wrapping her with it in a tight hug. She held on for so long that Koomis had to push her to leave.

"I love you too, Leaf. Now get going. You're wasting time now." This time, Leaf could hear the heart beneath the thorns.

"All right," said Ash. Her voice was back to its usual quiet, and she was standing to the side of the entryway. The setting sun cast its final light behind her. "I can't stop the others from coming after you, but I can give you a head start. You'll need to run fast."

"Thank you," Leaf said to her only friend.

"Yeah, well…" Ash couldn't meet her gaze, eyes lingering instead on the shadows on the floor.

Outside, there was a silence to the trees that told Leaf the Watchers hadn't come for her just yet. She would chase the setting sun all through the night and be out of their reach come morning. Leaf looked back at Ash, who was watching her feet from the top of the entryway. "What are you going to tell them?"

"The truth. That you left before I could catch you."

Leaf smiled at that, and it was clear in her voice. "Maybe you should try," she said playfully. It wasn't a statement really, but an invitation.

A silent heartbeat passed between them as Ash realized what she was asking. Then the wolf girl looked up, and for the first time that day, the first time in quite a long while, actually, she was smiling.

Leaf ran, and Ash followed behind. With every step, the sparse lights of the glade, starlight flies, and hints of fires from the burrows fell away into the night, replaced with Grandmother Moon's glow reaching down through the clouds. The underbrush rustled quietly as if they were both just another breeze lost between the leaves. Leaf felt Ash at her heels, the Watcher in the trees, the hunter, and the wolf in the moonlight. Behind her, the fears and confines of the Elderglade dropped away, and when Leaf turned back to look, she saw Ash in her shadow, breathing hard from her pursuit. She looked at Leaf curiously, wordlessly, and then a silent footstep forward dared them both to continue the chase.

The two of them laughed as they ran through the night.

6

REED

THE OLD DIGGER

"You look like you haven't slept a wink, kiddo," said Tarn, his balding head gleaming under a stack of boxes. Reed stood at the edge of Tarn's cramped quarters, keeping the door cracked open to clear the air. He could still hear the distant bustle of the merchants, and the scents of spice clashed with the stale smell of empty liquor bottles littering the old man's room. A rat skittered underfoot, and Reed discreetly lifted his boot, hiding his unease.

The old man's comment wasn't all that far from the truth; Reed hadn't slept much at all. He had no coin left for a place of his own after the haircut, meal, new clothes, and his little grift, and he had more than one reason to keep out of sight. "Too excited," he said, shaking the stiffness from his neck. "Got a big job starting today."

"That right?" The old man beamed. "Good on you. Just give me another minute here, would you? I know it's back here somewhere…"

The last of Fox's coin had been spent on a very small but very pricey bottle of rum. That was Tarn's favorite, and it wasn't easy to find. At least, it wouldn't be easy anywhere else. The Flotilla's marketplace had everything one could find on the seas, and none of the proprietors worried about where a coin had come from.

"Seems a little steep for one book," Reed said, shaking the bottle and watching its contents slosh.

"It's not the book you're paying for, son, it's the effort that went into writing it." Tarn emerged from his stack of boxes and collapsed heavily into a padded chair, leaning his head on the wall. The old man was somewhere in his sixties, Reed knew, but his frail arms, cragged face, and few remaining whisps of silver hair made him look somewhere closer to ninety. His expression was always sour, like he'd taken a bite right from a lemon, and the precious few teeth remaining to him shared the same color. Beside him was a nest of papers so thick that Reed could only wonder at the desk beneath them. "Here," the old man said, slapping a hardcover book into his palm and looking winded for the effort. His breath reeked of liquor, and his clothes hadn't seen a wash in a good few weeks, but Reed held his breath and smiled like he didn't notice. "Take a look through. It's the next best thing to having me there with you! Got everything I know in there, and believe me, that's a lot." The old man laughed himself into a coughing fit.

"I wouldn't be here otherwise," Reed said truthfully. He made sure to speak loudly for the old man's sake. "I don't think I know anyone else who's ever been to Turtle Rock."

Tarn smiled broadly, pushing deep laugh lines over his small, beady eyes. "Thanks, kid. Now, you're going to want to call it the Great Turtle, or just the Turtle, while you're there. That's how the locals say it, you know? It was a smart move coming to me. Smart move, indeed. Yep, always knew you were a clever one. Knew that right from the moment I met you. Heh, when that mother of yours started coming by the bar, I used to say—"

"I don't mean to be rude," Reed said loudly, knowing that if he didn't, the old man would launch into a story he'd rather not hear, "but I have a ship I need to catch. You know how it goes."

"Boy, do I. So, off to the Turtle, huh? Plenty of things to be found out there, if you know what you're looking for. You want gold? They coated their walls with it in their heyday. Gemstones? There's rubies as big as your fist. You can just go prying them right out of the eyes of statues, and believe me, they loved building statues of themselves. Vain, they were…" The old man rambled until he was out of breath, and then he was coughing long and deep. Reed moved to his side, but Tarn held up a hand until finally, he started breathing again. "Sorry about that. The salt air doesn't always agree with me, I think. That's why I don't leave the room anymore. Close that door, would you? I never should've retired. You're not done digging 'til you dig your last hole. You know what I mean by that, right?"

Reed was only half listening as he flipped through the book. He had no clue what he might be looking for in Tarn's journal, but there were pages and pages filled with scrawled notes and ramblings. There were drawings of plants and animals from his own journeys on the island. On one page was a giant spider, tall as a person to judge from the figure Tarn had drawn overtop it, and snakes that rose to twice its height. Great herds of cattle moved across inked plains like a walking forest, with moss and vine growing out of their wild beards. The old man was a decent artist, really, and that made Reed pity his current state even more.

"Right, of course," Reed mumbled. "Last hole."

"You've got exciting times ahead of you, kid, make no mistake about it. Just don't go off biting more than you can chew.

There are old diggers, and there are bold diggers, but there ain't no old, bold diggers, you hear me?"

He always loved to hear himself talk, Reed thought. If this was what an old digger amounted to, then he wanted no part of it. Snapping the journal shut, Reed wondered how much of the notes would still be useful, and how many would be horribly outdated. It had been a long time since Tarn ventured off to distant lands, or even beyond this meager room, but to hear him tell it, you might think these things happened just yesterday.

"This really has everything you know in it?" Reed asked.

"Everything I ever learned is in that book, I guarantee you," Tarn said, smiling proudly. "I've got more, you know, if you ever need some knowhow about other places. Kept a different book on every place I visited. That's a tip for you, by the way. Keep your thoughts written down. It'd be a damn shame to lose 'em."

"This one will be fine," Reed interrupted again. "Maybe I'll need another when this job is done," he offered more kindly but finished silently, *Maybe not.*

Tarn smiled his wide, nearly toothless grin, then held his hand out. Right. Reed took the bottle from his coat and handed it to the old man.

"Maybe you should cut back a bit," Reed said as Tarn took a long swig from the bottle. Looking around at the squalid cabin, it was hard to remember that Tarn had ever been a young man. "That stuff is going to kill you."

Tarn took the advice in stride, tilting the bottle to offer Reed a sip. "That's the thing," he said with a smile that no longer reached his eyes. "The way I figure, this stuff is all that keeps me going."

Reed nodded, not knowing what else to say. He was almost at the door before the old man called after him. "Take care of yourself out there, kid."

"You too, old man," Reed said, closing the door softly behind him.

The path from Tarn's quarters was a twisting maze of halls and corridors sunk deep into the hull of the *Free Man's Pride*. His footsteps on the iron floors echoed as Reed found his way back to the marketplace. Finally, he came to a second-story balcony, where he watched over the endless rows of stalls and tents set tightly together, small islands amidst the flood of the crowd. Something in his heart told Reed that he was going to miss this place, even though he'd rarely had the coin to be welcome.

"When I get back, I'll be rich enough to buy the whole damn market," he promised.

"That's good to hear, Reed," someone said behind him. Before he could even turn, a set of hands grabbed his shoulders, forcing him forward, far over the railing. Their grip was the only thing keeping him from falling over the edge. Fox sidled up beside him, leaning casually as he sneered, "You owe me some money."

Flicking a dull knife open in his bandaged hand, Fox pressed it into Reed's side until he could feel his skin threatening to split. "No apologies, no look of remorse. You're a real piece of work, you know that? Bet you thought that was pretty slick, what you did yesterday."

"I'm not sure what you're talking about," said Reed.

Fox flexed his bandaged hand and winced. "Sure, sure. And I'm sure you were just off for a quick run around the ship yesterday. Probably didn't even hear us calling after you 'cause you were late for another important meeting."

Did they know? Reed wondered how Fox could have caught wind of his journey with the *Dragon's Breath*, but he kept his face calm, not giving anything away. "Something like that," he said. He couldn't help but push his luck. Smirking, he asked, "What happened to your hand?"

"No more games," Fox hissed. "Here's what's going to happen. I want my money back right now. All of it. For every coin that's missing, we're going to have ourselves a little accident." He dragged the tip of the knife up Reed's side to his face, where a rosebud of blood bloomed on his cheek. "That'll add up pretty quick, I promise. Now, let's head somewhere a little quieter and get things settled. Then we can have a nice heart-to-heart about how things are going to be from here on out, got it?"

"Of course," Reed said. "No problem. I just have one question."

The hired muscle at his side threw Reed so hard into the railing that all the wind was shoved from his chest. While he gasped for air, Fox picked his pockets. They wouldn't find any coin, of course. It had all been spent. But there was the journal…

"How much do you pay your guys?" Reed wheezed.

"You're not buying them off, if that's what you're thinking. Not like your little runners on the docks. These guys make more with me than they ever would with a rat like you, so save the sales pitch, all right?"

"I wouldn't be so sure about that," said Reed. He smiled at the guy on his right, an impassive pug-nosed face glaring back at him. Reed dubbed him "Righty." "How much do you make with Freckles, here?"

"Shut up," Fox warned again. His pat down of Reed was getting more desperate.

"You know, I'm starting to think you might owe someone, too," Reed said more loudly. "Is that why you're feeling up my leg so hard? 'Cause I've got some bad news for you…"

"I said shut up, Reed. Shut up!" Fox's eyes were darting about frantically now, still looking for something valuable on him.

Reed shrugged. "You two might want to start thinking about a different career. If the bosses find out Fox can't pay what he promised, well, let's just say you don't want to be a 'known associate.'"

"Stop it!" Fox rose suddenly, knocking his muscle aside, and shoved Reed as hard as he could in the chest. Reed rode the momentum, letting himself fall over the railing, and by lucky happenstance, catching Fox on the chin with his boot as he went. The two goons were baffled by the loss of their quarry, but then they were gone, replaced with a colorful canvas tent that enveloped him with a soft, cushioned *woomph*.

A cloud of some exotic spice burst through the market, sending people around him into coughing fits while someone, presumably the proprietor, screamed angrily. Reed might have been able to parse the tirade if he wasn't so focused on catching his breath. At least he hadn't landed on his head.

"You okay? Can you move?" A nearby sailor poked Reed's arms and legs. "Anything broken?" Reed played up his pain, which wasn't hard, flinching at the man's touch and screwing up his face as a pair of market guards lifted him to his feet, keeping one leg high as if it were too painful to stand on.

"They tried to rob me," he said with a wheeze he hoped didn't sound too forced. He pointed up at Fox and the others, looking dumbstruck over the balcony. "I didn't have anything, so they threw me over the rail…"

One of the market guards who had come over yelled up, "Hey, you!" just as Fox's face dropped. He turned to run. "Get back here!"

"What about my wares?" a silk-garbed merchant moaned. He shot Reed a withering look.

“The Flotilla will reimburse your losses with whatever we take from those three,” the guard said. He turned to Reed. “Do you know who they were?”

“No,” he lied. He just wanted to get out of there before things got out of hand. “I was just on my way to work.”

“Where?”

“The Halfmug,” said Reed.

“Then get going. We’ll find you again once we’ve dealt with the others.”

Reed was out of there so fast that the market was long behind him before he remembered he was supposed to fake a limp. No one had stopped him, and he didn’t expect to be seeing any of them again, anyway. He picked up his pace when he saw the sun was rising above the sails that stretched over the sea. It didn’t take long to spot the tattered mess of the *Dragon’s Breath*, its bright oranges and reds standing out amidst the beiges and blues of other ships. He could see Finch watching from the side of the deck for him, eating something out of her palm.

“You coming aboard or what?” she yelled down between bites.

Reed bowed. “Permission to come aboard?”

Finch scoffed, then spit her pit into the water. “Not my ship, not my courtesies. Captain already said you’re crew. Don’t go ruining it now by bowing and saluting everywhere you go, this ain’t that sort of ship.”

“Point taken,” said Reed. He rolled his shoulders, side stinging. His shirt was starting to stain red under his coat. Tucking it closed and fixing his hair for good measure, Reed made his way to Finch, who was eyeing him suspiciously. Only then did he remember to wipe the blood off his face.

Once he was aboard, it was clear the deck wasn’t any more impressive than the sails. The ship was worn down and patched in so many places that Reed wondered if he might crash right through the mismatched floors. He took his steps cautiously, which made Finch break out in derisive laughter. She walked beside him, matching his pace with exaggerated caution.

"What? You never been on a real ship before?" she teased, leaning close and prodding Reed along. "She's sturdier than she looks. Captain says I'm to show you what's what, so hurry up. I don't want to be at this all day, yeah?"

The Flotilla had always had its share of small vessels, but those were usually private spaces. Reed was used to decks large enough to house markets and performers and crowds of roughhousing sailors. This boat wasn't the smallest he'd seen, but it wasn't near to the scale he was used to, either. It also wasn't much to look at. Reed was almost starting to wonder if the whole thing might slip under the waves one night, but with a vengeful Fox and his hired muscle lurking back on the Flotilla, he decided that a chance at sinking was better than a chance at a stabbing. Besides, they were heading to the Great Turtle. It wasn't like he'd need to be on this drowning bucket for long. So, Reed ducked his head low and followed Finch down to the cabins.

They passed a small galley where sharp spices and charred smoke had been baked into the walls from what must have been hundreds of meals. Their stores, however, were low and unvaried. "It's not much, but you won't be starving," Finch said, noticing his eye. "Captain was hoping to load up on fruit a while back, but that, eh, fell through. Hope you like hardtack."

A small stairway led down to the crew quarters, and even at a glance, Reed could see they were richly decorated. While the boat might not be large, the crew didn't have to be either, so everyone seemed to sleep with a room to themselves. There were spaces for storage set into the walls, and nooks all over the ship. *It would be a decent cargo hauler*, Reed thought, *but it's an even better smuggler.*

The door to the captain's quarters was closed, muffled voices on the other side. Reed thought the wood might be mahogany, and it was marked with a skilled, if rough, etching of a dragon in flight. Finch stood stiffly in front of a door he could assume was hers, waiting for him to pass it by.

"I signed on for the privacy," she said, giving him a stern look.

"Well, I didn't sign on to snoop, so that works out," Reed said, offering a smile.

"Yeah, right," she said, rolling her eyes.

Reed kept the smile even as she turned her back to lead him on. *At least she's not trying to stab me.*

Down the hall was an open door to something that looked more like a blacksmith's display than quarters. Ring, scale, and plate armors cluttered the room, some of them gleaming and smelling of oil, others coated in salt rust, and all fixed to walls or tables. A myriad of dull and dented blades had also been carefully secured in place. The pale, giant woman, Tamn, watched them both with cold eyes as they passed, nodding curtly.

"Tamn's room," said Finch. "She keeps us geared for all occasions. Captain is probably going to send you her way later, so remember where she is. You got a preference?"

"What?" Reed asked, eyes still lingering on the mountain of metal through the door.

"Gear. You prefer stabbing? Cutting? Smashing? You got any experience at all with that kind of thing?"

Reed had never worn any kind of armor before, and Fox's dull dagger in his side was the closest he'd ever come to a weapon, besides playing with brooms and broken bottles. "Swords," he blurted. The lie came to him before he could think it through. "Something light," he added.

"Can't handle the heavy stuff, huh?"

"I like precision," Reed countered. It was getting harder to keep his smile light. Was she trying to test him for something?

"I get that," Finch said, pulling a knife from somewhere he didn't notice and dancing it between her fingers. "But if you really like something lighter, this is the way to go." She spun the knife toward him on the back of her palm, offering the handle forward. When he hesitated, she dropped it from one hand and snatched it with the other. "Not too quick on the draw, are you, Reed? Talk with Tamn later and she'll get you set. Now let's get this over with."

Maybe she was trying to establish hierarchy, Reed thought. He often saw sailors jockeying for position under their captains, showing off to establish some dominance over their fellow crewmates. Reed was just happy to be aboard.

The hall was growing tighter with every step they made toward the prow of the ship. Scattered light through porthole windows kept the underside half lit, and lanterns filled in the gaps. Their flames were dulled through dusty red- and orange-stained glass and gave off a sour smoke that threatened to choke him. It turned the halls into the illusion of an inferno.

"Ridae welcomes visitors, but good luck trying to get a decent conversation with the nutcase," Finch huffed, slamming a door fixed with a metallic moth emblem. A light incense wafted out. "Help me keep that closed, yeah? I'm starting to smell that stuff in my sleep."

Another doorway belonged to Wright, who Finch explained had come with them the previous night. Apparently, his quarters were one of the nicer on the ship, saved only for important guests and the like. The door was locked when Finch tested the handle.

Wright came walking down the hall just as she did, stepping out from the captain's cabin and straightening his coat with a dignified air. He looked disdainfully at Reed as he approached.

"So, you didn't vanish off into another tavern ship, then? No more crowds to listen to your stories? There's still time to reconsider, if you're having second thoughts." He looked at Reed and seemed to pierce right through his new clothing, hair, and down to the unsure young man beneath.

"He's crew now," said Finch, surprising Reed in the quickness of her defense. Her tone was cold. "Captain made the call."

"Yes, he did, didn't he?" said the old redcoat. Reaching into his pocket for a key, he turned his back to them. "Well then, if you'll excuse me."

Wright slipped through the door and locked it behind him again before Reed could get a good look. It was becoming very clear that just about everyone on the ship desired privacy, which made him feel a little more at home.

"Eh, nothing exciting in there anyway," said Finch, irritation clear in her voice. "He barely brought anything aboard. I don't think he's even slept in there yet, him and the captain have been talking all night." She looked at Reed seriously. "Not that I was listening. Don't go repeating that."

"Who would I tell?" said Reed. With a last look at the redcoat's door, he followed Finch to the end of the hall.

The final door was at the very prow of the ship. "That's it," Finch said, shrugging. "We've got storage and some more places for sleeping, but we don't have much to store and we don't sleep too many. You could maybe share with Wright, but I don't think he likes you, yeah? Ridae would take you, but I don't know how anyone could sleep in there. Keeps that damn fire going all hours of the night, and whatever he's burning smells like hell gone rotten. So, that leaves you with this." She kicked the last door open, revealing what was little more than a closet cut triangularly into the wall. If Reed laid with his head in the topmost corner, he might have just enough room to stretch out.

"I don't need much," he said, trying to sound nonchalant. "Just a place to sleep."

"You're in luck, then, 'cause you're not getting more." Finch turned to him and made a face. "Well, that's everything. You eat yet?"

"No," said Reed, suddenly aware of the aching gnaw of his stomach. "Busy day."

"I bet," said Finch, glancing at his coat. A touch of red had leaked through. "And you're just getting started. Captain'll want to say his hello good and proper, now that he's free. Other than that, if you want something to eat, it's mostly salt beef and hard-tack stew, unless we manage to pick something else up along the way. Come up whenever you hear the bell."

"The bell?"

"For meals. You'll hear it." Finch rolled her eyes and walked off down the hall.

Reed took in his new quarters quickly. There really wasn't much to familiarize himself with. There was a small wooden bucket and crate on the floor filled with scraps of spare cloth that looked like sail trimmings. He supposed he could fashion it into a blanket. All in all, it was still a great step up from sleeping in the Halfmug's drippings, even if he lacked a proper bed, and he was definitely safer here than back on the Flotilla. Fox would no doubt be on the hunt for him even now.

Reed took a lantern from the hall and hung it from a peg on his wall, as there was no window in his room. The dull orange glow chased shadows well enough from the space. Closing the door softly, he took the journal from his inside pocket, where it was still safe and secure, and gave it a quick glance.

Property of Torrin.

Reed started at the name on the front page. Had he really been saying the old man's name wrong all that time? Reed supposed he did have a thick enough accent…

"Reed, you are inside, yes?" the muffled voice of the captain called from the other side of the doorway. Reed tucked the journal back into his coat and stepped out to meet him.

"Over here," said Reed. Captain Beldrick was standing outside a different door, further up the hall, knocking softly. He turned, shaking his head.

"There you are," he said with his wide grin. "I am not thinking to find you in a closet. Is Finch not showing you your room?"

"He said he didn't need much, Captain," said Finch, leaning out from her door next to the one the captain had knocked at. "Just a place to sleep is all." She smirked at Reed when the captain stopped looking her way.

"Still, I am thinking you desire a bed at least." Captain Beldrick shrugged at him and walked up the hall, beckoning for Reed to follow. "Come. We are speaking now, and I prefer that in my own quarters." Reed tried to hide his confusion. Another room? A bed? Finch gave him a teasing grin as he passed.

"Sleep tight," she mouthed, retreating into her room and shutting the door. A bout of muffled laughter quickly followed.

"I am being like you, when I am young," Captain Beldrick mused as they walked. The lanternlight sent the shadows dancing like flame over his burned skin. "No need for beds or pretty rooms. They are making you weak, is the thinking. A safe corner and a rock to rest your head is all a soldier is truly needing." He opened the mahogany door with the dragon etching and beckoned Reed to join him inside.

The captain's room was more densely packed and decorated than any Reed had ever seen. It was filled with trophies: antlers and skulls from creatures he had never seen, and pelts in exotic colors draped along the walls. Trinkets the captain had collected from his years on the Broken Waters were displayed on shelves. There were small engravings of symbols that Reed couldn't place, the rising sun, the wings of some great bird, mighty glaciers jutting from the sea, and many, many others. Flags and sigils of countries both known and unknown to him were displayed in neat rows along the wall, tattered in places, having been torn or taken from some far-off land. Perhaps they were nations the captain had once worked for, or even against.

A suit of fine leather armor was displayed on a stand. Its chest was covered with a decorative metal lining shaped into the face of a fearsome dragon, with long blades like hooked teeth that ran down the forearms. A set of long spears with many different heads rested on the wall behind it.

The most impressive thing to Reed, however, was the bed. It was large and plush, with sheets that ran a deep red, like blood. It had been built into the ship itself, and the faded paints, the careful way new wood had been blended with old, and the worn-away polish on its handrails in only a few places told the story of long years of use. Over the headboard hung a strange skull larger than any Reed had ever seen, with long, knife-like teeth.

"Is that…?"

"A serpent," said Captain Beldrick, taking a seat behind a desk strewn with maps and charts written in many languages. "The *Dragon's Breath* is just a name, you know. There are no dragons out there. Many ask, and many times I am correcting the curious on this matter." He smiled from his finely carved chair, which was made from the same polished wood as the door. The seat across from him, meant for Reed, was little more than a stool with a backing. "I am maybe spending too much on the chair," the captain admitted.

"It's nice, though," Reed said, gesturing to the room. "All of it."

"I am thinking so as well," said Captain Beldrick. "And the chair is good for the leg, I am telling myself. Always it is aching. I must either be pacing or sitting. Standing is never good." He turned his good eye to Reed. "So, be telling me more about the man I am seeing. Who is he? Where is he from?"

"Well, the name's Reed," said Reed. "You already know that. Born of the Great Turtle but Flotilla-raised. Guess you could say that makes me a sea turtle. This place has always been my home."

The captain laughed. "Always? You are never leaving?"

"Not as much as I'd like," Reed said truthfully. "This is the only place I've ever felt at home. The Turtle is a fine thing to visit, but I don't know if I could live there."

"And why is this being?" Captain Beldrick leaned forward, curious, his eye intent on Reed.

"Too many dangers," said Reed, thinking fast. "The wildlife will eat you alive if given half a chance. The stoneshapers are still bitter about the loss of their home and don't take too kindly to those who search through its bones. They think we're thieves." He tried to remember what little he could from Tarn's stories at the bar. There were a few tales from his mother as well, but he had to keep those thoughts from his mind. "The hill tribes are just as standoffish, but only to outsiders. Between the two, it's hard to find a place to settle down. And then you have the plant life. Eat the wrong sort with dinner and you won't be waking up for breakfast. Hell, you even touch the wrong set of leaves and you'll be itching for weeks."

"You will be pointing out to me these leaves as we travel," the captain said, laughing. He rubbed at the pit of his ruined eye. "My leg already aches, and my burns simmer even now. I am not needing more maladies." He reached down beneath his desk and pulled out a bottle of dark, smoky liquid, and two glasses. Filling them both, he handed one to Reed. "Drink."

"Thank you, Captain."

"Please, be calling me Keresh. I am never fond of titles. One of the many reasons I am no longer of home."

"Really?" Reed asked, curious. He swirled the dark liquid around in his glass, wary of what it was. "I've heard a lot of stories," he lied, "but where do you consider home?"

Keresh downed his entire glass and poured another, gesturing the bottle to Reed, who politely declined. "Somewhere far beyond your Broken Waters. A place better not spoken of." He noticed the surprise in Reed's face. "It is not a cursed land, I promise you, just a fallen one. In the years before I am leaving, it has as many names and rulers as I have fingers and toes. I decline to name my homeland only because I no longer know its name. There are only so many emperors-for-life you can be serving before you start to wonder how long a life truly is, and so I am leaving to find that answer myself. How long do you think that might be on the waters, Reed of the Flotilla?"

Reed was stumped. He knew the islands throughout the Broken Waters were dangerous, of course, and that the Flotilla had been formed out of necessity, but he had never truly considered the question before. He had enough trouble just making it through the day. There was never time to plan for a future just to dream that, someday, you might get a chance at something better.

"There's ways of getting by that can keep you a pretty long time," he said, thinking of Tarn. *Torrin.* "The real question, I think, is what kind of life do you want to live?"

Keresh was grinning now, bobbing his head at Reed's words. "I am liking you. I truly am. You have a feeling I am knowing very well." He dipped a finger into his glass and ran the dark liquid over the burned side of his face and his cracked lips. "Bravery and foolishness are the two sides of youth, my captain is telling me once. What are you saying to that?"

"That sounds right to me," Reed said honestly. "I'd say I'm a mix of both."

"Honesty is good, yes," Keresh said, nodding. "A mix of both."

Reed took a sip of the black liquid and nearly gagged. The taste was somewhere between rancid salt water and charred embers.

"It is burning the whole way through," Keresh said, laughing. "You will be having a taste for it though. Or not. Who is saying? It is one of my pleasures in life, and one can never deny themselves a good feeling. How about you, Reed? What are you enjoying?"

Eating. Sleeping. Not being stabbed. So far, I've failed at all three today. "Adventure," Reed decided, gazing past the captain and out beyond the window at his back. "I want to see what's out there."

"To this, I must salute." Keresh stood and motioned for Reed to do the same. The clink of their glasses rang through the room like a bell. "Stay with me, and you are seeing much and more of this world, I promise you."

The black-smoke drink burned through Reed's insides and left him wobbling down the hall by the time he left Keresh's quarters. He was glad not to have been asked much about the Turtle just yet because he hadn't read much of the journal, and his thoughts were too far and wandering to wrangle a decent lie. It was going to be some time before they made landfall, he knew, and he would use that time to learn all he could from Torrin's notes. Reed hobbled quickly down the hall, overcome by a sudden, desperate need to lay down. He was a fraud, he thought, but he would learn to be more. To be better.

He cursed Finch as he passed her door, unsure if it had been silent or not. The door to the unclaimed room was open, and the sight of its comfortable bed taunted him. She had played him, and now Keresh thought he was a soldier desiring sparse quarters. Reed wouldn't ruin that impression so long as it served the captain. It was back to the closet for him. The world rose and shook and fell under his feet as he walked. Somehow, he managed to make it all the way down the hall without falling over.

"Now that is impressive," Finch said in a bored drawl, swaying with the ship as she followed Reed. Her eyes examined him head to toe like he was some gruesome thing out of a menagerie as she walked to his door but made no move to open it for him. "Black smoke, right? My first glass had me throwing up before I even left the room. Not the best first impression I could've made. I actually thought the captain was trying to poison me. You have a bucket in there, yeah?"

"Yeah." Reed practically gargled the word, lurching for the door.

"You can still claim the other room, you know. It's closer to mine. You wouldn't need to stumble so far next time you want to share a drink."

"I'll keep that in mind," said Reed. He fumbled with the door, kicked the crate of tattered sail on its side, and fell into the pile, digging himself a nest on the floor.

"I'll leave you to it, then," Finch said, nudging his side with her boot. "I'd keep you company, but you don't have much space for guests." She chuckled all the way back down the hall. "And keep an ear out for that bell, yeah?"

Reed closed the door and held it shut with his foot, trying to steady the world around him. A moment's fancy had him trying to read the journal, but the letters slipped around the edge of his gaze and fell from his mind. He could study the journal later, he decided, tucking it near his heart. Maybe after a long nap, if the world ever stopped spinning…

7

ASH

THE SUNSET BRIDGE

Ash sat up, watching the distant moon race through the sky pursued by scattered stars, and waited for sleep to find her. She waited so long that thin rays of morning light were prying through the forest canopy just as her eyes started to close.

She had been late to bed anyway, spending half the night chasing Leaf through the dark forest. Surely the Watchers would know by now that Leaf was on the run. Perhaps they even suspected Ash was helping her.

When the last of the evening chill faded and the birds began to sing, Ash knew it was time to leave. Shaking the stiffness from her arm, she walked over to the thick branch where Leaf was nestled into the tree.

The green-haired girl was tucked into a tight ball, warm under her leaf-woven cloak, lost in a fearsome dream. Her closed eyes darted wildly back and forth as she rocked slowly in place.

Ash roused her gently. "Get up," she said, nudging Leaf's side. The green-haired girl mumbled something and rolled in place, pushing her away. Ash gripped her shoulder and started to shake. "Leaf, come on. We need to go."

Leaf woke with a sharp gasp. Panicked, she swung, her hand heavy with sleep, and Ash caught it deftly.

"Sorry," said Leaf, realizing what she had done. She looked only half aware, her eyes focused on something far beyond the trees. "Too many dreams."

"It's all right," said Ash, who never dreamed at all. "Come on. We have to get moving."

They collected themselves and climbed quietly down from the tree into the tall brush below, where the early morning mists were receding slowly into the soil. The Watchers would have many eyes and ears on the lookout, so, silently, they began to run.

Leaf, crouched low in her shrouded cloak, was almost invisible in the forest overgrowth. Ash felt rather exposed in comparison wearing her white wolf fur. Eyes much more often looked down than they did up, and so it had always been easy for her to hide between the leaves of tall trees. Now that it was Ash on the ground, she could only think of how much she would stand out.

They were traveling downhill toward the old ruin the clans knew as the Sunset Bridge. Their run through the night had taken them far, the furthest Ash had gone from the Elderglade since her arrival with the Old Wolf. A pang shot through her stomach—she'd left without saying goodbye to the Elder's sapling. Ash wouldn't be gone for long, she told herself, and she was helping a friend. The Old Wolf had taught Ash nothing if not the importance of friends and family, and so she would understand. It was a lesson Ash had thought would never apply to her again.

They didn't stop to hunt or forage along the way, sating their stomachs with the rations Leaf had brought with her. Everything Ash owned she carried on her back, and she hadn't stopped to grab anything on her way out of the glade. The Turtle would provide.

Leaf moved so quickly through the forest that Ash lost sight of her. Her legs were stiff and burning after their mad dash through the moonlit forest, sore from the whipping brambles and thorns, but she bore the pain quietly, as she'd been taught. Their run stretched on for hours through the morning, and Leaf hadn't stopped or even looked back until it was finally time to rest.

"Look," said Leaf, pointing to a gap in the trees. Ash glanced over her shoulder to the ruined tower, seemingly shunned by the forest. In the open air, the foliage peeled back to reveal the ruin, and the sunlight dimmed over the fallen stones.

"Stonefolk?" she asked, though no one else had built things like that on the Turtle. "I thought they didn't come this high up."

"We're pretty far down, actually," said Leaf. "The trees make it hard to tell, but Koomis taught me to watch the flowers." She pointed to a small, vibrant yellow patch growing between two trees. Ash hadn't seen them since her arrival at the glade, reminding her of a long-ago past, when she sat among the flowers, listening to the other children sing distantly. They had always sung without her.

"Different flowers like different heights," Leaf continued. "These ones stop growing when you get too high. I'd probably grab some for the medicine women if I was going back soon…"

"I'll bring some on my way back up," Ash said. It would be a weak apology, but better than empty hands.

Leaf nodded. "Good idea," she said, looking back to the tower. Her expression turned distant. "Should we check that out?"

"I figured you've seen all the ruins around here already," Ash said before shaking her head. "But you don't have time. The Watchers will be on the way."

Her eyes on the rubble, Leaf said, "Did you know I saw a mountain cat once?"

Ash frowned. "Did you hear me?" she asked.

"It was prowling the edge of the Elderglade," Leaf continued, looking past Ash, somewhere into memory. "It was still really young, so I didn't tell anyone. I didn't think it was dangerous or anything, just curious. I watched it for a while, and it got pretty close to one of the longhouses before it ran off." Her tired eyes came into focus again.

They didn't have time for this, but Ash was afraid to push Leaf past exhaustion. "Really?" she asked. "They don't normally come near the glade."

"That's what everybody says," Leaf said softly, her brow furrowing, "but I think that's only true for the adults. The cubs are curious, and they haven't learned to be afraid of people yet."

"All right," said Ash, "but what does this have to do with the ruin?" she pressed gently.

"Well, I was the only one who noticed the mountain cat that day. The other Watchers didn't do a thing about it." Leaf smiled almost ruefully at Ash. "I'm not that worried they'll be able to track me without you helping them."

Ash grimaced. *They're better than you think*, she thought, shaking her head. But when Leaf moved toward the ruin, Ash followed. All that was left of the tower was its base, half-swallowed by a newly growing tree. Mossy green hills had crept over the collapsed stone, and a small river ran through a broken window half buried in the earth. Water streamed down the tower in a sharp point that dug narrowly through the earth in deep channels that ran down the hillside.

Leaf sat on a stone ledge, inviting Ash to do the same.

Her legs felt hollow, screaming for her to rest, but she wouldn't so much as touch the cursed ruin. Standing this close was unnerving enough. "I'm all right," she said.

In the stillness, Ash's worries crept forward again. What would she tell the others when she returned to the glade? That Leaf had been too quick to catch? That she had failed to track her? If this was the one way she could serve the clans, where would she belong when they learned she had let them down? Ash would only take Leaf as far as the stone bridge, and only because they both knew the Watchers wouldn't cross it. Leaf might have grown up free from the taboo of the stonefolk remains, but the fear ran deep in the blood of the clans. If they could make it to the bridge, she would be free. Sitting still felt like wasting their chance to get her there in time.

Leaf bit roughly into a hard loaf of bread. "Want some?" she asked, her mouth half full.

"I'm all right," said Ash. Her nerves were on edge, though from the ruins or the Watchers, she couldn't say.

Leaf sat up, stuffing the other half into her mouth and chasing it with a large drink from her waterskin. Then, rubbing her hands on the hem of her cloak, she nodded. "All right. Ready." She was almost unintelligible through her mouthful of bread and water, but Ash was relieved she looked a little more herself. Her gaze more focused.

Sometimes, Ash thought that Leaf was more a stranger among the clans than she was. Leaf had none of the graces or respect for tradition that had been instilled in Ash. She had no fear of the ruins or the Deepwood. She didn't even know which clan she belonged to and never seemed to wonder about it at all. Ash often thought it was strange that a clanless nomad could so certainly carry herself alone through life, while she had always felt an outsider even amongst her own pack. Even Leaf's grandmother had lost her history to the stonefolk, and her grandfather had lost his life in their escape. As for her parents, Leaf never spoke of them. Perhaps, like Ash, she'd never known them at all.

The soft droning of insects dimmed as Leaf and Ash crept through the forest. In the distance, something louder bounded through the trees, heavy footsteps landing gracefully as they leapt through the tight twists of the upper branches. A silence followed that Ash recognized.

"The air," said Leaf.

"It's quiet," Ash finished. A silent predator.

Ash's arm tingled at the thought of a serpent. Bears and mountain cats weren't unheard of in the area either, but she didn't think it was either of those. The air didn't smell right, there was a sharp, sour scent to it, not the usual light, loamy breeze. No, the silence was from a hunter, and that meant either someone from another clan was in pursuit of a buck, or…

"Watchers," Leaf said quietly.

There was no use hiding now.

"They must've been running through the night," Ash whispered just loud enough for Leaf to hear. They ran, Ash letting herself fall some distance behind. She hoped that, from above, it might still look like she was pursuing Leaf, rather than helping her escape.

Shadows stalked them from the upper branches and trailed through the tall grass and tree trunks behind them. Three, four, maybe five, fast and in silent pursuit. They were skilled, Ash thought, to stay so silent over the terrain, but for them, this was just a duty. For her, this was a way of life. She'd learned to keep silent before they had learned to walk.

When the forest broke to open sky, Leaf leapt from the cliff rather than follow the ridge down, hanging in the air a moment before colliding with a great redwood rising near its edge. Below them, the forest spread wide, and Leaf lowered herself quickly through the leaves and along its trunk before jumping down between the lower branches, landing as silently as a fallen seed on the forest floor. Ash followed behind.

They'll keep their eyes on the forest ahead, Ash thought, waving Leaf back. At her look of confusion, she gestured for silence. Both fought to keep their breathing quiet. The tall grass would leave too easy a trail to follow, and for now, they were hidden from view by the rocky overhangs. Pointing upward, Ash led Leaf to circle back some distance along the cliff base, nestling into the grooves of the tall rocks, hidden behind pillars of shadow and earth.

Five nearly silent sets of footsteps treaded the grass high overhead. One by one, they leapt from the edge of the cliff, one was lithe and graceful, climbing down through the branches but rustling the leaves as she went. Another, large and bundled in heavy fur, was a shadow that blocked the sun and slowed his descent by embedding his knife in the tree trunk. The others slid and climbed down in turn, trying to muffle their grunts, their eyes on the forest ahead just as Ash had expected. Their descent was slower, she realized with satisfaction.

When the last of them, a large and fierce-looking Bear warrior, disappeared into the tall grass, Ash took a small rock and aimed it carefully over their heads into the forest beyond, where it landed with a sharp smack against a tree. One could almost mistake it for the sound of a snapping branch, if they weren't paying close attention. She watched as the grass bent and swayed from five separate directions toward the sound.

"This way," Ash mouthed, and began to move in the other direction.

They slowed their pace as they went, catching their breath and putting distance between themselves and the Watchers. Ash knew her little trick wouldn't fool them for long, so she and Leaf worked hard to make sure there wasn't a trail they could circle back on. She'd have to explain it—no one bothered to hide their trail in a chase—but that was a problem for tomorrow. Behind them, the forest resumed its usual quiet song, the soft-rustling creatures in the brush and birds' melodies in the branches, and Ash relaxed with them. The danger had passed for the moment.

"Why won't they just leave me alone?" Leaf asked quietly. Her jaw clenched with stubborn frustration. "I'm not hurting anyone. I didn't leave anything in their stupid camp."

Ash winced but kept her mouth shut. There was nothing she could say to change Leaf's mind, and there was only time to waste in trying.

"What's wrong?" Leaf asked.

"Just tired," Ash lied.

"I can keep going alone from here," Leaf offered. Ash looked at her, surprised. "They don't know you're helping me yet. You can go back home."

"It's fine," said Ash. The offer left Ash feeling hollow. Not because Leaf wasn't being genuine, Ash knew that she was, but because the deep guilt gnawing in her stomach was getting harder and harder to ignore. It needled her, too, that despite all her time in the glade, she still didn't think of it as home. "I can keep going."

"Okay." Leaf smiled. Ash looked away.

They didn't run after that. There was no point. They weren't sure just how many others might be in the forest looking for Leaf, or where they might be, but they knew that hunters and Watchers were probably still nearby. It was better to move quietly and conserve their strength in case they had to run again.

They passed through large stretches of quiet wood, where deer drank from whispering streams and pranced through the brush. Bleating goats climbed rocky rises in the distance. Ash could see hints of their gnarled horns through the canopy, sure-footed, standing upright on sheer cliff walls. She wondered how long it had been since she'd last seen their kind. Those herds never wandered close to the Elderglade.

Broken branches of old road snaked up through the land, like dirt and gravel tendrils cutting through the forest. The trees grew shorter here, and slimmer, having only grown since the stonefolk vanished. The forest was still recovering, but already a wealth of wildlife had returned to the grounds, the soil thick with humus and fallen leaves.

They passed a ruin of an old campground as they walked. It was clan, not stonefolk, so Ash was unafraid as they walked between burned husks of longhouses and the charred skeletons of tents that still stood, silent witnesses to the brutality of long-ago occupation.

"Who were they?" Ash asked as they passed through the ghost village. Wolves only settled in caves and spent the rest of their time on the move. If these were Beavers, they would have built closer to the water, and Crane or Loon would have hidden higher in the hills. Bear and Marten, she knew, preferred the denser forests down in the valleys.

"Raven," said Leaf.

"Really?" Ash asked. The blackened remains took on a new interest as she tried to make out lost detailings in the fallen campsite.

"This used to be their territory, but the stonefolk chased them out a long time ago."

That was a surprise. "I've never met a Raven," said Ash, wondering how Leaf had learned such things. She thought of the young boy yesterday with his black eye markings, but he was a Magpie. She thought of all the people who'd passed through the Elderglade and couldn't remember a single one who had named themselves Raven.

"And you never will," said Leaf. "Koomis told me they're all gone. Killed off by the stonefolk. The ones who lived here went into hiding in the Deepwood. A few intermarried into the other clans, but the name was lost over time." A look of wry amusement crossed her face. "I tried to go looking for them once, down in the Deepwood. Koomis caught me before I could start climbing, though."

"And now you're headed there anyway," said Ash, smiling sadly.

Leaf nodded. She hadn't spoken about leaving her grandmother yet, and Ash wondered when she might. She'd stop by Koomis's burrow on her return, she vowed silently. Tell her what had happened. That Leaf had gotten away, and that she'd made sure of it.

Leaf stopped before a small patch of land. The charred remains of the village were arranged in a circle here. Ash realized this was where the Ravens had danced and celebrated together. She could almost hear the echo of drums as she imagined all the dancers in their feather and jingle dresses, their ghosts dancing deeper below into the hills before vanishing into the black expanse of the Deepwood.

"Who is this Woods Witch?" Ash asked. She had been so focused on staying one step ahead of their pursuers that she hadn't had time to consider what Leaf was truly stepping into, but the Raven clan's vanishing in the Deepwood led her to wondering what exactly had happened to them. What had they found down there?

"Koomis told me about her, once," said Leaf, that far-off look in her eyes again. "She's a traveler, like us, except she's not from the Turtle. Koomis said she came here from somewhere far away, over the black salt waters, because she supposedly looks nothing like us." Leaf turned to Ash and raised her hands. "I mean," she added quickly, "like the rest of the clans. Well, I know you're of clan and I'm not, but…you don't look like us. I don't mean that in a bad way."

"I understand," said Ash. She drew her wolf's head lower, sudden shame twisting her stomach. The words always stung no matter who said them—a reminder that she had no right to stop Leaf from doing what she wanted to do. Ash might be of the clans, but Leaf was of the people, and there was nothing she could ever do to bridge that distance.

"Anyway," Leaf continued, hurrying on, "Koomis says she lives down in the Deepwood, and she keeps things collected from the stonefolk ruins. She isn't unfriendly, exactly, but she doesn't talk to others much, and almost nobody ever goes down to see her. It's too dangerous, they say, since the Ravens vanished. But if anyone would know what I found in the ruins, it's her."

Ash wondered what had set Leaf so fervently on her path, but she couldn't bring herself to ask. "How did Koomis know about her?" Ash asked as they left the ruined clangrounds behind. "I've never heard of a woods witch."

"We used to meet a lot of people before we settled in the glade," said Leaf. "Dad even knew someone who came here from over the water. Then they had me."

"Wait," said Ash, stopping suddenly. Maybe they weren't as different as she thought. "Do you mean your mother wasn't from the Turtle?"

"Maybe, or maybe she went over the water after having me," Leaf said, and shrugged. "I'm not sure. Koomis didn't like talking about it much, and I never really knew either of them anyway."

Ash couldn't wrap her head around that. For someone so curious, Leaf didn't at all seem bothered about not knowing her parents. "Do you ever wonder what they were like?"

"Sometimes," said Leaf. "I can remember my dad a little, when I really try. I know he was tall, and he would lift me up really high." She smiled briefly at the memory, before her face fell back to flat acceptance. "But I can't remember much else."

"Do you ever miss him?"

"It's hard to miss someone you never knew," said Leaf, somewhat shortly. "I can't even picture his face. Anyway, he's gone now, just like the Ravens."

Ash wanted to ask more, not just for Leaf's sake but her own, but as Leaf picked up her pace, it was clear she didn't want to speak further. Ash wondered if she would have another chance after today.

Silence normally didn't bother her, but now it was weighing on her near as heavy as the wolf cloak. Leaf was going to be gone soon, truly out of reach of Ash, the Watchers, and the clans, with no promise of ever returning. The Deepwood was a dangerous place even for experienced hunters and warriors, and Leaf was neither. She was good at climbing, and sneaking, and digging into places where she shouldn't be, but if a serpent should happen upon her, or a spider, or a spirit...

Ash let her thoughts wander until the wind drifted an old, familiar scent across the grounds, carrying her to memories of long walks with the Old Wolf.

"Why do we watch over the roads?" she'd asked Ash once.

"To see who might still walk them," Ash had answered, her new axe gripped tightly in her hand. "There are those who would do our people harm, and we stand ready to protect against them."

She still cherished the pride in the Old Wolf's smile.

The sun had fallen low by the time they reached the rim of the mountain. From the cliff's edge, Ash could see beyond the tree line to the expanse of distant hills and peaks that stretched across the horizon. They were so tall they dwarfed the ledge Ash and Leaf were standing on, cutting like a white knife through the sunset-reddened clouds. Others sank so deeply into the valleys that Ash could blot out their great lakes with her thumb. How could she ever protect it all? From here, the distant forests of the valley floor were like carpets of moss growing along the rocks. And somewhere beyond it all, waiting in the deepest crevices of the valley floors, was the Deepwood.

"There it is," Leaf said, shielding her eyes from the sun setting between two mountain peaks. A long pathway bridged the gap between them, held on the backs of two carved stone titans who grimaced under the weight. Even at a distance, Ash could clearly see the pain etched into the face of the titan on the far side, jaw gritted and features twisted at the monstrous effort.

Ash turned to Leaf. In the sunset, the bridge looked unnaturally dim, with midnight shadows defying the bright sun. It had always been an unnatural sight from a distance, and from up close, it was even stranger, like slivers of night had cut their way back into the day. Whatever the stonefolk had done, it had been anything but natural. But Leaf was unafraid, walking onto the old stone road to the bridge before she seemed to remember Ash and turned back.

In the distance, a raven cried out.

"Oh, right," Leaf said. She was trying to keep her voice light, but she sounded sullen to Ash. "I guess…this is it, then."

Ash nodded, not knowing what to say. They had made it to the bridge. Leaf was free. And it did nothing to keep the guilt from eating her insides.

"You know," Leaf started, her voice smaller than usual, wondering and hesitant, "you could always—"

Something crashed in the woods behind them, and Ash and Leaf turned, drawing their axe and bow. Ash's arm stung, and she braced herself for a serpent. To her horror, not one but three figures emerged from the wood.

They could have been mistaken for Watchers but for their fur cloaks and sharply honed axes, vicious points curled like fangs. *Wolves.*

"That's as far as you go," said their leader. He was tall and lean-muscled, with the deep brown skin of the trees. A familiar face, though more lined than Ash remembered, turned to her with a curt nod.

Her heart raced as she fought to keep her breath steady. This was all her fault.

"We're not here to hurt you," Ohnah said. His long hair was tied back in a knot, and Ash noticed how much of it had turned to snow. "The Watchers informed us someone's been bringing stonefolk relics to the Elderglade. Was it you?"

One of the Wolves looked past Ash like she wasn't even there, reigniting an old, burning shame. The other, however, looked right at her, and his eyes held nothing but contempt.

"You've failed in your hunt, Ash," said Grey Moon from beneath his hooded pelt. His face had grown more lean, and his smile reminded her of a hungry wolf. "Why am I not surprised?"

"She did better than you," Leaf called out. She'd backed onto the bridge. "I'm already out of your reach."

"Don't count on that," said Grey Moon, raising his bow. "You could be halfway to the sunset and I'd still drop you like a fox."

"You wouldn't," hissed Ash, raising her axe.

"He wouldn't," agreed Ohnah, giving the youth a stern look. His eyes slipped past Ash to Leaf. "Nothing has been done that calls for violence. Give us what you've taken so we can dispose of it, and then we'll all return to the Elderglade."

"No," said Leaf. "I'm not going back. The Watchers don't need to worry about me anymore. I'm not their problem."

"You see? She has no respect," said Grey Moon indignantly. "Not for her elders, and not for tradition. But that's no surprise from a clanless. No family to teach her better." He looked at Ash with the same malice she'd known well in childhood. "Then again, teachings don't always stick."

"Perhaps not," said Ohnah, glancing at Ash. "Perhaps you're beyond the reach of the Watchers now, but protecting the Turtle is the Wolves' sacred duty, and our hunting grounds stretch from shore to shore. Continue into the ruins, and we will find you, one way or another."

Ohnah was the same as he'd always been. He and the Old Wolf used to argue long into the night, often about Ash. She wondered if he'd finally risen to clan leader, as he'd always wanted. If so, she suspected he'd volunteered for this hunt only to shame her, as had Grey Moon.

"That's enough," said a third wolf, a soft-voiced older woman. "I know you," she said to Ash. "Do you know this girl? A Wolf doesn't play with her meal, child. If you were hunting her, you would have captured her already."

Ash didn't know what to say to that.

"Please," the she-wolf continued. "Talk sense into your friend. Convince her to return with us peacefully."

The guilt was twisting in Ash's stomach. Everything that happened, everything that would happen next, would all be her fault.

"I'm not going back!" Leaf called from the bridge.

"The clanless has made her decision," Grey Moon said, raising his bow again.

"Put it down!" Ash yelled, stepping in front of his shot.

"You see? She defends her!" Grey Moon yelled. "You're no Wolf," he sneered. "And you never were."

"Enough," said Ohnah. The head of the pack took the bow from Grey Moon but reached for his own axe. Finally, he looked at Ash, and she held his gaze. "You would raise a weapon against the pack? I shouldn't be surprised, but I am disappointed. I'd hoped Ingan saw something in you that I couldn't, but it seems you were her one failing after all."

The sound of the Old Wolf's name stung. When duty divided the pack, how was she always stuck between? Ash held a shuddering breath. Win or lose, this wasn't a fight worth having. She set the axe back down, drawing the wolf hood low over her eyes.

"You don't deserve the Chief's pelt," called Grey Moon, echoing doubts she'd long carried herself. The sting held in the long, cold silence that followed.

Then a hand was at her shoulder.

"Hey, are you okay?" It was Leaf. Ash hadn't heard her come back across the bridge, but Leaf was moving to stand between her and Grey Moon.

The Wolves shifted, ready to strike. Ash moved on instinct. As Ingan had once done for her, so Ash would do for Leaf. "I am," she said quietly, holding her arm in front of Leaf to keep herself between the two sides. "I am a Wolf," she said more loudly, "and I won't let you hurt my pack." A shiver crawled up her spine as she felt the cold road of the stonefolk at her heel. The Old Wolf had taught her to watch for dangers on the road, and now she would walk it.

"You're going to come with me?" Leaf whispered. She sounded hopeful, and when Ash looked at her, her face was lit like the dawn.

"I am." Her heart was a frenzied drumbeat, guilt and shame and excitement as well, rolling in waves as she fought to steady her breathing.

“And so, you turn your back on clan,” said Ohnah. Grey Moon went to retrieve his bow, but the old hunter held it from him. “I warned her this would come to pass, you know.”

Ash ran her thumb over the axe crafted by the Old Wolf. Her first gift, and her first teaching. “There are those who would do our people harm,” she said, staring down the pack from her cloak, “and I stand ready to protect them.”

Grey Moon scoffed, trying to rouse the others, but Ohnah would not pursue them over the cursed stone of the old kingdom, just as Ash had expected. Near every instinct she had was screaming at her that this was a mistake, that the curse would fall on her as well, and that she had just doomed herself to whatever fate had fallen on the vanished stonefolk. But Leaf was there with her, and when she saw her smiling friend, her sense of duty won out. She was going to make things right.

The pack prowled the edge of the roads, howling their hunter’s call as Leaf and Ash crossed the stone. It was a promise, but one they couldn’t make good on just yet. Ash and Leaf ignored them as their howls fell to silence and walked together into the sunset.

8

FINCH

THE NIGHT MARKET

Howls of laughter roared over the decks and waters below, bouncing beyond the rising swells and endless masts of the Flotilla.

Finch couldn't stand the sound of it. There were too many voices, speaking in too many languages, about too many things for her to track. The small crowds crawled over the deck of the *Dragon's Breath* like an army of insects carrying the crew's newly traded provisions aboard, stacking crates and barrels and taking the ship's long-aged goods in exchange. Captain Beldrick stood overtop them all from his place at the helm. A small gaggle of other senior sailors had gathered around him, trading news and stories, and now and then the captain would lead them in another round of laughter, shaking hands and clapping each other on the back in their small, private circle.

"At least we'll have proper supplies," Finch muttered. A boy with a mess of bright, wiry red hair stopped and squinted at her. "I wasn't talking to you," she said, spitting at his feet. "Get moving."

She didn't like having strangers on her ship. Well, the captain's ship, but it was her home, and given that she had nowhere else to be in this world, every foreign footstep on the deck felt like an assault. Pressing past the throngs, she worked her way across, ducking under crates being carried by heavyset men, dancing around the ambling crowds, and then stopping abruptly to duck into an impromptu alleyway between their newly stacked goods. She wondered about swiping something before it could be properly inventoried, but quiet breathing betrayed that she wasn't alone back here.

"A good place to duck out on working," said Finch, punching Reed on his too-thin arm. "Not that you've got much to work with. Did you get stuck back here?"

A barrel thudded heavily, shaking their hiding place. "Just keeping an eye on things," said Reed. His eyes glanced back and forth over the deck before he shrank himself even lower.

"Yeah, I bet you are," said Finch, remembering what Ridae had said. Reed really was just a rat, scurrying away, hiding wherever he could. "See anything interesting out there?"

Reed thought for a moment, a look of concern crossing his face before he pushed it aside. "It's what I'm not seeing that concerns me," he said. At Finch's irritated look, he continued, "Do you usually allow so many people on deck? The crew's outmatched six to one."

"What? You think they might try something?" asked Finch. She ground her teeth together. The worry had been lurking at the back of her mind all day, and hearing it put a twitch in her hand. "Captain says that sort of thing doesn't happen on the Flotilla."

"Not *on* the Flotilla, true," Reed agreed. He ran a hand over his eyes, as if to clear off hair that didn't seem to be there. "But there's no law beyond the bounds of the boats. Who's to say what happens once we're over the waves?"

Finch lowered her voice. "Is there something you're not telling us?" she asked, leaning close.

From the bounce of his lip, Finch could see Reed was fighting to keep that calm façade. "Nothing I haven't already warned the captain about."

Rat. "Warn me."

Reed lowered his voice to match hers. "Most folk on the Flotilla aren't out to rob you," he said, glancing at the men moving beyond the crates, "but there's plenty who'll sell you out just fine to the sort who will. I warned the captain that there are eyes everywhere on the docks, learning what they can about us. Who we are, what we're carrying, where we're going..." He scratched his side nervously. "I know you're capable people. You wouldn't be operating with such a small crew if you weren't. But there are others out there who won't mind chancing those odds, and they'd take a shot at us the first chance they got."

A disdainful laugh crept through Finch's chest and shot out her nose. She jabbed a finger into Reed's chest and found it was surprisingly tough. "Let's be clear. There is no *us*, turtle boy. You're not crew. Not really. You're just a guide that the captain hired, and if you can't deliver on what you promised, you won't be leaving that island alive."

Reed rubbed his hand over his heart where she'd jabbed him and seemed to search for something to say. He never had the chance to find it.

"Is this the beginning of a fruitful friendship I am seeing?" the captain's voice called jovially over the deck. The sailors beside him chuckled as he waved to Finch and Reed. "Or perhaps it is the attempting of two to hide away when there is much work to be doing."

Finch went to drag Reed from his hiding spot, only to find that he was already carrying a large bundle of loose ropes stacked over his head.

"Hah! And as for you," the captain called out to Finch, "Tamn is taking stock of all we are to hold. You are to be helping her below."

"Aye, Captain," said Finch. She gave a curt salute, then shoved her way past a freckled arm to head below deck.

"We can feast once on well-spiced pigeon, or eat nightly with salted fish," said Tamn dully. Her eyes never left their stock of cargo.

The ship's swaying was softer below decks, nearer toward the center like a gentle cradle. The soft warm fires that lit the dim, and the long, monotonous wash of the waves nearly lulled Finch to sleep.

"Still, couldn't we have held onto something, at least?" she asked through a yawn. "I get enough salt in my air and water. Does it need to be in my food, too?"

"Salt preserves," said Tamn, matter-of-factly. She tapped Finch's barrel. "How much?"

"Fifty-six salted cod, confirmed." Finch rubbed her hands on her trousers. Her fingers came back dry and cracked from the counting. "Fourteen each."

"Nine each with leftover," Tamn corrected her. "You're forgetting Wright and Reed."

Finch muttered to herself in irritation at the thought of someone else eating her food.

"Does Wright even eat?" she asked. "He hasn't come out of his quarters once since he arrived."

"If you live, you eat," said Tamn, bluntly. She rolled another barrel to Finch and tapped its side. "Count. Seventy-seven in this one. Confirm."

"What do you know about this whole journey the captain is planning?" Finch asked as she dug her hands into another pile of salt and fish. "Turtle Rock. I'd never even heard of the place until we got the job. What sort of treasures does the captain hope to find to make this whole thing worth it? And what is he expecting to be there that we need to hire a guide? I mean, what do we even know about this guy Wright?"

"As much as we knew about you when you came aboard," said Tamn. Her speech was abrupt and stiff, head lost in her numbers. The words had been meant to prevent more protest, but Tamn's icy tone only sparked fire in Finch.

"As I recall, you were in desperate need of hands at the time," she argued. "The ship was a wreck, your supplies almost gone. And hadn't you just lost a couple guys?"

"Five," said Tamn, her tone unchanging. "Captain called it the unfortunate tithe of the deep. Now count."

"Twenty-seven, twenty-eight, twenty-nine," Finch said pointedly, digging her hands through the salt. "So, when you brought me on, it was out of necessity. But these two, do we really need them? One is paying us with a share of our own work, and the other…" Finch bit her lip. She couldn't find the right words for her misgivings of Reed, not without admitting to Tamn that she'd let the rat trail them right from the start. "Do you trust him?"

"I trust the captain."

And that was that. Tamn was like a mule: loyal, reliable, and stubborn to a fault. Finch knew she wouldn't make any progress this way.

"At least tell me what you know about Wright," she said, switching tracks. "You think he's on the run from something, maybe? You've got to admit it's at least a little strange that he ripped any loyalties off his jacket."

"People make enemies," Tamn said bitterly. "And not all lost causes are worth wearing. I trust the captain's decision."

"Why?" Only a fool trusted blindly. Finch watched Tamn carefully but found no fault through which to gauge her feeling.

"Why do you insist on talking when you should be counting?" Tamn dropped a heavy barrel of hardtack in front of Finch. "One-hundred and eighty. Confirm."

Enough for a month, Finch thought. *That is, if nothing happens to the others along the way.*

The sky was turning a bruised purple through the window, water dappled with red and golden points that rolled softly toward the skyline, when they finally finished counting the goods. The deck no longer thundered with as many boots, but the low rumble of stragglers remained. Finch could hear their laughter above as the captain regaled them with yet another story of his years on the sea.

Finch had few stories to share herself, and even less will to share them. If Tamn had any words beyond those of duty, she kept them silent in the wake of Captain Beldrick's shadow. All she'd ever learned of the ironclad giant was that her homeland was somewhere very cold, and that the war she'd fought with the captain left the ruins of her upbringing buried beneath the snow.

Finch wondered whether that was better or worse than to see your home drowned. Sometimes, her thoughts returned to swollen tides, the manic, bubbling, drowned words calling to her through a fog of memory, saltwater so strong she could almost taste it. Shivering, she let the smell of incense flooding the halls drag her back from her counting-lulled delirium, and left Tamn and her inventory behind.

"Ridae, keep your damn door shut if you're going to burn that noxious spew," Finch shouted, slamming the door of the lantern keeper's quarters. In truth, the smell wasn't that bad. The deep, herbal blend sang of places far beyond the Broken Waters, but it caught and lingered beneath the deck, bringing a tickle to her throat. She raised a hand to cough, and then an eyebrow when the sound came first from the far end of the ship.

"That you, turtle boy?" she asked, walking lightly toward the sound. It was hard to see through the smoke in the halls, but she could make out the shadow of a young man, tall and thin, leaning against a doorway. At the sound of her voice, his coughing cut abruptly. That raised her suspicions. By quick tally, Wright, Tamn, Ridae, and the captain were all accounted for in their quarters or on deck, and if it wasn't Reed, then someone was hiding on their ship. A stowaway, perhaps, or even a thief. Her hand went to the knife at her belt. "Best speak up now," she said, waving a hand to clear the smoke. "You don't want to know what we do with stowaways on this ship."

"I'm not a stowaway," said a small voice. They were young and timid sounding, but with an irritating undertone of arrogance. A freckled, bandaged hand emerged from the dark and smoke, and then a thin young man, squinting so hard his teeth were showing. "I was moving cargo and got turned around in the smoke," he said.

"Impressive, in a one-way corridor," said Finch, eyeing the boy skeptically. He gave only a shrug in response. "Who are you supposed to be with?"

"Calloway," the youth offered. "We traded salt cod for your mint."

His hand twitched at his waist, his eyes glancing to the door beside him, and Finch knew there was more to his story than what he offered. "You're leaving," she said, grabbing him tightly at the wrist.

For a moment, he looked almost ready to fight her, but the defiance vanished at the sight of her knife. She frog-marched the young man down the corridor over his protests. She'd already been tricked once by the lying rats of the Flotilla, and she wouldn't let it happen again.

"I'm going, I'm going!" the freckled youth protested.

"Not fast enough, you're not," said Finch, giving his arm another twist. "Move it."

She'd get him off the ship before the captain felt any sympathy for another stray. She thought for a moment of bringing him to the railing and offering him to the waves, but instead marched him back to the docks on the very off chance that he really was just a lost ship hand. Before she let him go, she pinned him between the edge of the dock and the hull of the *Dragon's Breath*, his feet teetering perilously at the edge of the dock.

"I told you I was going," he whined. His hands were pressed flat against the hull of the ship to keep from falling over.

"Not before we see what you're hiding," she said, shouldering him in the back to keep him off-balance. Then she went for his pockets.

"Help! Help! I'm being robbed!"

"We've got a stowaway here!" Finch yelled over him. If the crowds of busy ship hands and sailors cared one way or another, nobody showed it. It didn't take long for Finch to find the dulled knife tucked into the youth's pants, but it took a little more searching to find the paper tucked in his boot.

He almost fell into the water at her shove. "What's this?" Finch asked, unraveling the note.

"What's what?" he asked, steadying himself on the edge of the dock. "I don't know what you're talking about."

Looking over the words as if she could read them, Finch managed to recognize the scrawl of Captain Beldrick's name.

"If you don't know what this is, then you won't mind if I keep it," she said, giving him a final shove away from the ship. She tucked the note into her pocket as he caught himself. "Get out of here."

"Gladly," said the freckled youth, sneering as he left. Finch watched as he walked along the docks, gritting her teeth. He walked away alone without rejoining his supposed crew.

She returned to the deck and leaned over the railing for a time, watching the comings and goings of the ships and people as the sun fell lower through the sky. The ocean rolled and swelled beneath them all, at times rushing between the planks of the floating docks to flood sailor's boots with seawater. They sloshed along regardless, seeming not to notice their soaked trousers sagging and pulling, weighing them down. *A lifetime of hard work for hard men breeds apathy to hardship*, Finch thought, and not for the first time wondered if the weight of the world would ever catch up with her long enough to press the life from her eyes, as she saw in so many ship hands. Surely these men had been young once. She could see the life still in the youth roaming between the ships, the eager, hungry eyes of scavengers looking for any morsel of hope they could find, and when the saltwater tried to pull them down, they pulled back, fierce in the face of unearned hardship rather than accepting of it.

A sudden touch of warmth hit the air, and the return of smoke and incense alerted her to Ridae.

"Needed some fresh air, yeah?" Finch asked as they settled at her side.

"I preferred the warmth of a familiar sun," said Ridae. The lantern hanging from their gnarled walking stick swayed softly in rhythm with the rocking ship. Finch looked up at the only sun in the sky, bright and orange and falling low, and wondered what it was the lantern keeper was on about this time. "We set sail to paths unknown at noon tomorrow," they continued, their soft voice muffled beneath the gentle wash of waves.

"That's why we've got a guide," Finch said with a sardonic smile. She rolled her eyes. "Hey, let me ask you something, and try to give me a straight answer for once, yeah?"

The lantern keeper nodded.

"What does this note say?"

Finch unfurled the paper taken from the boy and handed it to Ridae, who held it still before their lifeless mask. When they shifted to better read by the lantern, its flames set the shadows of the mask moving, twisting into features almost like an expression.

"The name of our ship, a good deal of cargo, our final destination, and the name of the captain." Ridae sighed. "Could it be that we all need a reminder of who we are?"

Maybe Reed was telling the truth, Finch thought, *about the Flotilla's eyes. But maybe he only said it because he arranged for it to happen. Another ploy to gain trust.*

Ridae nodded in time with the waves. "Good thing we have someone to guide us," they said solemnly. "Be it flame or moon or star or knowledge, we all are lost without light to lead the way."

Finch sighed. They always had to make things weird. "Why didn't you speak up about Reed following us yesterday?"

"I did." Ridae turned to her, shadows flickering in confusion over their mask.

"What I mean is, why didn't you tell the captain?" she asked, gritting her teeth.

"Why didn't you?"

Finch slammed the railing and sent it shuddering. If the lantern keeper could dodge questions, then so could she. "If the captain knew we were being followed, he might not have been so eager to bring in someone new."

"He brought you in, didn't he?"

That was different, Finch thought, bitterly. Her face must have spoken the words for her because the lantern keeper started to laugh.

"Be it snoop or thief or murderer, the captain knows no fear. The brightest fires throw the longest shadows, and through their dancing dark, our lives are shown for what they are, if you've the eyes to see it," Ridae said ponderously. Finch groaned and lowered her head. "The captain is a clever man. What he needs to know, he knows."

Finch thought that, in many ways, Ridae was something akin to a bloodsucking insect. Their words were an annoying, meaningless whine that buzzed in her periphery, flittering beyond her, touching skin only when you've already looked away. She hated the way the lantern keeper used so many words to say so little, and like with any insect, she wanted to deliver a swift, satisfying smack.

"The little Finch is thinking herself a bird, perhaps, to be watching so intently the horizon!"

Finch snapped to attention as the captain laughed to himself from the helm, a large grin cracking the burned side of his face. At his side stood Tamn, gleaming in her armor like an iceberg that had burst through the bottom of the ship.

"Some of our supplies are being yet unseen. You are going with Tamn to find why of the delay, yes?" he asked in that way he always did, as if his orders were a question.

"Aye, Captain," said Finch in a dull drone. She left the lantern keeper to stare alone at the Flotilla, flame burning softly with the sun.

"I am telling you many times to be calling me simply Keresh," the captain chided with a playful look. Finch rolled her eyes before setting off with Tamn along the docks.

After weeks of calming wind and waves, the crowded sounds of the night market were almost too much to bear. Small ships and larger barges encircled the massive central floating dock that almost served as a vessel itself. Several layers of shops and stalls had been built into its main structure like a hive, rope walkways and rickety staircases swarmed with patrons haggling for strange and exotic goods. Finch followed in the wake of men scattered by Tamn. The armored giant drew many glances as she walked, although not as many as Finch had suspected. There were strange sights in every stall, from spined lizards that sprayed venom against glass containers, to living plants whose slow tendrils reached out for insects, and even fire breathers bathing the central causeway in green and purple flames. Even the other travelers were just as strange as Finch and Tamn must have seemed to the people of the Flotilla. Robed preachers screamed in broken tongues so harshly over one another that Finch could only make out one word for every three, mostly about doom and death and ultimate deliverance, blaming the sins of man, of mere existence, for the calamitous nature of a dying world.

"You're only dead if you give up," Finch said, shoving her way past them.

"You! You!" someone yelled. "You want to buy this bird!" A tall, thin man built like a dying tree stood in her way, holding a red- and yellow-plumed squat of feathers in a case. "She sings the most beautiful songs, I promise you! There is no other like her in all the seas. You buy her!"

"Get away from me," Finch said, pushing him roughly aside. For a second, it looked like the cage might fall and send the bird flying free, but he pulled back fiercely, puffing himself up before starting his same pitch on another woman walking the other way.

It's probably for the best, Finch thought. Even if the bird had broken free, where would she be left to go all alone in the middle of the sea?

The interruption wasn't long enough to lose sight of Tamn, but Finch had to fight to press herself through the crowd already closing behind her. Finch was careful to keep her hands at her pockets as the river of travelers flowed around her, though no pickpockets came her way. She caught sight of her destination before she managed to catch up with Tamn, a small schooner-turned-fishing boat called the *Free Lance.* Its bright yellow sails emblazoned with a red sunburst shone in the market lights. To get around the crowd, Finch climbed up the side of a merchant's stall and lifted herself to the swaying walkway above, then ran the length of the market overhead to drop beside Tamn as she arrived.

"You fell behind," said Tamn.

"I caught up," Finch countered, waving off her concern.

The walkway of the *Free Lance* was guarded by two squat but massive men, and a third lean man with arms that fell almost to his knees. On seeing them, he lit up with an apologetic smile.

"Your goods, I know. My most sincere apologies," he started, arms held wide in false helplessness. His words dripped out the sides of his mouth like oil, and Finch thought he walked too proudly to seem truly cowed by anyone. "Sorin," he said to Tamn. When she gave only a stare in return, he continued. "It would seem the good men of the Flotilla felt they had reason to inspect our cargo before sending it along. We would have sent word to you about the delay, but we expected the ordeal to be over and done with by now. Regardless, you have my assurances that all of this will be well sorted before you depart."

Finch watched Sorin carefully, but she left the giant to do the talking.

"What are they searching for?" Tamn asked.

"The guardsmen?" Sorin asked, eyebrows soaring in bewilderment. "Why, I haven't the slightest idea. Many things come through the markets, you know, substances, mechanisms, even messages the Flotilla authorities feel warrant a careful watching. They could suspect any one of these illicit happenings. None of which, I assure you, they will find aboard our vessel, and certainly not within your cargo."

"We need this loaded by tonight," said Tamn. "We leave in the morning."

"Then perhaps you'd best try reasoning with the good men in our hold," said Sorin, bowing to allow them onto his ship. As she walked past, Finch noticed his bright white teeth were stained at the edges with green. His skin was dark like the captain's, but unblemished or burnt. He was very well put together, with long dark clothes that wrapped elegantly from torso to forearms, draping out like wings as he strode behind them. Finch was surprised when he spat a hunk of leaf into the waters.

The *Free Lance* was far less nice than Sorin's appearance implied. The ropes tying the sails down were all frayed and knotted several times over. The deck had gone unscrubbed for some time, and algae and barnacles and all manner of parasitic dwellers were crawling along the dark corners. The few men above deck sat sullen along the railings, spitting hunks of green leaf into the water as they eyed Finch and Tamn. Finch watched her step carefully, glancing back and forth between the sailors as Sorin led them below deck, where soft red candles sat in glass enclosures, providing a dim light along the darkly stained wooden hallway.

He brought them to a room lined with several rows of barrels and crates and satchels, large leather bags loosing puffs of powders as their footsteps rattled along the floorboards. Around one large barrel stood three guardsmen clad in light chainmail, digging with their hands through a stack of salt beef while keeping the grunts of the ship at bay.

"Is this meant to be yours?" one of them asked, pointing to Tamn. He was an older-looking man with a wild black beard gone a patchy gray.

"Yes," said Tamn.

"Your name?"

"I'd like to know who we're talking to, first," said Finch. The words escaped her before she thought them through. Something was off, but she couldn't say what it was. Her hands slipped casually to her pockets and the unseen knife at her belt.

The guardsmen might have taken offense to that, or maybe even suspected she was up to something, but a glance at Tamn, her armor, and the greatsword at her back kept them quiet. "Lieutenant-Commander Alden, guardsman of the Flotilla Council. Now, again, what are your names?"

"Tamn," said Tamn.

"No surname?"

"Just Tamn."

"Well then, Just Tamn, tell me, which vessel is it you serve on? And are you its captain, or merely a ship hand?"

"I am Tamn, second-in-command to Captain Keresh Beldrick of the *Dragon's Breath*, and I am here to collect the cargo we've paid for."

"That cargo being?"

"Sixty pounds of salted beef."

The guardsmen looked between themselves, but Alden raised a hand. "And that's all?"

Tamn gestured to the barrel. "Count it. Confirm."

Alden huffed indignantly. "We have. And we've found nothing out of place. It could be our information was mistaken. Or it could be you're better at hiding things than we suspected. Either way, you're free to leave, but know that we'll be keeping an eye on you and the—*Dragon's Breath*, was it?—for the duration of your docking."

Tamn was an expressionless statue, but the weight of her set the room to silence when she spoke. "We'll be gone tomorrow."

The Lieutenant-Commander hesitated, looking to his fellows, then nodded. "Very well, then. Take your cargo and go."

"The cargo was to be brought to us," said Tamn.

Finch looked around the room, the subtle tension rising. There was almost an excitement to it. The men of the ship didn't look like they were planning an ambush, scam, or anything else illicit, but there was a strange sort of hesitancy about them, like dark clouds not yet ready to storm. They all looked to Sorin, who in turn looked to Tamn and Finch and bowed, smiling. "The good lady is right," he said. "I will, of course, be having my men carry your goods to your ship."

Tamn gave a single nod, looked once at Lieutenant-Commander Alden, and left without a word. Finch followed hesitantly. She wanted to understand. Three men to guard over a barrel of salted beef they'd already searched only to give the all clear after hearing their names?

Our names, Finch thought. *They wanted to know who we are. And now they know when we're leaving. But do they know where we're going?*

When they reached the docks of the night market, Finch excused herself to Tamn saying she wanted to browse before returning. "When will we ever be back here, yeah?" Tamn continued to the ship alone while Finch climbed the stalls of the night market again, but this time sticking to the proper bridges and ladders so as not to draw any attention to herself. It was by the vendor of a large collection of glittering gemstones that she found her vantage point over the *Free Lance*.

It took either far too long or far too short for the Flotilla guardsmen to leave the boat. Either they should still be searching, or they would have left immediately after finding no suspicion with Tamn. But to wait several minutes meant they must be talking with Sorin about something, and when the tall, lean man discreetly handed them a small leather satchel that must have been filled with coin, Finch's suspicions were confirmed. The whole delay was a ruse to lure them in. She gritted her teeth as his men lifted their barrel of salt beef for the long walk back to the *Dragon's Breath*. She might have followed them to eavesdrop, but she decided to watch the *Free Lance* a little longer.

And then she spotted him. That squinty, freckle-faced rat that was crawling around in their ship. *Reed was right.* She wasn't sure whether he was frustratingly impressive, or impressively frustrating. At the very least, Finch now knew that his advice wasn't completely useless. The freckled rat scurried out with a satchel smaller than what had been paid to the Lieutenant-Commander, then raced off somewhere into the darkened recesses between the drifting ships.

The last thing Finch saw worried her most of all. *Someone out there knows where we're going.* A single bird, with paper tied to its leg, was loosed from the *Free Lance*, flying to the distant horizon, its image quickly diminishing between the fires of the night market.

9

LEAF

THE COMFORT OF QUIET RAINS

Stained glass closed like bloody fingers over the setting sun, the light like shredded slivers through the distant mountain peaks. Even inside the dream, Leaf knew that horizon was forbidden to her. She was just one of the many children being marched through the halls of the old home, kept in orderly rows by stern men and women dressed in strangely colorless robes and speaking a stranger tongue. Leaf broke from the ranks, her eyes stopping on the window just a moment too long. A tall shadow appeared at her side, his hand falling swiftly on her.

That home is not our history.

When she rose again, it was with another's hands, climbing through thick thorns that bit deeply into their skin, smearing sharp red over the black wood of the forest. They clutched at something hanging from their neck. Leaf thought for a moment it was the ember, but the weave of the spiderweb charm ensnared their fingers instead, and its patterns pulled them deeper into the comforting memory of long hours crafting with their family. Then the canopy broke overhead to the brilliant night sky. The lost children of Grandmother Moon trailed in her wake. Mountains rose in heavy black shadow against the sky, but between them, there was more light than they had ever thought there could be in all the world. With still-bleeding hands, they climbed ever higher.

These scars are not our history.

The midnight trees turned to marble beneath their hands, rising into columns around her, and the star-filled sky turned to stone. Leaf walked down a long, darkened hall, dying flames holding onto the last of the light. Someone had fallen to the floor in a panic, while others pushed and shoved around her to escape as the ground rumbled and cracked. Leaf walked calmly against their current, pale hands gripping something hidden at her chest. Could she make it in time?

That stone is not our history.

The floor gave way to water, and then she was alone, struggling under the weight of a vast dark sea. Beside her, a serpent slithered along the surface, prowling between the waves toward a rising black mass, peaks piercing the storm above.

There were two moons in the sky, like two great eyes watching her from the heavens. The eyes of the Turtle were upon her, watching as she drowned.

Did you not understand?

Leaf woke with a start, flailing her arms as water fell on her from above. *The sea?* The thought left as quickly as it came, the dream-dark depths fading in faint morning light.

"It's all right," said Ash, sitting at her side. "It's just a carving. It scares me, too."

Carving? Leaf's eyes were still bleary, struggling to make sense of the shadows. They'd made their shelter in a small cave overnight. Looking up, she could see now that it wasn't really a cave at all, but the remnants of some long-fallen statue. The walls around them were rubble, coated with creeping moss and vine, and the ceiling was the face of an aged, sorrowful man.

Curious, Leaf sat up, wiping droplets of water from her forehead as she ran a finger along the great stone face. Water pooled and fell from its eyes like tears, and the patter of rain whispered from outside.

"Should we travel in this?" Ash asked, gesturing out through the mouth of their meager shelter. Cold fingers of wind reached through the opening, tracing her skin. In the far distance, Leaf could hear thunder, but she couldn't see the lightning. She let out a loud, cracking yawn, her empty stomach rumbling.

They ate together after making a small fire, listening to the water trickling slowly over the rocks, landing in soft plinks on cold stone. Even as a child, Leaf had loved the sound of rain. It meant long days at the fire with Koomis, sharing meals and telling stories. Rain was made for huddling under blankets in caves and groves and the other hidden places of the Turtle. It was a respite from the outside world, if only for a few hours, and it brought life to the land.

But since this was only a gentle rain, Leaf didn't want to wait it out, and the two of them slid through mud and sludge as they moved down the mountain. They traveled with cloaks up, Leaf under her shroud of woven foliage, and Ash under her wolf's head. The sunset bridge had bought them time, but Ash was certain the Wolves would still follow them. There were mountains and hills and valleys beneath the bridge, and Ash was sure they would pick up their trail on the other side. There was history enough between them that Leaf didn't doubt her.

It had been seven days since Ash decided to follow her over the bridge, and Leaf still didn't know how to thank her. Ash had broken taboo, stood against clan, and walked over forbidden ground to follow her. It was a gesture not easily made or matched, but they were bound now. It was more than Leaf knew how to put to words.

"That was a place of worship," Leaf said, bundling her hood as they passed the sunken walls of a broken church. It had been swallowed almost entirely by mud and overgrowth. A crooked steeple with a rusted bell hung piteously at the top, plinking softly in the rain, and fragments of shattered glass and a cracked, armless statue littered the earth below.

"What did they used to worship?" Ash asked. She was still skittish around the ruins, but at least she listened to their histories. Leaf didn't know if Ash was genuinely curious or simply trying to fill the hollow silence permeating from the ruin. Still, her reluctant interest was more than anyone else in the clans had ever granted her, and Leaf was eager to share everything she knew.

"They worshipped the stone," she said. "I think. Our ancestors live on through the trees, right? I think theirs were supposed to live on in the statues. That's why so many of them look like people and faces and things." She thought of the sorrowful man carved in the cave and wondered who he might have been.

"I guess that makes sense," said Ash, although she didn't sound convinced.

"They used to ask it for forgiveness," Leaf added. "I guess they thought they were disappointing their ancestors. Or maybe the spirits of the rock, I don't know. They definitely believed something was in there, though."

"Where did you hear that?"

"From Koomis," said Leaf, though she hadn't learned it directly. Like most things about her grandmother, that tidbit of knowledge had been pieced together through years of careful listening. Several times, Leaf had caught her grandmother praying with gestures unfamiliar among the clans. Koomis would press her palms together on the nights she thought Leaf was sleeping, and murmur to the broken moon and stars above. Whenever Leaf asked about it, her grandmother insisted she'd been dreaming. But when she found the same gesture years later in the statues of the old kingdom, Leaf knew she hadn't made it up. By then, she was also old enough to realize that Koomis didn't talk about it for a reason.

Ash nodded, but her eyes slipped from the ruins. She still thought them cursed, as the others did. Leaf could recognize her fear, but she couldn't understand it.

"Why are we following the stream, again?" Ash asked, gesturing to the shallow water snaking through the forest.

"Water flows down," Leaf explained, in that voice she often used when explaining obvious things, such as how to climb trees, where to find the best frogs, and which plants were safe to eat. "We follow the water, we find the Deepwood."

Ash shivered.

The Deepwood lay in the lowest valleys of the Great Turtle. Even in the time before the stonefolk, the clans had learned which paths brought them safely around that dark forest. Dangerous creatures roamed its depths, giant serpents and spiders, and other things as well. Facestealers, some said, waited to snatch any travelers foolish enough to descend. The Thing Behind the Trees, invisible in the pitch-black wood. Every sort of haunting figure or spirit children could conjure was said to be hiding down in the Deepwood, but Leaf was never one to believe those stories.

"What's that?" she asked. Her mind had wandered so far that she had missed Ash's quiet voice beneath the rain.

"I asked why you think this Woods Witch is even down there," Ash said. "And if she is, how do you plan to find her? We're going to need light, which means fire, and that's going to attract all sorts of things."

"Maybe she'll be one of them," Leaf whispered, wriggling her fingers at Ash. Then she patted the lantern in her pack. "I've got light, though. We shouldn't need to worry about fire. And I think the Ember might be able to help us, too."

The name of the strange, glowing stone had fixed itself in her mind, growing as she pondered its nature. It had even started appearing in her dreams.

Ash didn't seem to think much of her answer, though she didn't argue either, simply shaking her head.

Their journey through the hills took them through more territories of both clan and stonefolk. They stuck close to the ruins' shadows, as venturing too deep into the forest risked being spotted. They nearly stumbled into a group of Beaver fishermen who were following the rivers in their longboats, but their furred hoods were pulled high against the rain, so Leaf and Ash had passed them undetected. The two kept low in the growth, in case word could pass back to the Watchers or the Wolves. They passed other places like the broken church, but Leaf held back her desire to explore them, even as they walked beneath a crumbling keep leaning out of the hillside. Trees grew out its windows like worms from the dirt, its roof a mix of stone and wood and leaves. She knew it would make Ash deeply uncomfortable to explore those places and didn't want to seem ungrateful to her only companion.

The mountain began to level into a valley, somewhere still high above the water. Gentle slopes of rock smoothed out to wide, low grass, until Leaf and Ash found themselves on the outskirts of a large, overgrown field. Charred wood stuck out like great black bones from the soil, wild fields of fruits and vegetables of all sorts grew in the tall grass, and Leaf recognized the burned grounds where the Buffalo had once gathered. The stonefolk had made their farms here after running the Buffalo out, and the clan had not come to reclaim it. The land was cursed now, everyone said. Stepping over patches of wildly growing berry bushes and sprouts of wheat, Leaf found it very difficult to believe. The land was healing. She was sure the clans only avoided it out of fear.

Ash raised a hand and hunkered low in the grass. Leaf did the same, looking out to where she nodded.

Something large and heavy trundled through the grounds ahead. Leaf could see glimpses of brown fur moving between the green, and she grinned.

While the Buffalo clan had not reclaimed their old lands, the buffalo themselves held no reservations. The young male in the grass before them let out a short grunt, oblivious to their presence. They were close enough to hear its rumbled breathing, the smell of its wet fur thick in the air. When it trudged forward, its hooves squashed through the mud, and Leaf and Ash followed to where the rest of its herd was grazing. Their numbers had fallen low during the time of the stonefolk, low enough that some feared they might never climb back again. Leaf had never seen one this close before, or seen so many at once, and wanted to see how they moved together, but a look from Ash reminded her that this was not what they were here for. Sighing, she gave them a wide berth. It had been a long time since the herd walked beside the clans, and the last people they remembered probably hadn't treated them too kindly. "We could use the meat, though," Leaf said.

"Not that much," said Ash with a nauseous look.

"But if we just got a small one..." Leaf wondered aloud. "It's going to be a while before we reach the Deepwood. Who knows how long it'll take for us to find the Woods Witch once we're down there?"

Ash shook her head. "We'd never get one away from the herd. Especially a little one. We'll find something else."

Sighing, Leaf nodded.

"Should we go back to the trees?" Ash asked. "There's more cover. We can find the stream again once we reach the other side."

"No," said Leaf, watching the sky closely. "We'll stay low through the field. If there are any clans about, they won't see us in the grass. We should be out of here before too long." At least, she hoped. The soft gray clouds overhead were slowly darkening, drowning the world in heavy shadow. The wind was following them now, too, and in its wake, a trailing storm.

Bits of broken homes rose everywhere through the grass. After forcing the Buffalo out, the stonefolk had quickly established their own farms in the grazing lands. Leaf and Ash crossed a path of old road that still stood in defiance of the wild overgrowth, its stones dark with rain. It webbed out between the tall grass to the many ruined homes. Their doors and windows had all been barricaded, covered by long-rotted boards fixed into place, or were blocked off with hulking objects inside. Each home Leaf passed was another itch in her mind, strings of thought and curiosity weaving together into imagined tales of what she might find within. Even with the storm chasing them, each ruin left unexplored felt like a weight at her heels.

They made good pace, but they couldn't outrun the sky. Leaf and Ash went from stalking low through the grass far from the buffalo, to walking hurriedly, to running full tilt as the winds swept the fields and thunder rumbled. Large shadows rolled over the valley, and the storm seemed to swallow the light, rain falling so heavily that Leaf could scarcely hear beyond it.

Ash yelled something at her.

"What?" Leaf called, running to keep up with her friend several steps ahead. They pressed their hoods together, huddled from the rain.

"We should go back," Ash said. Even this close together, the wind tried to steal her words. "Find somewhere in the forest and shelter until the storm passes."

"We can't," said Leaf, pointing at the mountains behind them. They were swallowed entirely now by the dark weight of the storm, hazed behind the heavy rain. "We'd just be running into the thick of it! We'll find better cover if we keep going."

Leaf couldn't help but think Ash looked nervous and small under her cloak. Her eyes darted back and forth to the far-off woods on either side of them. "We could make it," she said weakly.

"It's too dangerous," Leaf said, taking her friend by the hand. "Come on!" She pointed further off into the valley, where the river snaked toward a small farmhouse of stone nestled against a small hill. "We can take shelter there!"

It was hard to read her feelings beneath the cloak, but Leaf thought Ash shuddered before trying to yell something over the storm. Her words were lost in the howling wind. A crash of thunder boomed in the sky above as lightning struck somewhere in the distant field, the air filling with frightened caws and black feathers taking flight.

The ruin wasn't far. Through the tall grass, Leaf could see that the thatched straw roof had collapsed long ago. A tree grew out from its center, and the stream wound through the dirt to its side, pooling by the walls of the old stone home, where a great wooden wheel still treaded the gentle current.

Leaf nearly lost her footing in a slick of mud, sliding into the cracked doorway of the house. Ash's steps slowed, and Leaf could feel her hesitation, but another crash of thunder sent them scurrying inside. The door was gone, but Leaf still whispered a small "excuse me" as they entered.

Through the heavy stone, the crash of thunder fell to a dulled rumble, and the rain quieted to a low murmuring in the walls. Leaf could hear her own thoughts again. She could also hear something moving inside the darkened home. Looking cautiously about, as stories of stonefolk and spirits and scuttling things that lurked in shadow briefly flit through her mind, she found a small piece of wood spinning in the darkness.

"What's that?" Ash asked.

"Must be connected to the wheel outside," said Leaf, studying the wall behind.

"But what is it doing?" She gave the wood a suspicious look, keeping far from its reach.

Leaf shrugged, walking to the base of the tree. Water trickled from the leaves overhead and pooled on the floor, but it wasn't as bad as outside. She took an old wooden chair and tested it before trusting it with her weight. "I saw one before, once, but the wheel was different. It rode the air instead of the water. I couldn't figure out what it was meant for, but it's strong enough to leave a good bruise if you get in its way."

Ash sighed, backing into the wall to give the spinning wood even further distance, and flinched from the cold stone. "So, what do we do now?"

"Wait out the storm, I guess," said Leaf. "Maybe we could get a fire going."

The laid stone floor would have held a fire if they needed it to, but some scrabbling through the darkness revealed a small fireplace set against the wall. There wasn't much in the way of dry kindling, so instead, Leaf took the chairs and tables and anything else she could find made of wood. The place had mostly been emptied years ago by foreign travelers digging through the grounds, but they must have found the furniture uninteresting. Together, Leaf and Ash managed to get a small fire going. They even found a bottle of something dark and red.

"What's that?" Leaf asked when Ash pulled it from beneath a collapsed section of roof.

"I thought you would know," said Ash. She set the bottle down next to the fire cautiously, as if it might bite her or shatter in her hands. "A stonefolk drink?"

"Oh, maybe," Leaf said, suddenly very interested in the bottle. The warmth of the fire fell away as she examined it. The liquid was quick and fluid like water, darkly colored, but clear and free of debris. "You know, I think I might have heard of this stuff before. Some of the travelers who used to come through here would go looking for it, sometimes. Apparently, it's some kind of old fruit drink."

"Who would go digging for old fruit?" Ash asked, shaking her head.

"It's supposed to be really valuable," Leaf said. She smiled deviously at Ash. "Want to try some?"

"Not even a little."

"Come on," said Leaf, prying at the top of the bottle. Some kind of wood had been jammed tightly into its mouth. After some struggling, Leaf managed to pry it out with a loud pop, and it shot off somewhere into the dark.

"Is it supposed to do that?" Ash asked, her axe raised.

"Probably," said Leaf, watching a small trail of vapor fade along the rim. She brought it to her lips and sniffed, grimacing horribly at the sudden sting in the air. "Oh, that's awful," she said. "Here. Try it."

"I'd rather not," Ash said, but at least she was smiling, holding back her laughter. Grinning back, Leaf held the bottle closer, leaning toward Ash.

"Come on!" Leaf teased. "Just once. Try it!"

"No," Ash said, laughing, pushing her back. "Get away from me!"

They tired quickly, Leaf's body aching, and settled by the fire. Leaf took another smell of the bottle. It was sweet, but overpoweringly so, with a sharpness like needles stinging the inside of her nose.

"That's awful," said Ash. She was holding her nose closed. "I can smell it from here. It must have gone bad."

"That's how it's supposed to smell, I think," said Leaf. "That's what the Bears told us, anyway. Well, they told Koomis, and the Bears heard it from travelers, but anyway, it's supposed to get better the older it gets."

"I still think it's gone bad," said Ash.

Leaf took a small sip from the bottle. The liquid was cool on her tongue, but it tasted of fire. Sweetness and sulfur and something sharp raced down her throat, and she pulled away quickly, holding the bottle out as if it might burst into flames.

"Maybe it's not old enough," she said.

Ash took the bottle from her, studying its contents with a wary eye as its scent slowly filled the room. It sloshed in the glass like water, droplets trickling along the inside of the bottle like the remnants of the storm drippling down from the tree in their shelter. Leaf nudged Ash's shin with her foot, nodding again to the bottle.

"You're not going to let up on this, are you?" said Ash, who took a wary sniff. She wrinkled her nose before laughing.

"Misery loves company," said Leaf, laughing with her.

When Ash drank, her reaction was much the same as Leaf's, only with a few extra sputters. They passed the bottle between them, taking small sips as the storm grew outside. As strong as the drink was, it wasn't entirely unpleasant, its spreading warmth was new to them both, welcome against the chill. It wasn't poisonous, either, and it wasn't very often they had flavored drinks. Sometimes, the clans made sweet water with berries and fruits and syrup from the trees, but none of them were nearly as strong as this. The bottle was emptied sooner than either of them expected, and by then, Leaf and Ash were huddled near the fire.

Ash's wolf pelt was draped over an unbroken chair, set out to dry. Leaf could see her long red hair in full, its damp ends curling into rings. Ash caught her staring and shrank into herself, tucking her chin behind her knees, so Leaf let her gaze drift on, as if she had always been focused on the shadows on the wall cast by lightning through the tree.

She ran her hands through her own hair, feeling at the roots where her natural color had started to come through again. It was usually stained with a mix of berries and roots from deep in the hills, helping to cloak her in the forest, but it had been some time since she'd attended to it, and in the days since their escape from the Wolves, she hadn't thought about it at all.

Leaf pulled off her pack and dug through its contents. There was still a chill in the air, even with the fire going, and the cold had sunk deep into the bones of the house. Her blanket was tucked safely at the bottom of the bag, but when she gave it a sharp pull, it sent the rest of the contents spilling across the floor and into the dark corners of the room.

"I'll help," said Ash, standing shakily, but something knocked her legs from beneath her, because she stumbled back to the floor, laughing. Leaf giggled as well.

"Here," said Leaf, handing over the blanket. Her eyes followed along the many freckles running over Ash's pale arms, which looked so unlike the rest of the clan. She'd rarely seen Ash exposed without the heavy wolf pelt.

"I'm all right," Ash argued, looking away. She said it in the same way Koomis always had. Although she didn't understand the reasons, Leaf knew that sometimes people argued for the exact opposite of what they needed. Leaf kept the blanket up, dangling it in front of her face until she relented. Ash wrapped it tightly into a makeshift cloak.

"Thank you." Her voice was small and quiet, but grateful.

"Did you know they warned me about you?" Leaf asked, changing the subject. People didn't like when you lingered on their discomfort. "Back when I first got to the Elderglade, I mean. The kids had all these stories about you. They said there was a stonefolk hiding in the trees."

Ash looked down her makeshift hood at the fire.

"I wanted to meet you *so bad*," Leaf continued, and from a sliver gap in the hood, she saw Ash's frown curl at the edge, threatening a smile. Or maybe a smile being pulled into something else. It was too hard for her to read.

"I heard," said Ash, still watching the fire. "You know, I hear everything that happens in the glade. I sit around all day just *watching* people." She throttled the empty air. "I was there when you first arrived with Koomis. The children whisper about you too, you know."

"I do," said Leaf.

"But it's not just the children," continued Ash, her voice rising. "It's the adults, too. And even the *Elders*. They say you're always going off into places where you shouldn't be. Some of them," she dropped her voice to a whisper, "some of them think you might even be a facestealer."

"What?" Leaf said, mock-appalled. "I don't steal faces. This is the only one I've ever had, and it's mine."

"Well, they know you're always going places you shouldn't," said Ash, her voice slightly off-kilter. "They tell stories about you sneaking off to the ruins, and then those stories grow, you're finding hidden caves, or hiding deep underwater without coming up for air, or even..." She raised her eyes gravely from beneath the hood. "...sneaking off to the Deepwood." She held her expression stern for a moment before breaking into a fit of laughter. "*Facestealer*," she said, still laughing as she shook her head.

Leaf laughed with her. "I don't get it," she said. "Just because I'm not like them, they think I'm a monster?" People were very strange creatures, and most of them couldn't even see it. "They always talked like that about you, too," she continued, frowning. "That there's a girl in the trees who looks like stonefolk, and that I had to be careful about you." Leaf's frown deepened. "But they also said you were protecting the clans, and so maybe you were a facestealer who took skin from the stonefolk, but really you did it to protect us, and..." Leaf bit her lip, trying to catch her thought, but it was gone. "I don't really know what I was saying, anyway."

Ash had gone silent beneath the cloak, tucking her freckled arms beneath the blanket.

The storm raged outside, rain washing the world into heavy silence. Her grandmother used to shrink inside herself like this as well, and Leaf sometimes thought there was nothing she could say that wouldn't dig her even deeper. People were complicated, fragile things, always breaking in unexpected ways.

"So, you were there that day, huh?" Leaf asked.

"What day?" Ash asked, shifting sullenly under her cloak.

"The day Koomis and I arrived at the glade."

"Oh," said Ash, nodding. "Yeah. I mean, always watching, right."

"We weren't supposed to stay long," said Leaf. She bit anxiously at her nail. "I mean, it was clear we weren't really welcome, being clanless and all. Koomis wouldn't have come unless she had to. I think the elders even got into an argument about it."

"I remember," said Ash.

"They only let us stay because Koomis used to know some of them, back in..." The image of the darkened children's home loomed in Leaf's mind like mountains. "They said she helped them, and now it was their turn to help her. I don't think they would have taken us otherwise."

The harsh wash of rain over stone drowned out her heartbeat, and Leaf relaxed her fist, letting her frustrations fade into the rumbling of the storm.

"I heard that, too," said Ash. "The elders said they wouldn't have gotten away if it wasn't for her. They couldn't turn her away after that."

Leaf nodded stiffly, swallowing a lump down her throat. "She was too hurt to go anywhere else. I bound her leg, but I don't think I would have even made it to the glade with her if it weren't for the Bear clan."

Ash lifted her head from the hood just slightly, a long strand of hair catching the firelight. "What happened?"

Thunder rolled low over the home, and a gust of wind rippled through the tree in the ceiling, sending raindrops scattering over the floor. The fire wavered but didn't die.

"It was stupid," Leaf said, her voice falling flat. Everything felt limp as she retreated into herself. "We were just climbing the hills, no different than any other day, but I guess the rock must have been slippery from the rain, because suddenly...well, she was on the ground, and yelling pretty badly, and when I went to check her leg, it was bent the wrong way. There was a lot of blood." Days had turned to seasons, and still she lived in that moment, as if somehow she could reach back and make everything okay.

"I'm sorry," said Ash.

Leaf shook her head, rocking on the floor. "It was my fault. I should have scouted the path better."

"That's not your fault," said Ash. There was an unexpected bite in her tone. "Not to be rude, but Koomis is pretty old, isn't she? Almost older than anyone in the glade. She shouldn't have been climbing anymore anyway."

"Why not?" Leaf asked, a little defensively. "Just because she's old doesn't mean she should have to stay in one place forever. That's what the stonefolk did to her. She was supposed to roam all over the Turtle, until..." Something burned inside her. Her frustration stoked to anger, and her words choked, her face flushing red. It was a long moment before she could speak again. "She'd still be roaming now if she hadn't slipped. She wasn't supposed to end up in the burrows."

A sudden warmth gripped Leaf by the shoulder, pulling her close. Ash had lifted the blanket to let Leaf in. Comforted by the intense warmth from Ash and the blanket and the fire, she started to cry.

"It's so stupid," Leaf said weakly. The anger had burned through her and left nothing but cold exhaustion. "I don't even know why I'm so sad about it. The glade's been nice enough, but it's just—it's not—"

"It's not the same as what could have been," Ash finished. "I know. I didn't plan to stay in the Elderglade either. It's just where I ended up."

Leaf looked up at her, but Ash's face was shrouded beneath her makeshift hood.

"What happened?"

"Ingan died," Ash said simply. The fire cracked. "I brought her body up the mountain with some of the other Wolves, and when they left, I just sort of...stayed behind."

"Why?" Leaf asked. A life of wandering left her perplexed as to how anyone could choose to stay in one place, or pass on knowing their history. "Didn't you want to go back with your clan?"

It was hard to guess if Ash shivered from the cold or something else, but when she spoke, it was quiet, her voice too even. "They weren't my clan anymore. Ohnah made that clear. Once the Old Wolf was gone, the *new* was in charge. I knew I couldn't stay with them anymore, so I went to the Watchers. It wasn't all bad, though. No one really notices me up in the trees, and Ingan taught me plenty about hunting and hiding, so I did well, and I could still visit her tree, so…" The hint of a laugh, a bitter snort, really, shot through Ash's nose, and came back a sniffle. The shadows off the fire twisted her face into a smile that was bitter and full of longing. "So really, maybe it was the best place for me."

"I'm sorry," said Leaf. She dug her nails into her palm, pressing again and again. "Sorry for taking you from her."

"Don't be," said Ash, shaking her head. The firelight reflected in her eyes. "She taught me the most important thing you can do is protect the people around you. She doesn't need me to look after her anymore. And I think she'd want me to be here with you."

Leaf wiped her eyes and smiled, warmth rushing through her cheeks. She had to turn away. Then she laughed, the sound sharp and light. She didn't mean to, she didn't really even understand why, but it became uncontrollable. Her body shook as she tried to contain herself. Ash watched her strangely for a moment, eyes wide, before her mouth turned up, and then it gripped her, too.

"Why are you laughing?" Ash asked, even as she giggled herself. Giddiness sank into Leaf's stomach and made her feel light inside. "I really meant that!"

"I know," Leaf said, wiping her eyes. "I'm just…I'm really happy you came with me. It's been me and Koomis my whole life, and with her not being able to travel anymore, it's been…" Leaf struggled to find the right words. "The forest felt different alone, but now it doesn't have to, you know?"

"I do," said Ash. She held a hand over her mouth to hold back laughter or crying or something else, and when she pulled it away, her expression was flat, as if she'd pulled her heart out with it. "It was just me and Ingan, too. I've been on my own ever since."

"Then," Leaf said, her head light and her thoughts spinning, "then maybe we can be alone together. I mean—you know, if that's what you want."

"I do," Ash said, nodding solemnly. "I do want that."

"I don't think I can go back to the glade," Leaf said, her laughter now tinged with a dour note. She hadn't even realized it until she said it, but now it was out there, and she knew it was true. "I don't know when I'm going to see Koomis again. She isn't going to leave the burrow, but I guess I thought I'd stay, at least until she…you know… And now I have no idea what I'm going to do after I figure out what this stone is," she said, holding the Ember aloft. The soft light of dawn shone brightly, captured in the stone. The rest of the farmhouse remained dark save for the fire, and brief flashes of lightning receded in the distance.

"I can't go back either," said Ash. Leaf could feel her tense at the admission. "Not after I stood against the others like that. Not that I regret helping you," she added quickly, her voice slurred strangely, like she was half asleep. "And I definitely didn't mind showing up the Wolves, but they're going to tell the Watchers what I did. And I won't be welcomed back."

Leaf felt herself nodding, her head gently lolling back and forth faster and faster until she was nodding furiously. That was her fault, like Koomis's accident had been her fault. Another moment she couldn't reach back and fix, and this time she hadn't even realized she was doing something wrong. She nodded until her head was dizzy, and felt Ash's hand steadying her. Suddenly she was very tired, and wanted nothing more than to sleep. Her limbs were growing heavy, and her insides were warm. With the fire crackling softly, and the rainwater trickling gently through the roof, the Elderglade felt very far away. Her worries melted softly in her mind, washed away in the comfort of quiet rains.

"I'm sorry," she said as her head fell to the floor. It landed in Ash's lap.

"Don't be," said Ash.

"But I am," Leaf said. She tried to apologize again, but her words slurred. She gripped the blanket tight.

Ash lowered her makeshift hood and let the blanket fall over them both.

"It's my fault," Ash said. Leaf wasn't sure if Ash said anything more, but if she did, it was lost in the haze of rain and fire and sleep. As night slowly fell, her wandering thoughts drifted into dreams, and she fell asleep soundly in the arms of her only friend.

10

REED

THE *DRAGON'S BREATH*

The *Dragon's Breath* skimmed sun-dappled waters, racing toward the horizon. Beside them, a large school of dolphin leapt in the waves, keeping pace with the ship and cackling endlessly among themselves.

"You are seeing, Reed, that they know better than us which way the current is changing," said Keresh. "And so we are setting course to follow."

Reed savored the cool ocean spray on his face against the bright sun as he helped man the sails. He knew the Great Turtle was isolated, but they were on their seventh day of open ocean now, and the bare horizon was starting to make him uneasy. Without any ships or landmarks to gauge their speed, it felt like they were floating in place, adrift on an aimless sea.

A sudden wind swept over the waters, nearly wrenching the rigging from his grasp. The makeshift tattered canvas looked ready to take off into the sky.

"Hold!" Keresh yelled as he worked his end of the sail down. The wind picked up again and Reed pulled hard against it. His new coat hid his small frame well, and he had fooled Keresh into thinking he might actually be man enough to help on deck.

Reed braced himself against the sweeping winds. With the jib turning, the waves came at them even harder, the deck threatening to slip from under his feet as it lurched to and fro. His coat caught on the rising wind, pulling him sharply one way as the deck slid another, and then the sail was free, flapping dangerously in the wind as Reed grasped empty air, head ringing.

"I have you!" Keresh yelled. The burned man ran along the deck as Finch took the wheel behind him, leaping over the midship railing, and grabbing Reed by the arm before he could fall over the edge.

"I have you," Keresh said again, grinning broadly as he helped Reed to his feet. "It is my fault. I am not tying the rope tightly enough. You are to be resting below deck now."

"I can help," Reed said, finding his feet. He leaned up against the wall, trying to hold the contents of his stomach in, and felt for the weight of the journal in the pocket at his chest.

"I promise you, I am handling this." Keresh smiled again and clasped him on the shoulder. Reed flinched at the pain in his arm. "Go and rest your bones. You are not wanting to be like me, aching all of the time. Rest now. The waters onward are being only worse, I am afraid."

Reed wasn't about to argue with the captain, but it was hard to hold himself proudly after his embarrassing display. He'd finally been trusted enough to help around the ship only to end up right back where he started as a shut-in in the closet.

His coat mostly hid the bruises covering his body. The *Dragon's Breath* wasn't anything like the sturdy ships of the Flotilla. While it sailed gracefully over the waters and was well-suited to weathering the heavy waves of the open sea, it did very little to dull their impact. Reed had woken in his closet-quarters from violent sways too many times to count. Even in his dreams, the world was unsteady. Last night, he'd dreamt he was climbing a mountain as it crumbled beneath his feet, doing its damndest to buck him off. His anxiety over the Turtle was only growing with every new page he read in Torrin's journal.

He wasn't the only one who spent most of the hours in his cabin, however. Ridae, a strange-robed priest he'd met only once, was often filling the hall with incensed smoke. It did help him to feel like less of a shut in, but he'd taken to closing the lantern keeper's door whenever he passed by, both to get on Finch's good side, and because the smoke had started to find its way into his dreams, too. Once, he woke thinking he was on fire.

Tamn and Keresh were always about as well, fixing or planning or talking about their plans to fix things. Reed hadn't had much chance to speak with the pale woman yet, although from his observations, she didn't seem all that talkative. So far, the only two words he'd managed to get out of her were "Not now."

Wright was even more elusive than the rest. Reed had been worried about their next meeting, given the man's clear disdain for him, but now he wasn't even sure they'd see each other before landfall. The old redcoat hadn't stepped from his cabin once since the journey began. Occasionally, the captain knocked softly at his door, and the two men spoke in muffled tones while Finch hung around pretending not to listen. Other times, someone would bring Wright food, but they were only ever met with a curt nod and sent on their way.

So far, this duty had not been entrusted to Reed.

Finch was the only person who had any time to speak with him. She was waiting outside his closet as Reed wobbled along the hall. Despite his longing for a comfortable bed, he'd refused to admit he'd been tricked.

"How'd it go?" Finch asked.

"Fine," said Reed, straightening his back against the aches.

"That's good. Wasn't sure about you at first, but you really impressed me out there," Finch said, a sly smile just starting to crack her face. "I've never seen anyone swab the deck with their back like that before." At Reed's glare, she erupted into a fit of laughter.

"The wind was stronger than I thought it would be, all right?" Reed spoke over her, slumping against the closet wall to the floor. "I just…got a little carried away, is all."

"Slipped away is more like it," said Finch. "You were almost shark bait. You're lucky the captain is as good as he is."

"Why do you do that?" Reed asked, trying to change the subject. "Keresh said he doesn't like being called 'captain.'"

"Yeah, well, the captain's weird like that. Besides, it's a respect thing. If I was a captain, I'd be damn sure everyone around me knew it."

For some reason, it amused Reed to think that Finch's greatest ambition might be to command this scrapheap of a ship. She must have mistaken his smile for warmth because she slowly slipped down the wall until she was sitting beside him.

"You go see Tamn yet?" she asked, stretching her legs out. She was short enough that she could. Reed had to brace his feet and back on opposite walls, or else curl like a cat on his pile of canvas. More than once he'd woken and stretched, only to hit his head on the wall.

"No, she's been busy," said Reed. The truth was he hadn't even tried. He found the pale woman intimidating and could never quite tell what was going on behind her ice-cold eyes. She always looked upset about something, and it was better that it not be him.

"Tamn's always busy," said Finch. "You've probably noticed things around here are a little haphazard. You gotta make her make time, yeah?"

"Thanks for the advice."

"Come on," said Finch, sighing. She grabbed Reed by his coat and hefted him to his feet. "No sense thinking on it. Let's get you geared."

The door to the pale woman's cavern was closed, but Reed could hear clanging metal through the iron-banded wood.

"Tamn," Finch yelled, knocking. When she didn't answer immediately, Finch doubled down with her fists, yelling louder. "Tamn, open up!"

The door opened a crack. Cold eyes watched impassively through the gap down at Finch, then Reed.

"New guy needs arms," said Finch, slapping Reed on the shoulder and pushing him forward. "Well, that's my part done. Couldn't even knock on a door yourself, huh?"

Reed fought to keep from turning red. He had never met someone so intent on burying him in little humiliations.

Tamn studied him cooly, letting out a small sigh through her nose. Wordlessly, she opened the door.

Reed walked carefully into the armory, following Tamn's massive shadow. She was always wearing some sort of armor, and right now she looked ready for full-on battle. Reed didn't often see people in full metal plate on the seas, as it mostly got you drowned, but Tamn moved as if it was silk, stalking around the room as she examined weapons secured to the walls and tables.

The air was thick with the smell of rust and polish and paint. Reed admired a long line of polearms displayed on the wall, but

Tamn stepped between them immediately. "Captain's," she said briskly, shaking her head. She pointed her chin to a display of two-handed greatswords. "Mine."

That was fine with Reed. He doubted whether he could even lift one of those great steel monsters. He couldn't believe that Tamn always kept hers on her back.

"You've got a fortune in arms here," Reed said, impressed. "If you sold a few of these, you might even be able to afford some real food." He was trying to make light, but their steady diet of hardtack and salt beef was taking its toll.

"Can't equip armies with apples," Tamn said, brushing away the thought.

Reed shrugged. "You got me there."

Even the air around Tamn felt cold, though it might just have been her off-putting demeanor. Reed tried very hard to make the people around him comfortable, mostly as a matter of survival, and the standoffish, armored giant left him uneasy. He supposed you didn't need to be polite when you were armed.

"Dominant hand?" Tamn asked him. She turned to one of the workbenches, studying a nick in a small knife.

"Uh, left," said Reed, flexing his hands as if he weren't quite sure which was which.

Tamn grunted and set the nicked blade aside. She moved quickly through a pile of what looked like scrap wood. Glints of rusted iron banding revealed they were, in fact, shields.

"Experience?"

Reed stared at her, confused. "Sorry?"

"Combat experience."

"Oh, uh…little. But I've had some sharp things in my side before." The wound from Fox's knife had healed nicely with a bit of looking after. At first, Reed had worried about infection, but enough time had passed that he figured he was in the clear. Fox might be a dirty rat, but at least he kept his weapon clean.

"Not like this," said Tamn, reaching for the greatsword at her back. It was sharper and more polished than anything else on the ship, even more so than Keresh's spears. Whenever she wasn't patching a hole or mending the walls, Tamn could be found sharpening her sword or polishing her armor. The dark blue metal gleamed and rippled in the sunlight when she was on deck, making her look like a walking glacier. Reed had no idea what she looked like beneath all that armor, all he could guess was that she was very, very strong.

"Try this," said Tamn. She handed him a blade longer than his arm. Reed managed to lift it, but it wobbled gently in the air. "You need weight behind your swing," she said, clicking her tongue.

"Maybe too much weight," said Reed, lowering the weapon onto a workbench with a loud *thunk*. A thin metal spear caught his eye, but she handed him another longer sword of pale silver. It curved in a dangerous crescent.

"Lightweight. Adaptable," said Tamn, examining his stance. She prodded his arms and knees, nudging him into position. "Good for cloth and clearing brush."

"That's good," said Reed. "I expect we'll be seeing more trees than knights." He waved the sword through the air softly. It was still heavier than he liked, and Tamn narrowed her eyes at his clumsy swing. He could feel the giant's judgment bearing down on his every twist even as he tried not to embarrass himself more than he already had.

"Hm," she grunted.

Reed put the curved blade down before Tamn could hand him something else. "How about this?" he said, pointing to the thin metal sword. Its hilt was covered in curved metal leaves that acted as a handguard.

"That?" Tamn said, picking up the thin blade as if it were a toothpick. "No weight. No heft. Penetration is concentrated to the tip. I could snap it in two with this," she said, tapping at the greatsword.

"I'll make sure not to pick a fight with you, then," Reed said, giving her his best smile. Her flat face didn't even twitch. "Could I give it a try?"

Tamn thought for a second, but she nodded and rolled the sword from her hand to his. It landed somewhat more solidly than he'd expected, but Reed still found it very light. *Well balanced.* His hand slid into the handguard as if it were an extension of his arm. He swung its fine point around the room, rays of sunlight catching red across the dyed steel.

"Clumsy," said Tamn, straightening his posture with her hands. "Keep the tip pointed forward."

Tamn took a similar blade off the wall and assumed a duelist's stance. Reed had seen more than a few back on the Flotilla, and although they were mostly braggards, he had witnessed a few real fights. Tamn mimicked their swaying posture even through her armor.

"Strike me," she said.

"I don't know," Reed started, "maybe I should practice—"

She lunged, swiping the flat of the blade at his arm. Reed blocked just in time. "This is practice. Strike me," she demanded.

Reed blocked the next blow, and the next. Tamn pressed her advance, swinging wide and leaving Reed just enough time to react, but not enough to catch his footing. His arm was wearing quickly. Even in armor, Tamn was tireless, moving faster than him, predicting his every step. It quickly became clear that if this were a true duel, he would already be dead.

"Clumsy," she repeated after knocking the sword from his hand with a heavy thwack. She shook her head in disapproval.

"He is being our eyes, not our hands," Keresh said from the open doorway. He was leaned across the frame, arms crossed over his bare chest. A wide smile cut across his face. How long had he been watching?

"No awareness of his surroundings, either," Tamn concluded.

Keresh strode across the room and reached for the fallen sword. "An excellent choice," he said. "Not so much for the man I am winning it from, of course, but where is he to complain now?" His laugh was loud and booming.

"Who's manning the sails?" Reed asked, slightly worried.

"I am having Ridae and Finch take care of it. They work well together, even if they are not knowing it. Myself I find overwhelmed with curiosity when hearing of your meeting with the quartermaster."

Reed sighed to himself. Finch probably went right to the captain after she left. "I'm a little out of practice," he said, shrugging. "Especially against such a skilled opponent."

Keresh's broad smile didn't falter, but his eyes softened. "Of course. You are excusing me for a moment, while I am speaking privately with Tamn."

"Oh, sure. I mean, yes sir," Reed said, saluting. Tamn handed him a scabbard, and Keresh gave him the sword.

"Return later," said Tamn. "You need more work."

While Reed didn't relish the idea of facing her again, he nodded politely as he turned to the door, trying to ignore the pain where she had slapped his hand.

"Now, that was smooth," said Finch. She was sat in the stairwell, looking very pleased with herself.

"Shouldn't you be on the sails?" asked Reed.

"Ridae has it handled. Easy stuff when you know what you're doing."

"I'm sure the captain appreciates you deciding that for him," Reed said, walking briskly back to his closet.

"What, so now it's 'the captain'? What happened to Keresh?" Finch asked, following behind him. "You might not have noticed yet, but the captain isn't a big stickler for formality. If you're on this ship, it's because he likes you."

"At least someone does," Reed muttered.

"What, Tamn give you a hard time?"

He threw open the door to the closet and blocked the opening with his arms. Finch walked right into him, then looked skeptically through her heavy-lidded eyes. She backed up smiling, and pulled an apple from her pocket, wiping it on her vest before sinking her teeth in.

"Where did you get that?" Reed asked.

"Flotilla," she said through a mouthful of mush. "They're all over the place if you're quick enough. Last one, though."

"Thanks for sharing."

"I'm sure I'm not the only one keeping secrets on this ship," she said, ducking under his arm. She took a seat on his crate. "You don't see me trying to pry them out of everyone, either."

"You're listening in on the captain every chance you get," Reed scoffed. The captain's laughter roared in the hallway outside as he passed, and the solemn heavy footsteps of Tamn followed. "Not that's it hard. You know, I'm starting to get the feeling you don't like me very much."

"I wouldn't be talking to you if I didn't like you," Finch said, rolling her eyes. "I'd be ignoring you like our guest down the hall. You ask me, and you don't, by the way, that guy hates the lot of us. You especially, though. I think the only one he even kind of respects is the captain, but only 'cause he needs our ship."

"Doesn't matter, though, does it?" Reed asked. "He's paying, isn't he?"

"He's paying us in shares," Finch said, "which means he's paying us with our own work. Whatever he's been talking about with the captain, it must be pretty promising to make a journey like this on faith. Either they know something we don't, or he put a hex on the captain and stole away his mind. Personally, I say we go and take whatever he's after without his help and split the profits five ways instead of six, you know?"

Reed sighed. She would do well with Fox and his gang, and probably their bosses, too. "How do I know that doesn't become a four-way split once you've got what you want from me?"

"See that?" Finch said, punching him on the shoulder. "We'll get you thinking like a proper sailor yet. Don't worry too much, though, that's not how the captain operates."

"Certainly not," said a voice in the hallway. The masked face of Ridae appeared at a crack in the door. Reed had seen only glimpses of the lantern-keeper so far, and nothing of whatever might lie beneath their robes. "If he were a different man, our happy family would have fractured some time ago."

"Sorry, I didn't notice you there," said Reed, which was hard to admit about someone who walked around with a lantern all day.

"Few do," said Ridae. "To my great dismay, I find most people are dreadfully unobservant." Their voice was like a faraway whisper, muffled under mask and cloth.

"You got that right," said Finch, waving the core of her apple before throwing it into the corner. When Reed scowled at her, she shrugged. "What are you down here for, anyway? Didn't I leave you on the sails?"

"The fire needed tending," said Ridae, opening the closet door further and gesturing to Reed's lantern. He could see that the others in the hall had been relit as well. "Dreadfully unobservant. Everyone takes the light for granted with no thought for who put it there."

Reed's thoughts were on the hall, however. Even with the fires lit, it was darker than it should have been. It was too early for the sun to have set, which could mean only one thing.

"Storm's coming," said Finch, reading his thoughts.

"Exactly right," said Ridae. "Keresh and Tamn are on the sails now, leaving me free to tend the fire. A duty more crucial than a slight wind."

"That's a little self-important, don't you think?" said Finch.

Even through mask and robes, the lantern keeper's look at her was pointed. "I could see how you might think that."

"Are they all lit from the same flame?" Reed asked, trying to change the topic.

"Don't ask," Finch moaned.

"We're all lit from the same flame," said Ridae, as if that were a perfectly reasonable thing to say. "Our shadows cast together on the wall. But yes, I tend to them all with this flame, if that is the question you meant to ask," they added, patting their lantern. "Do be more specific next time, please."

"Right. Sorry." Reed tried to smile, but Ridae's insect mask gave no hint of emotion or intent, and he had to pull himself away from the draw of its carved, spiral eyes.

"You done with the sermon?" Finch asked.

"Never," said Ridae, stepping back into the hall. "But the fire carries the message well enough. I'll leave you to interpret the shadows."

The sky only grew darker as the day went on. A storm rolled in quickly, big gray clouds blocking out the sky far off over the horizon. The captain decided that this was a good sign, and that they must be getting closer to the waters around Turtle Rock, which were always stormy. Reed was less enthusiastic, not because he was hesitant to begin their land journey, but because the waters had become even harsher. The bowels of the ship rocked and threw him about. He kept his sword sheathed in the overturned crate, bracing it against the wall with his feet.

The very notion of dinner was enough to make him sick, so he ignored the bell when it echoed down the hall. Reading was out of the question as well. Shrill winds shrieked around the walls, and a low rumble of thunder shuddered over the ship. He didn't want to guess how high the waves might rise, there'd been times on the Flotilla where he had seen entire ships taken under massive swells. Some managed to resurface, but most stayed beneath the waves. He wondered how the *Dragon's Breath* would fare. Captain Beldrick was an experienced sailor, he reminded himself, and surely couldn't have survived this long at sea without learning to handle storms.

Despite all his rationalizations, sleep only claimed him for a short time. Even in his dreams, his legs wobbled beneath him, stumbling along the deck of his own magnificent ship. He realized too late that it was already taking on water, and suddenly he was drowning. When he tried to break the surface of the ocean, ink-black water filled his lungs, and something slithered out from the depths, wrapping tight around his legs and wrenching him sharply down to the dark abyss.

When he woke, he was tangled up in scraps of sail.

A crack of lightning struck somewhere outside, very close from the crash shuddering through the hull. Reed stood shakily, trying to force himself steady on the wall. This storm would be bad even for a Flotilla ship. The journal had warned him about this, but he'd hoped that his lifetime at sea had taught him to handle a little rain. He was starting to realize just how in over his head he really was.

The raging seas swayed the ship back and forth, threatening to steal his feet from beneath him as Reed made his way down the hall. The crew would need help dealing with the storm. All hands on deck. Behind closed doors, he could hear the contents of various rooms and cupboards and stowaway nooks clattering about. He worried that Tamn's room would be a hurricane of swords and knives, but hers was the quietest of all. All he could hear was the mild rattle of armor and weapons struggling against secure bonds.

Reed held tightly to the railing as he climbed the stairs. The galley was locked down as well, save for a few empty barrels that had broken free and the contents rolling along the floor. The storm was even louder up here, and the shrill wind worked its way so thoroughly through the walls that he could have been standing on open deck.

"Captain!" he shouted, but his words were stolen by the storm. "Captain!" he yelled louder, straining his voice as he pressed on the door to the deck. Through the crack in the door, and illuminated by flashes of lightning, he could make out a tall, slim silhouette that could only be the captain manning the storm sail. He was in the air nearly as much as he was on deck as he swung about the ship doing his damndest to keep the sail from flying apart.

He yelled something back at Reed, but his words were lost in the wind. Reed leaned forward, just enough to hear better, and a sudden gust of wind caught him under the coat, trying to drag him out the door. Too late, Reed realized what the captain was trying to tell him.

"Stay inside!" Keresh yelled, waving his burned arm frantically. "Be checking—" and then his words were gone again.

Reed braced against the doorframe, waiting for the wind to shift. *Check what? The galley? The supplies? For leaks?* The last thought worried Reed the most. Even on the worst boats of the Flotilla, he had always felt safe knowing he could just jump ship if one started sinking, but they were alone on the ocean. Out here, your only options were to sink or swim.

"You heard the man," came a voice from behind Reed. Tamn's steady hand gripped him by the arm and pulled him inside. "Check on the others. I'll help the captain." She strode past him onto the deck, still clad in her full suit of metal. Reed wondered if she slept in it or put it on before braving the storm. Either option seemed completely insane.

"I'm on it," Reed yelled through the wind, although he wasn't sure she could hear him. Part of him was disappointed, but mostly, he was relieved.

He managed to stumble back down the stairs without falling.

Half the lanterns in the hall had fallen from their hangings, and the few that remained had all gone out. A faint, eerie red glow lingered among the embers, and he could make out Finch, busy strapping down loose cargo that had broken free of its holdings.

Reed had to brace himself against another set of punishing waves. A peal of thunder cracked so loudly that, this time, he thought for sure the ship had been struck.

"Give me a hand!" Finch yelled. She was sitting atop a loose collection of crated goods, struggling to keep them from flying back off down the hall.

Reed lay over top of them until she managed to strap them back together, and they worked at securing them back into storage. After that, Finch went racing up the stairwell to help Tamn and the captain and didn't bother asking Reed to follow. He was grateful she'd left so quickly, because another set of waves sent him sprawling to the floor. The front of the ship rose against an oncoming wave, higher and higher, until Reed was sliding backwards down the hall. The corridor was quickly turning into a long fall, and he scrambled desperately for something to catch himself on.

A hand gripped him tightly by the wrist. Ridae was leaning out from their doorway. "It would seem, to my great disappointment, that you are not the sort of turtle who swims." Their lantern was still lit, shaking wildly with the rocking ship, which righted suddenly with a heavy crash. "You've been entrusted with duties, I expect. It would be unseemly to leave them unfinished."

"I need to check on everyone," Reed said, more for himself than Ridae. The world was starting to spin. Absurdly, he wondered if sailors drank to spin it back the other way.

"Well, task complete then, I'd say. Well done. I'm going topside to help the others."

Reed nodded as Ridae strode out of the room, racing through the halls like a sapphire wind, the lantern at their back still swinging wildly.

The others were all on deck now, helping the captain. All of them save for Wright. Reed had to get his bearings as the world continued to spin, the crude dragon on the captain's door and the clattering metal behind Tamn's whirling together.

"Wright," he said, looking at the door down the hall.

Ridae's room had been left open in the storm, and heavy clouds of incense poured along the floor in thick, pooling clouds. Despite everything else going on, Reed took the time to close it.

Wright's door was unlocked when he reached it. Inside the room was dark, save for the soft red glow of a probably dying lantern. The old redcoat's things had been strewn about by the storm. Clothes and maps and notes were laying about the cabin, flying back and forth with every sway of the ship. Wright himself was almost motionless, his back to Reed and head tilted to the ceiling as he leaned over something at a small desk.

"Wright," said Reed, grabbing for the man's coat. "Wright, are you okay?"

The old redcoat turned slowly to him, his eyes growing tired as the red glow behind him died. He looked as though he hadn't slept in years, and he certainly didn't look happy to see Reed.

"I was busy," he growled in his broken-glass voice.

"There's a storm," Reed said stupidly. Another wave hit the ship, sending it lurching so far to the side that Reed had to brace himself between the doorway to keep standing.

"I'm well aware," said Wright, his face a stony mask. He scratched roughly at his beard. "Captain Beldrick is a capable man. I'm sure he'll see us safely through it." Another wave took the ship, sending the desk sliding against the wall without Wright to brace it. "They are not requesting my aid, so I can only assume they do not require it. There's nothing for me to do but wait for the storm to pass."

"Of course," Reed said. His eyes, however, were stuck to Wright. Something about the man looked off, his eyes or skin or *something* shining a little too clearly in the darkness. "It's…the captain wanted me to check on everyone. Make sure everybody's okay."

"Well, as you can see, I still endure," Wright said, buttoning his coat. "Let Captain Beldrick know I appreciate his concern. Are we finished?"

"Oh, yeah," said Reed, trying to figure out what he'd seen. Was there a candle lit that he had missed? "Yes sir, we're finished. Sleep well, sir."

Wright nodded curtly, then stared Reed down until he turned to leave.

The door slammed shut behind Reed after he returned to the hall. Wind and thunder howled as the ship lurched. He wasn't sure how he managed to get back to his closet, but somehow, he didn't stumble even as the storm grew worse. He couldn't say for certain when he finally fell asleep, or if he managed to sleep at all. The storm seemed to rage for an endless age before it finally broke, and then the sun was back, prying through the crack below the door as the morning bell beckoned everyone to breakfast.

Reed wondered at first if what he had seen in Wright's cabin was some strange, fading dream, or if he had somehow hit his head while being thrown about the ship. He couldn't imagine why the old redcoat had done it, but he could have sworn that there wasn't a candle at his table at all. Instead, Wright had held a small red stone with the fierce, unmistakable glow of a burning, bloodred sunset.

11

ASH

THE DEEPWOOD

Ash hadn't expected the sheer sense of desolation left in the wake of the stonefolk.

In her travels with the Old Wolf, she had been immersed in the upper reaches of the Turtle. The sprawling, old-growth forests had long served as a refuge, only occasionally broken by the towering spires through the lower canopies, hints of the stonefolk far below. Now, walking beneath those very canopies, even in a crumbling, decrepit state, the stonefolk's works towered above her, villages and walled keeps wedged in between the great trees of the forest. Crooked steeples kept watch over them as they made their slow crawl through the Turtle's lower valleys. It had been seven days since they'd waited out the storm at the old farmstead, and seven more that Ash still had not apologized.

The tall grass and forest brush rustled in the way that told her they were truly alone. It was too early in the season for most of the clans to venture this far into the valleys. Anyone who might still be tracking them—her mind went to Ohnah—would surely have lost their trail by now, as Ash and Leaf continuously crossed the stone roads and bridges that divided the Turtle. The clans wouldn't dare to, especially not proud Wolves. Still, during sleepless nights, Ash often wondered whether she was hearing their distant howls in the air or sinking into bittersweet memory.

And then there was Leaf, who was still having terrible dreams. They seemed to be getting worse to Ash. Night after night, she rolled fitfully, almost falling from the branches when they made camp in the trees, or kicking up plumes of dirt when they rested beneath their great roots. She had trouble finding herself in the morning as well, with a glazed look in her eyes that was taking longer to fade. Every morning, Ash was having to speak with her more and more, her words grounding Leaf, luring her from the terrible things she'd seen during the night.

Ash wasn't well practiced in telling how high or low you fell on the Turtle by sight alone, but she could feel the difference in the warmth and fullness of the air. The earthy moss and peat from the decaying ruins were hard to ignore. A sweetness drifted over the fields, so different from the cool bite of high mountain air. The stream they had been following ran warmer as it descended through the hills, newly hatched fish swimming deeper through outlying ponds and lakes in great schools. Sometimes, Leaf would catch one to eat over the fire.

Aside from the towns and keeps that lined the river valleys, they passed through older, long-abandoned clangrounds. Leaf noted their tree markings and how the branches twisted together during their slow growth, marking pathways through the wood, and Ash studied their curved roots that formed rooftops for burrowed shelters. Leaf explained there had once been vast warrens dug into these lands, but they had been collapsed or flooded by the stonefolk. Fox Clan, too clever by half, tried to outwit the invaders with underground passages but had been rooted out. Their scattered survivors now carved out the burrows of the Elderglade.

The stream finally vanished into a furrow of tall grass during the early morning hours of another day of travel. Before them, the remnants of a long stone bridge spanned the gap between two high hills, like islands floating amidst a sea of grass. The bridge had collapsed in its center, and the titans whose arms held it aloft were gone to the elbow. A makeshift rope bridge crossed the gaps between the stone, but that wasn't what drew Ash's attention. Below her, the sea of false grass spread between the hilltops and beneath the broken bridge, revealed only for what it was by the lack of debris that should have been sitting below. Her stomach sank as far as the depths of the black forest hidden beneath their feet.

"So, that's the Deepwood," said Ash, marveling at the seemingly tranquil field. "You wouldn't know looking at it."

"The stonefolk definitely didn't," said Leaf. "Not at first. Koomis told me a whole army tried marching over the grass before realizing what it was. They thought we were pulling some kind of trick on them."

"But they built bridges," said Ash. "You'd think they'd just raze it all to the ground like everything else."

"Maybe the old king liked having it around," said Leaf, shrugging as she examined the stream, watching where it seemed to fade into the grass. She felt carefully with her foot for the hidden edge of the cliff. "Or maybe they didn't know what to do. Trying to burn it down would be like trying to dig out a mountain. There's just too much for anyone to move."

Leaf took careful steps before she seemed to find it, then waved Ash over. Ash followed hesitantly, feeling for where the grass of the hilltops turned to moss and leaf. Every step that sank a little too far leapt her breath from her chest. "Anyway, Raven Clan went into hiding down there after they were attacked. Maybe they kept the stonefolk out. We just know they stopped trying to go down eventually."

"Maybe it was for a good reason," Ash said quietly. She thought that crossing the long-broken bridge into the heart of stonefolk territory wouldn't be half as terrifying as descending into the black forest, but guilt was laying on her heavily, and she couldn't say no to Leaf. She'd made her decision, and it was her duty now to help.

"You ready?" Leaf asked. Her eyes were wide but held no trace of fear.

Ash took a long breath as she watched the almost lazily swaying false grass, looking so peaceful and harmless in the daylight. She thought of the serpent hidden between the black trees, who had ventured so far through the hills, perhaps in a desperate search for food, and the memory bit into her arm again. The scar hadn't faded, nor had the fear of its dagger-like fangs or bloodred eyes. Even the thought had her instinctually twitching for her axe, and she looked protectively to Leaf. There would be more like it waiting below, and Grandmother Moon only knew what else.

"I'm ready," she said, trying to make herself believe it.

Leaf's lantern was their only light. Ash watched as she dug through stores of carefully preserved berries, smearing them against the inner glass. The scent woke nearby starlight flies, and they drifted up from the grass until they were packed nearly wing to wing inside the lantern. Leaf sealed it gently, and then fastened it to her back.

Reaching the forest floor would be difficult. There were few places where you could walk into the Deepwood. The edges were sheer cliffs, with few places that had low enough handholds to climb. Most who stumbled on the Deepwood did so unknowingly, their rapid fall through the hidden canopy both their first and final look at the strange world beneath. Even in the few places rumored to have a tight, narrow pathway that cut into the hills, a false step would mean your end.

Leaf and Ash decided to climb down over the trees. It was daunting, but Leaf was a good climber, and Ash even better. She knew branches better than cliffs. Fastening a rope harness, they tied them off to one another. It provided only a small bit of imagined safety. Ash wondered if it might be more dangerous than it was worth, but kept her worries silent. The Old Wolf had once told Ash that fear would eat the ground beneath your feet more surely than anything during a climb.

She went first, stepping slowly into the false grass and feeling blindly for the cliff's edge. Drawing a deep breath, she sank into the world below, first through tall grass and into soft moss, and then beneath the dense leaves supporting it all. Daylight disappeared. Sharp bristles scratched her skin, and warm rivulets of blood dripped in thin lines down her exposed arms. She held her eyes shut tight, fingers feeling for grooves in the cliff edge, finding gaps to grip, and lowering herself slowly but surely, one step at a time. Ash could hear Leaf climbing above her, but she was lost in the thickness, the lantern light with her.

Ash had braved cold mountain peaks with the Old Wolf, stood against clanmates in defense of her friend, and faced off against a horned serpent, and yet, somehow, descending through the top of the black forest was the most frightening thing she had ever done. The rustling branches were loud in her ears, and all she could see was darkness. Her fingers strained to find a hold in the rocks, and her bare toes reached blindly for purchase, her boots safely in her pack. Occasionally, she could feel tension in the rope growing taut between her and Leaf, slackening slowly when they made their way back to each other. Finally, they found their rhythm.

It was some time before Ash brushed against a thornless branch at her side, still too thin to support her weight. One anxious footfall followed another down the grooves of rock and earth and dirt as they pushed through the last of the Deepwood's ceiling, the thick moss and thorned branches finally giving way to open air. Daring to open her eyes, Ash looked over her shoulder to the beauty of the dark forest.

Her first thought was that there were so many stars. The upper canopy was dotted with thousands of tiny lights, stretching into the distance. The rift in the earth felt ancient. As if she were climbing down through the sky itself, descending through stars and infinite blackness to where the earth lay somewhere far below. They weren't truly stars, of course. Bracing herself against the cliff, Ash craned her neck closer to one of the nearby glowing lights; a large, luminescent mushroom growing from the side of a tree.

A moment later, Leaf descended alongside her, her lantern finally showing through the shroud. In the false sky, her light could have been the sun. It turned shadowed bark to bone, revealing the strange pale trees and leaves of dark red overhead. Ash's fingers were ghost white, almost ethereal, and yet somehow, when she held her hand to the trees, she felt at home. Leaf looked strangely out of place, her bark-brown skin and green hair a stark contrast against the almost colorless forest.

Somewhere far above was the gentle whisper of the valley winds and the slow-trickling stream. But here, she could only hear the sound of scattered mist falling deep into the canyon. Low-whistling insects buzzed through the branches, and in the distance, something large cried out, faint and shrill and unknown.

At the lantern's edge, the larger branches sprawled beneath them into long, twisting pale roads, dark shadows dancing along their edges. Pinpoints of yellow light—eyes, Ash realized—watched them curiously. Ash drew closer, and a large flock burst in a storm, fleeing the lantern. Only one lone, curious bird remained, cawing at their approach.

"Ready?" Ash asked, jutting her chin toward a tree. Leaf nodded, bracing against the cliffside. It wouldn't be too far a leap, but a fall at this height would be fatal.

"All right," said Ash. "Together. Ready…now!"

They leapt in sync, reaching for the same heavy branch. Ash could only hope it would be enough to hold them both. The tree rumbled with a sturdy sound like striking a massive hollow bowl, barely swaying at their landing. The grooves of the bark felt rough under Ash's fingers, cold and sharp and altogether too stiff, closer to rock than wood. The remaining bird took off, protesting fiercely as they pulled themselves to stand.

"How far down do you think we'll have to go?" Leaf asked, peering into the dark below.

"No idea," said Ash.

Leaf stretched and cracked her fingers with a loud snap. "You as good at climbing trees as rocks?"

Ash smiled. "Better."

With their eyes adjusting better to the dark, Ash could see higher above them now. The forest canopy almost glowed with its own eerie light. It was faint, almost nothing, but against the dark, it hung over them like a red-purple sky.

Undergrowth crawled up the trees, perhaps trying to find the sun. Moss climbed up trunks, nestling along the bark in soft cushions, and thick ropes of bone-white vine wrapped around them like so many snakes. Ash misliked the white vines, they seemed to wriggle strangely in the moving lantern light, so she took great care to avoid them. Wordlessly, Leaf did the same.

Leaf led the way this time, holding the lantern forward. She stopped a few times to examine the dark red flowers blooming in the branches, the petals curling outward in five sharp-pointed leaves. She plucked some by the stem, carefully tucking them one by one into her bag before deciding she was satisfied. Ash waited impatiently. There was too much climbing left to be done. A short distance away on a nearby branch, a squirrel was watching them intently. It leapt into the air below when they got too close, white fur vanishing suddenly into the dark.

The air had grown warmer as they descended the mountain, but now that they were below the canopy, Ash was boiling. There was no wind, and the air was thick and moist, tasting almost like bitter syrup, rich with the smell of earth after a fresh rain.

Bird calls echoed from the black. Some were familiar to her, like the light *deet deet deet* of nearby chickadees, but others weren't. They made harsh *craw*s more like screams than songs, and likely far larger than many of the birds in the mountains, larger than any creature had a right to be. A massive branch snapped so loudly that Ash thought it was a crack of lightning, silence echoing into the forest. Leaf grabbed Ash's hand—she'd seemed unshakeable, but Ash was grateful. It was a long while before the drones of insects resumed.

The branches eventually led to the trunk of a massive tree. Ash couldn't see its edges beyond the bounds of light, and she wondered just how large it really was. There were spaces big enough to make a burrow just in the folds of its bark, wide grooves that were easy to grip as they started to climb again. It would go easy enough if the bark held the whole way down, but they climbed for so long that Ash was starting to wonder if the tree even had a bottom at all.

It was impossible to gauge the passage of time in the sunless forest, even as Ash found herself trying to read patterns in the false starlight sky. She knew only that they had been climbing a long while when Leaf fed her lantern another smear of preserved berries. They couldn't risk losing their light.

The moss growing from the side of the tree felt familiar, even if it was red. She didn't want to trust her weight on it, maneuvering instead around its long curtains, down and around to the side, past both it and the snakelike vines enwrapping the tree. But Leaf stayed right above her, no matter how quickly Ash moved, and followed with effortless leaps and falls, keeping the rope slack between them. The moss grew thicker the lower they went, seeming to loop endlessly around the tree.

The lantern barely scratched the surface of the vast darkness beneath them. There was no telling just how long they still needed to climb, but there were limits to their stamina. Not wanting to lose the day finding the safest way around the great swaths of moss, Ash dug an uncertain foot into the wall and rested her weight on it. She could still reach the bark with her fingers, but the thick mush was too much for her toes to breach, and most of her weight was held by her arms.

"Are you alright?" Leaf asked, the rope tension taut.

"Yeah," Ash lied, barely clinging to the bark with her fingers, her feet dangling limply. "Watch your step. The moss gets thicker from here."

"Okay. I'm right behind you." Leaf said it cheerfully, as if the climb so far had cost her nothing. Ash grimaced and swore silently to keep her pace steady.

They continued slowly, Ash forcing her footing. She saw only the vast stretch of red moss engulfing the tree, its bone-white bark buried somewhere beneath. Vines fell around them in great ropes and snakes, but she wouldn't trust her weight on them, either. So, Ash led them around the moss, climbing sideways as much as down for what might have been hours, given the strain in her arms, but it was probably only minutes. Every grip and step consumed her mind.

A great, rending crash came from above, and several vines whipped past her. Ash ducked, pressing her face into the strangely sweet-smelling moss, and her stomach dropped when the rope went loose. Time seemed to still as Ash caught every detail of Leaf's surprise, her fingers grasping toward the bark as moss ripped from the side of the tree. Her eyes wide, and her feet desperately scrambling to keep hold.

The world rushed back to life around Ash. She swiveled to the side as Leaf fell past her, grabbing tightly onto the bark with one hand and wrapping the rope around her other. It burned through her hand before snapping taut, and then the curtain of moss crashed down on her. Everything went dark as it tried to pry her loose along with it. She could have sworn the vines retreated back down the tree like serpents as they fell, glowing in Leaf's lanternlight before they fell out of sight. Ash held strong, her entire body screaming as her arm try to pull from its socket, and then Leaf was swinging upside down below her, dragging at Ash, and flying in a large arc that sent much of the contents of Leaf's bag dropping into the abyss below. She managed to catch a lip of bark on her return, scrambling quickly to the tree before Ash's hold failed her.

The lantern, both could see, had shattered against a branch, the starlight flies dispersing, vanishing into the dark. As the light shrank to a dim glow, the last thing Ash saw clearly was the frightened look on Leaf's face as she stared up at her.

"Are you all right?" Ash called down. Her voice caught, betraying her fear.

There was a sound of frenzied scuffling and heavy panting before Leaf answered shakily, "I'm alive. Thanks to you."

It was only in the dark, knowing no one could see her face, that Ash let herself frown. Doubts and fears and determinations were taking voice inside her, drawing lines on just how far she should be willing to commit to this foolishness. They should never have descended into the Deepwood, they said. She owed Leaf to see it through. If they didn't die on the climb down, they would die on the climb back up. How many more chances could they really afford to take?

How many chances did Ash owe Leaf?

"Let's keep climbing. It can't be much further." Ash tried to sound confident, even though she hadn't heard anything from Leaf's bag hit the forest floor, and the lights of the starlike mushrooms still reached far below. She couldn't let her doubts get the better of her now. One way or another, they would make it to the bottom of the tree.

"Yeah," Leaf said, her voice a strange mix of confidence and fear. "We can do this."

"We will," vowed Ash.

Without the lantern, the climb was far more difficult than if they just had to deal with the burning in their arms or the stiffness of their fingers. The gentle forest starlight seemed to play tricks on their eyes, turning the dim shapes of trees and branches into living, hidden things. Ash kept hers closed to block out the wriggling vines and shifting surface of the bark. She felt carefully with her fingers, and progress slowed. Ash could gauge her distance from Leaf by the tension in the rope, and together, they took the tree at a pace they both could handle, coaching and encouraging each other down all the while.

Sometimes, they would find a solid branch to stand on, letting their arms rest briefly and relishing in the solid footing. Sometimes, Ash would feel her head start to drop, and she would jerk her chin up just as suddenly. It was so warm down here, and dark, and they were so very tired. It would be such an easy thing to try to sleep curled on the branches, but even easier for both of them to fall should just one have a dream or nightmare visit.

Leaf clearly felt it, too. Sometimes, Ash could hear her sharp breath, like she'd suddenly become aware again and was forcibly staving off her own exhaustion. It seemed they came to a silent agreement that whenever this happened, it was time to climb once again.

The temptation of sleep followed Ash from those moments of rest into the exhaustion of the climb, every drip of sweat down her arm, every strand of hair slick to her face, every stiff limb trying to seize as she pulled herself again and again over the bark like another beginning of the same thought.

How far do we have to climb?

The harrowed fragments of time coalesced into minutes, and then hours, and then what felt like days before time found her again and Ash's foot found solid earth. Not moss, or a wide branch, but soft, spongy earth. It stretched as far as she could feel, and when Ash was finally sure that they weren't just on some wide, mossy branch, she collapsed with Leaf onto the ground.

"That wasn't so bad," Leaf said breathlessly. Ash thought she could hear her laughing.

"We almost died," she said, keeping her voice low. She wasn't sure what might be lurking nearby in the dark forest, but the heavy silence in the air only heightened her fears.

"We didn't, though."

She couldn't see Leaf to tell if that was supposed to be a joke. "What are we going to do now?" she said, her voice louder than she meant it to be. "We can't find our way through the Deepwood without any light."

"Ash—"

There was a howling inside her yearning to get out, and her concerns flew freely with it. "I don't know how you were planning to track down the Woods Witch, but I think that's out of the question now."

"Ash—"

"And we can't make the climb back up. Not today, anyway. I don't have the strength for it, and I doubt you do either. Maybe we should camp here and try to find our way out tomorrow. We can come back with more light."

"Ash!" Leaf hit her hard on the arm.

Ash might have seen red if it wasn't pitch-black. "What?"

"Open your eyes."

It had been dark for so long that she forgot she was even doing it, but when Ash opened her eyes, she was shocked. Sunlight and fungus still twinkled distantly like stars far above, but there were others, too. A rainbow glow emanated from clusters of mushrooms hidden beneath broad, dark leaves. There were so many of them, Ash could make out the edges of the trees.

Ash raised her hands, and although she still couldn't see herself in the light, she could make out her silhouette eclipsed against it.

"Oh."

Leaf laughed, and Ash could see her dark shape shaking in the light. Then, just as quickly, it was up and moving.

"Wait," said Ash, tugging at the rope that still bound them. "We shouldn't touch anything. We don't know what might be poisonous."

Leaf, a curious hand straining toward a cluster of mushrooms, stopped. "Right," she said, slouching disappointedly. After a moment, she perked back up and reached into her half-emptied bag. Ash recognized the shape of the leather pouch, and watched as Leaf flipped it inside out and, with her hand inside, and picked up mushrooms before flipping it right ways again. "I can test them later," Leaf said happily.

Ash didn't see what the use of that would be but didn't argue. There were more important things to worry about. "Do you have any berries left?" she asked.

Leaf's shoulders slumped as she felt around her bag. "They must have fallen out," she said, her voice was only a whisper.

Ash muttered a curse. She hadn't thought to split the berries between them, because there'd been no need, but hindsight taunted her. At least she still had food and salves, but they desperately needed proper light. Who knew what lurked in the dark? The serpent's wound burned in her arm. *You do not belong in this place*, it told her.

"This is my fault." The words left her almost against her will. The climb had left her with nothing but her thoughts, and the darkness gave canvas for all her imagined dangers to play out. If they only had *light*. "Leaf, I'm sorry, I—"

"It's not your fault," said Leaf. "I'm the one who fell."

Ash sighed. Leaf noticed so many things that sometimes, Ash was surprised at how she could miss the obvious. Maybe it didn't matter. The only thing they could do now was try to solve the problem in front of them. "I should have found a better way," she said quietly.

"And I shouldn't have slipped," said Leaf, sitting down. "But I did, and you didn't make that happen."

"I might have loosened something while I was climbing," Ash argued hollowly. She needed something to be her fault. "I could have looked for a better path around."

"Maybe you would have found one," said Leaf, "and maybe not. Koomis always told me I shouldn't worry about the what-ifs. All I can do is try to solve the problem in front of me and see what comes next."

Ash let out a breath. There was no sense arguing.

Leaf continued, "The way I figure things, either we need to find more berries and see if we can call the starlight flies, or we figure out what down here might give us enough glow to see by."

It was as good a plan as any. Ash sat up.

Leaf wandered between the flora while Ash kept her eyes on the surroundings. Sometimes, she thought shadows moved in the distance, and occasionally a far-off glow would vanish briefly, reappearing a moment later. She kept one hand at her axe, and the other raised to Leaf, ready to pull her back should something strike. They weren't the only creatures lurking in the Deepwood, she knew, but she wasn't certain exactly what else might be down here with them.

A large something came stumbling toward them through the brush. Ash pulled Leaf behind her, even as Leaf pushed forward. *She's fearless*, Ash marveled. The creature didn't come closer, walking slowly by them in a wide circle. When its head passed over the glow of a cluster of mushrooms, Ash recognized the shape of curled horns. It had to be a goat of some sort, but monstrously huge, thick with the smells of wool and moss from the trees. It looked like a walking shrub. Ash jumped when it bleated, before it started nibbling at a small patch of grass. Leaf moved to try and pat it, or perhaps to grab a clump of its wool, but it threatened to butt her, and so she and Ash moved along.

Ash kept one hand at her axe the entire time. The shrill cry of a bird called out suddenly, and then stopped just as quickly. Were she still in the hills, she might have thought it taken by some hunter's arrow. Down here, however, she didn't know what sort of predators were at play.

Eventually, they heard water trickling nearby, and followed it to a small grotto where the stream above had fallen. The luminescent water was pale, easily visible against the dark forest. Ash ran her fingers through it, savoring the feel of the water. It was cool and refreshing against the sickly, moist air of the Deepwood. Beneath her fingers, tiny shadows of fish and frog scattered into the deeper water. Suddenly, she removed her hand, realizing what she'd done. Her exhaustion was overwhelming her caution.

They followed the edge of the shore, stepping carefully, their pace slow. A few times, Ash spotted the strange, pale vines creeping near the water and stepped over them warily. A particularly thick one managed to catch Leaf's foot and sent her crashing into the dirt. Ash was quick to hack at it with her axe.

"We might need to find somewhere to rest for the night," she said. Her eyelids were heavy, and the more she pushed against them, the heavier they seemed to grow. For the first time in her life, she had no idea what time of day it was. "I can barely see anything. The grotto branches off into a river, and if we follow it, we might lose the cliffside."

"We can't lose the cliffside when we can just follow the water back," Leaf said. She peered up at the blackness. "Do you think it's night?"

Ash wondered how much of that was wanting to explore, or whether Leaf was just trying to avoid her nightmares. "It might not be night, but I'm exhausted," she said. "Aren't you?"

Leaf sighed. "Well, maybe some rest would—"

Something rushed through the darkness between them, whispering over the grass in a quick hush. Ash fell silent and raised her axe, trying to track its source. Leaf went quiet as well, her shadow clear against the water. She was weaponless. Ash went to stand beside her, but stilled at the sound of a sickeningly familiar rattle in the air. Leaf gasped, her silhouette shuddering in the dark, and then she screamed.

The rope fell limply at Ash's waist, and she sprang forward. "Leaf!" she yelled, chasing after her cries. She couldn't see much beyond the glowing fauna and empty shadows, but her feet found solid earth. Ash kept her eyes focused on the few lights that remained to her. When one was blocked, she ran for another, each time making sure to follow Leaf's yells. She stumbled, branches scratching her face and burrs digging into her clothes, drawing blood. Passing a patch of glowing mushrooms, she scraped up a handful without slowing down.

Then Leaf went silent.

"Hold on!" she screamed. "I'm coming!" She ran blind in the direction Leaf had last cried.

Something sharp, like a tree branch, caught Ash heavily in her side. She swung with the curved end of her axe, smacking with her other hand. A long smear of the glowing mushrooms marked the dark side, and the thing writhed away from her.

The faint, moving light flickered in and out of the darkness as it twisted between the trees, trying to lose her. Twice, Ash nearly fell, scrambling and rolling through the brambles, but she kept it in sight. She refused to lose it now that she could see it.

"Leaf!" she called again. "Where are you?"

The creature turned, circling left through the woods, then back around her silently, revealed only by quick flashes of the faint glow through the far-off trees. It could see in the dark, she knew, because it could see *her*, circling but not coming closer, but it probably didn't understand that she could see it now as well. It circled around her once, twice, three times, keeping low and trying to gauge her reaction, and Ash played blind, moving her head about while keeping it locked in the corners of her eyes. After the fifth rotation, it stopped at her back, raised up, and lunged.

She spun, caught the thing with her axe, deep and heavy as it crashed down on her, the weight like a fallen tree. The back of her axe pressed so hard into her chest that she worried her ribs might crack, but the serpent shuddered and then stopped moving. Warm liquid dripped onto her face as she fought to pull free. The dying rattle slowly came to a silence.

"Leaf!" Ash called more desperately, fingers clawing into the rough scales. She kicked at its weight, digging into the dirt to try to get out from under it. "Leaf, talk to me, please!"

"Yelling will only put you in further danger," said a new voice. Ash spun. It seemed to come from everywhere at once, echoing in the dark wood. The voice was like wind whistling over fallen leaves, soft and hoarse and beautiful.

"Who's out there?" she asked, holding up her axe.

"Introductions are best made properly, not by the end of a weapon. Lower it, and we may speak freely."

"How do I know you didn't set that thing on us?" Ash asked, still gripping the handle. "How can I trust you?"

"Did you think you killed it yourself?" the voice asked. "Felled it with one mighty blow, is that it?" There was a sickening silence, and the darkness seemed to yawn at her. "If I wanted you hurt," the voice came again, "I would have let the serpent kill you, and you would never have known I was even here."

Ash's hand wavered. The serpent back at the Elderglade had barely flinched after she'd struck it with her axe.

In the darkness of the Deepwood, held under the weight of the great dead serpent, Ash still couldn't let go of the axe. She dug its end into the earth, using it to pull herself free, blood mixing with dirt to form a thick coating of mud on her arms. She was dead on her feet. It was only when her arms refused to lift that she finally let the axe hang limply at her side, her breaths ragged.

Lights began to appear from the surrounding forest, slowly at first, and then more freely, moving like tiny rivers through the air. They drifted forward in a familiar stream of starlight, coalescing around a figure on the other side of the stream.

She was a full head taller than Ash, at least. Her face was milk-white in the starlight, with a sad, haunted look, and a tangle of brittle-looking hair. It wasn't the pale blonde of the stonefolk, nor the aged silver of the elders, but true white. Shadows carved deep into her features, and dark rings ran wide around eyes shining like twin moons. Her skin was marked in inks of stars and the silhouettes of many animals, her spindly limbs poking from beneath a thick heap of mismatched furs.

"My name is Rue," she said, her arms spread wide. She kept her palms to the sky in welcoming, looking for all the world like a spirit. Ash wasn't sure that she wasn't. "Who am I speaking with, who has braved such a dark and uninviting place?"

"My name is Ash," she said, her voice spilling in unsteady breaths. "Please, let me borrow your light. I need to find my friend."

Rue gestured to the stream, and rivers of starlight flowed from her fingers to where Leaf lay by the water. She looked almost peaceful, as if she were only taking a nap, and Ash ran to her side.

"Leaf. Leaf! Wake up. Are you okay?"

By the flies' light, Ash could see that Leaf's eyes were open, but they were glazed over, unfocused, or looking at something that Ash couldn't see.

"Your friend is poisoned," said Rue, watching from across the stream. "She won't survive without help."

Ash gripped the dirt, biting her lip, thinking over her options. There was no climbing out of here, not while carrying

Leaf, and she realized bitterly that she knew little of the medicine women's ways. Even if she did, who could say that she even carried an antidote to the serpent's venom? There was no one else she could turn to.

"Can you help us?" Ash asked uncertainly.

Rue's voice was calm. "I can."

"What was that serpent?"

"You have many questions, I'm sure, to risk coming here," said Rue gently. "I do as well, but this is not the place to speak them. There are many dangers in these woods, and it would be better to speak in safety. May I approach?"

Ash watched the strange woman, who looked so different from both the clans and stonefolk, yet not so different, she thought, than her. Still, her skin crawled at the sight of the unsettling stranger. There was something in the way the woman moved that unnerved her, but what if her fear was the same fear that fueled Grey Moon? The woman was tall and pale and unlike anything around her. Ash refused to harbor that feeling in herself. Cautiously, she nodded to Rue.

The ghost woman waded through the river with surprising grace, the water barely stirring beneath her. When she emerged from the other side, she knelt over Leaf. Leaf looked even more frail, as if a single touch might snap her like a twig.

"We will carry her together," said Rue, gesturing into the woods. "There's a home not far from here."

"Yours?" Ash said.

Rue gave her a considerate look before answering. "For a time."

"I'll carry her," Ash said. Leaf was light, and fell worryingly limp over her shoulder, but she was still nearly too much. Ash had spent everything in the climb and the fight, and was now forcing herself ahead through stubbornness alone, concern for others overwhelming any consideration for herself. "Just show me the way."

The darkness retreated from the pale woman, who seemed to glide through the tight brush and nettles of the wood. Ash followed her path carefully, but branches nicked her limbs. Exhaustion weighed in her bones, and she lowered the wolf hood to better breathe.

They walked through vast stretches of the black forest, passing trees she thought at first were the sides of the cliff, and crossed over the surface of stilled waters using great twisted tree roots. Rue led them in silence.

A question was growing in Ash's mind, but it was quickly becoming a certainty. The stonefolk had never settled the Deepwood, and the Raven Clan who'd hidden here was vanished. The pale woman was a mix of both, the appearance of one and the customs of the other, making her unique in all the Turtle. Eyes still careful on the surrounding forest, Ash said quietly, "We're looking for someone. A woods witch. Do you know anyone like that?"

Rue sighed, and a queer sort of smile crossed her face. Ash's stomach tightened. The pale woman watched her with twin moon eyes, irises milk-white and blind, but still somehow piercing.

"Two children descended into the wood searching out a ghost story," she said, looking deep into Ash, into her core, and beneath. "And, for better or not, it seems they've found one."

The forest echoed with the cawing of ravens.

12

REED

THE SHADOW BELOW

A monstrous raven with eyes as dark as midnight loomed over the text, black-ink wings rendered in astonishing detail. Reed was impressed by Torrin's work. The raven was only one of the many creatures depicted within the journal's pages, and Reed flipped over them slowly, committing each to memory.

The whistling winds cut through the hull and whined down the corridor outside his door. There was a great roll of thunder, a sudden lurch, and then Reed was almost on his side again. He gripped the journal tightly, bracing boots and back against opposite walls as he tried to keep upright.

The waters were only growing worse the closer they got to Turtle Rock. The captain, the only one who knew how to navigate these currents, was now spending so much time at the helm that he seemed to sleep while standing, eating only the spray of saltwater off the sea. Reed wanted to go up and help somehow, had offered many times in fact, but ever since his failure at the sail, the crew always seemed to have other matters for him to handle below deck; lighting candles, mopping the hall, bringing Wright his meals. Right now, he was to be listening for leaks in the hull, a task often given to the children of the Flotilla to keep them out of the way.

"We are needing your guidance over the land," Keresh had told him. "You are leaving to us the trials of the sea."

And so it was that Reed found himself spending all his hours reading the journal in his closet-quarters. *The birds always gave them away*, he read. *Our guide was quick to point out the difference between flying in hunt and flying in fear. When the shadows of the hill tribesmen watched us from their mountain forests, black wings betrayed them every time. Rarely did they come close enough for us to spot properly, though. We only saw them by silhouette, standing like midnight shadows in the boughs of their ancient woods and watching us from the windows of that ruined kingdom...*

The old man had loved to wax poetic whenever he got good and drunk, and Reed wasn't surprised to find his writings were much the same. Without Torrin there to answer questions, however, it was difficult to separate fact from his fancy. Was a bear "taller than the tallest man" only a head larger, or twice as tall? "Horned serpents that swallowed men whole" could mean any number of things. Were they scavengers preying on the dead? Did they kill with some sort of venom? Or were they large enough to attack groups of travelers with fang alone, swallowing their meals whole before slithering back to the dark? Reed had seen a giant snake only once before on the Flotilla, in a curiosity collection of exotic creatures. The children, himself included, had screamed in horror as its jaw unhinged to swallow whole a captive boar. If the serpents of Turtle Rock were anything similar, then this journey would be perilous indeed.

The more he read, the more he found that Torrin took a very dim view of the islanders, both forest and city dwelling alike. He wrote arrogantly of the "ruin dwellers" too timid to reclaim their homes, and the forest tribes who "fled at the sight of civilized men." From his telling, one could get the impression that the Turtle's inhabitants were only obstacles in the way of a prize promised him by rite of birth. Between the vagaries and dismissals, however, the journal imparted valuable wisdom, too. His etchings, for example, were immaculately detailed, and although his written descriptions were fanciful, his drawn diagrams often detailed elements he'd neglected to write about entirely, like the knife-like claws of the great, many-patterned cats that roamed the deep forest. Their eyes gleamed like tiny stars through the wood as they watched travelers pass in the night. There were massive herds of lumbering creatures Reed had never seen before, looking something like a mound of carpets with hooves and antlers as wide as a man's spread arms. He saw leagues of bears fishing along the rivers in salmon season—*they'll leave you be so long as you don't venture near their food, or one of their young.* If you did happen by one of their cubs, however, all you could do was pray you weren't standing between them and mother bear.

A peal of thunder rolled over the ship, closer than the last, sending a deep rumbling through Reed's chest. A moment later, the swell rolled below them, careening the ship far enough to port that Reed thought they might actually capsize, before rolling back just as violently the other way. He smacked his head against the wall on the return.

Blinking harshly, his vision blurred as he tried to read on. There were sights even stranger than the creatures, drawing Reed deeper into Torrin's memories. The old man's expedition had lost members as they traveled. Some to accidents, others to malnutrition or misadventures, but sometimes, someone would simply vanish, lost around the corner of a ruined hall or after venturing into the trees for a moment of privacy. There was one time, he wrote, where a missing crewmate returned days later with a strange, glazed look in his eyes. When asked what had happened, the man had replied only with nonsense words, screaming about things none of them could understand. In the end, he had tried to kill them, and the crew decided he must have been poisoned by foraged goods and delirious. Reed wondered if there was something more going on than a simple poisoning, but he didn't know what exactly that might be.

"Are you alive in there still?" a soft and muffled voice murmured through the door. *Ridae*. The lantern keeper's voice was always dulled beneath their mask, but somehow their words always carried clear.

"Yeah," Reed called back, stretching the stiffness from his body. "Is something wrong? Does the captain need me? I'm ready!"

He tucked the journal into his chest pocket and left his closet-quarters before Ridae could say anything more and found them standing alone in their lamplight. The soft incense of the lantern filled the corners of the corridor.

"As I said, I was checking to see that you were still alive," said Ridae, their insect-eyed mask tilting at Reed. "You've been so long lost to us that I might have mixed up the when of it all."

Reed shook his head, masking his irritation by stretching his neck. "There's not much to do but sleep right now," he said, shrugging.

"For you, perhaps that's true," said Ridae. They nodded to the topside of the ship as another peal of thunder rumbled, waves rocking beneath them. "You might even be doing the best thing for yourself by staying locked away, but I think there is work to be done still by living hands. Care to join me?"

"Doing what?" Reed asked, more to make conversation than out of curiosity. He followed the lantern keeper down the corridor, working to keep his footing steady, and proceeded upstairs to the galley.

"Hard work requires a good meal," said Ridae, "and who better to tend the cookfires than I? Alas, by these lights I have but two hands, and so needs I go in search of more."

"I take it you haven't asked Wright," said Reed. He hadn't seen the old redcoat again since their last meeting in the man's quarters. Food was brought to him sometimes by the captain when the two would speak in private, but usually it would just be left by his door. Reed accepted that he planned to hide away for their voyage on the ship, but he was starting to wonder how the old man would keep his distance once they began their journey overland. Would he stay just as sullen and silent when there was nowhere left for him to hide?

The galley heaved with a heavy wave, and Reed braced himself on a bar set from the counters. Ridae handed him a pile of onions from a barrel.

"Cut away the worst of the corruption," they said, taking a long, rectangular knife and chopping roughly through the salted beef. "Best we use these up before we reach the island. Once you're done, you can add them to the pot."

"Stew again, eh?"

"Stew always," said Ridae. "Unless you prefer your beef and bread to break your teeth."

Reed got to chopping. His knifework was getting better from his time in the kitchen, and soon, tears brimmed in his eyes from the fumes, but his skills still paled in comparison to Ridae, their knife a blur in their hands.

"Tell me if you can, guide, what exactly we can expect on arrival at the island," said Ridae, gesturing their knife pointedly at Reed. "I prefer not to walk blindly."

"What do you want to know?" Reed asked, summoning stories from the journal.

"Oh, a great many things," said Ridae, stirring the pot. "But from you? Well, can our crew expect a warm arrival on the island, for one?"

"That depends on if you mean from the ruin dwellers or the hill tribes," said Reed, trying to remember what Torrin had written about the harbor town on the south-eastern shore. It was one of the only places where ships could shore away from sheer rock cliffs. "There's a sort of circular bay ringed by cliffs and a small settlement. The houses are mostly abandoned, but there's a core of people still living in the ruins by the docks." From Torrin's etchings, it looked like the mountains over the bay had been carved into great, stone faces of the old kings looking over their fallen land, and so that's what he told Ridae. "They'll take our coin well enough at the docks, and though they've never been known to cheat anyone, they're not exactly friendly. We might think ourselves explorers, but they'll only see thieves coming to plunder their lands."

"So long as they're not trying to kill us, I'll consider it a welcome reprieve," said Ridae, nodding as they added strips of beef to the stew pot. Another wave caught the ship, and Reed watched the stiff iron pot roll to keep even with the horizon. He'd seen this setup before at the Halfmug and a few other ships. Ridae held a lid over the pot with a long arm, waiting until the ship settled, then resumed stirring. They sounded almost bored even with the storm outside, their footing sure and steady in the sway. "And what of the world beyond the docks?"

"Well, the hill tribes will eye us, but they keep their distance," said Reed, trying to remember what else Torrin had written. Even Torrin's guide, who was of the tribes themselves, was nameless in the old man's notes. "Sometimes you'll see shadows in the trees."

"And what are these shadows?" Ridae asked. They turned to look at Reed, the bug-eyed mask staring into him.

"You mean the hill tribes?" Reed asked, confused.

"Do I?" Ridae's hand shook, banging the ladle several times so that no drops fell outside the pot. "You should always seek to say what you mean. People are people, and shadows are shadows. It is very dangerous to confuse one for another."

"I only meant that you might see them hiding in the dark," said Reed. He felt unnerved by Ridae's sudden intensity, his skin crawling as the lantern keeper leaned closer. Their mask watched him carefully, light from the cookfires painting expression-like shadows over its grooves. First curiosity, then delight, then fear, and all the way back around again until Reed reminded himself he was only looking at a mask.

"I've seen beyond the flames and shadows to the drifts of darkness that walk like men," the lantern keeper said in a quiet, almost reverent whisper. "Tell me, what do you call a reflection without a viewer?"

"I—I don't understand," said Reed.

"Nor do I, yet there they stand," said Ridae. "Be sure to check the next time you see your shadows in the wood if any men are attached at their ends."

Reed puzzled over that as he finished with his onions, scraping them into the pot to boil alongside the salted beef. A small loaf of hardtack was taken out for each of the crew members, waiting for broth to soak it into being edible.

Tamn strode through the door, like an emissary of the storm as lightning crashed behind her, her armor gleaming blue in the dim light. The wind howled as it swept through the galley, bringing a wet chill as it swirled Reed's onion scraps into the corners of the room. Tamn pulled the door closed. Her heavy footsteps clanked along the floor as she took the offered bowl, threw her loaf into it, and quaffed an entire mug of ale. Then her eyes flit back to the door.

"How bad is it out there?" Reed asked.

"Bad."

"Maybe I should lend a hand."

Tamn ignored him, drinking from her bowl of boiling stew and crunching at the barely softened bread. She ate until she was done, then grabbed a second helping for the captain still at the helm. As she went to leave, Ridae stopped her at the door, blocking her way with their lantern pole.

"Even at risk of drowning, you wear that armor," they said. "This means you fear something worse. Tell me, are we still being followed even through the storm?"

Tamn nodded. Then she left, glowering as she pushed her way past Ridae into the shrill scream of the high seas.

"What does that mean?" asked Reed, nearly nicking his finger. Possibilities bubbled up in his mind, half-forgotten tales told long ago on the Flotilla. He'd expected rough, punishing waters, maybe even a run-in with seaborn brigands, but this was something else. "Why would someone follow us through a storm?"

"Either they mean to go where we go, and know the captain is the best man to follow through a storm," said Ridae, who had returned to stirring the pot, "or they mean to go where the captain is, and will brave the storm to get to him. When things like these are left to doubt, it's best to prepare for the worst." They handed Reed a bowl and mug and ushered him to the door. "Here, take these to Wright. See that the old snake doesn't die before we reach the shore, would you? It would be a terrible shame to all of us."

Reed had to work to keep his footsteps even, bracing his elbows against the wall to fight the swaying of the ship. Somehow, he managed his way down the stairs and through the corridor while only burning himself once with spilled stew. When he reached Wright's door, he had to knock by tapping it with his foot.

"Food!" Reed called out.

"Leave it," Wright barked gruffly through the wood.

"It's going to spill all over the place," Reed pointed out, "and I'll be the one who has to clean it up. Do me a favor and open up, would you?" He tapped the door again, and through the gap, saw the harsh red glow of the setting sun shadowed by Wright's silhouette. The old man waited silently. "Besides that," Reed called, "I hear we have trouble coming."

The door cracked opened. Reed could see Wright in the darkness, pupils shrinking from the light of the hall. "The storm?" he spat. "I'm well aware of the danger we're in." He took the bowl and mug and turned to close the door, only to find Reed's foot wedged in the gap.

"Not the storm," Reed said, trying to get the old redcoat's attention. Wright scowled at him. "There's a ship following us. They've been at it for two days now." Reed tried to keep his face even, as if he were only delivering rather than worrying about the news. "Ridae thinks they wouldn't be braving this storm unless they wanted something from us."

The old man seemed to grow taller with his impatience, shoulders broadening as he breathed in heavily, but Wright's face was a cold, stone mask. After a long, tense silence, his nostrils flared on the exhale. "And what am I to do with this information?"

Reed bit his lip. He wasn't exactly sure. "Prepare yourself for the worst," he decided, realizing he should do the same.

While Wright huffed and sealed his door again, Reed ran to his own, taking the journal from his coat and tucking it into the bundle of canvas that served as his bed. He suspected he would end up on deck soon and didn't want his only source of information on Turtle Rock to be soaked into an unreadable mess. Then he went to Tamn's armory to find the leaf-hilted sword he'd tried before but found someone else was already there.

"Captain," said Reed, stopping to salute.

"We are not having time for formalities," said the captain. His hair hung over his shoulders in long ropes still wet from the storm, and saltwater glistened between the cracks in his burn scars. His back was to Reed as he stared over the array of arms set on the wall, weighing his options carefully. "Lucky being for us that Tamn always is keeping our tools so sharp."

"Are you expecting trouble?" Reed asked, surprised at the squeak in his voice.

"Imminently." Keresh rubbed his fingers deep into the burned flesh of his shoulder, inhaling through his teeth. "I am not being the man I was before," he said, still not turning to look at Reed. "My bones ache with this rain and cold. My movements are fast, but not as fast as they once were being." He reached for a long, slender spear made of a wood so dark it was almost black. "But old and young alike, I am the same man still, and guilty of the same crimes. It would seem one has come to demand its due."

The captain twirled the spear effortlessly in hand, testing its balance, and gave a crooked, bitter smile at some distant memory. "The same spear, are you knowing this? No, you cannot. It is only fitting."

"The same as what?" Reed asked. He searched the armory for the leaf-hilt sword and found it secured among the weapons Tamn was working to sharpen. Wood and leather clattered as he dug for a proper scabbard to carry it.

"Not what, but when," the captain said. He had a spear in hand, a knife in his belt, and a steely look on his face as he turned to Reed. He didn't bother to look for armor. "There are two ships now on the horizon. One before us, and one behind. Do you know what this is meaning for us?"

Reed didn't at all like that thought. "An attack," he said quietly, fingers twitching.

"An attack," the captain agreed. "And as we are carrying a fortune only in salted meats, so you know what it is they must be coming for."

"For Wright?" Reed asked. The old man must be running from something.

"Hah!" the captain laughed at Reed's confusion. "For *me*. The old man is having much time with which to make enemies, I am sure, but it is through deeds that I have earned my multitudes. You are saying once you are hearing the stories of me. The Burning Waters, yes? Tell me, what do you know, truly?"

Reed had to think about it. Was this a test? Reed had never mentioned specifically what he knew about the man, his crew, or his history. He'd heard of plenty of battles happening across the sea during his lifetime, however. Some were heroic, but sometimes the same stories were a tragedy. Sometimes, men liked to brag about feats of valor, while others chose instead to hide away from their memories in the bottom of a bottle. As Reed saw it, more than anything else, each story was written in blood, and the Broken Waters was a red ocean of misery, threatening to drown those caught in its tides. War was not a heroic thing.

"Not much," Reed admitted. He'd never been one to hesitate in telling a lie, but somehow, with the captain's eye on him, he couldn't help but feel ashamed. The captain had shown him nothing but kindness, and Reed had served him nothing but lies. "I know a lot of people died."

"A great many," the captain agreed. His steely-eyed determination softened to something solemn at the look on Reed's face. "Men on both sides, all of whom might still be alive if not for me."

The storm raged outside, winds shrieking and thunder rumbling as Reed mustered his nerve to meet the captain in the eye. Keresh Beldrick didn't seem a cruel or wicked man, but smiles often hid the worst intentions, and the heaviest of regrets. How had he not seen it before now? "What did you do?" asked Reed, almost afraid to know the truth.

The captain shifted on his feet as the storm tried to throw the ship, and chuckled to himself as Reed leaned on the counter for support. "Perhaps someday, if we are surviving this, I am telling you the tale of the Burning Waters in full. All you need know for now is that, at that time, I am believing I am in the right. The Broken Waters will always be a dance of death, and fool was I to think I can stem the bleeding."

Reed tied a scabbard tightly around his waist, wondering if it were on the proper side. His breathing picked up.

The captain took Reed by the shoulder and looked him in the eye. "Some men are being pursued by regrets, always running for fear they will be caught and drowned. Others can do nothing but stay fixed on the past. They believe their lives were better then, and if only we could undo the terrible now, we might be returning to some imagined glory. Both of these men are being wrong. We must keep an eye in both directions. One on the past, so we can learn from our mistakes, and one on the future we must hope to build. Remember this." He fixed Reed's scabbard, cinching it properly, before guiding Reed's fingers to grip the hilt. "That is better. I am sorry to say my young friend, but the lottery of time and place has bequeathed you my sins through no fault of your own. Now, you must be fighting for your life. I showed no mercy to the men I once faced, and I am sure they are having none for me and mine."

Reed jumped as Finch crashed through the door, and he might have lunged at her in fear if not for the fact that she'd already shoved him out of the way. "Enemy close, Captain!" she yelled. Her voice was trembling, her fists clenched in anger rather than fear. "They unfurled their flags. Yellow with a red sunburst. I knew that guy Sorin was trying to pull something."

"Not Mr. Sorin with his salt beef," the captain said gently. "Not directly. But his friends, or family, or their ghosts perhaps, have come to collect their due." He spun his spear in hand. "Come. Let us be making them work for it."

The sky was black under the weight of the storm, the dark only broken by cracks of lightning that painted the deck a blue so deep it was almost violet. They rode through screaming winds, rain striking like pebbles on Reed's flesh, their impact leaving motes of cold growing over his skin. His hand gripped nervously on the leaf-hilt sword still in its scabbard.

Captain Keresh Beldrick stood tall and proud at the helm, spear in one hand, the other on the wheel as he leaned into the rage of the storm. Reed kept his free hand tight on the railing as the ship rose and fell along the waves like some great whale leaping across the ocean. Peeking over the white swells, he could see the enemy vessel in the distance ahead doing the same, although their ship heaved dangerously to the side compared to the rocking of the *Dragon's Breath*. Supposedly, they wore red sunburst on yellow sail, but beneath the storm, the entire ship looked gray.

"There is no going around them!" the captain yelled. His voice battled the wind, Reed straining to hear him. "The currents are deciding our fate. We must be dealing with the men ahead before the men behind are catching us. They are trying to board, to kill, and we are not letting them! Tamn, see to it that any man who steps on our decks meets steel. You must be the glacier into which they are crashing!"

"Aye, Captain," said Tamn. The iron giant clanked starboard where the ship on the horizon was banking. Reed could see now, the many men aboard bracing themselves against the railings, curved swords in hand as they watched the approach of the *Dragon's Breath*.

They really are trying to kill us, Reed thought.

"Ridae! Your eyes are seeing more than any I have ever known. Show them then, those who would harm us, what it means to be the marksman!"

"Aye, Captain," said Ridae.

Reed was shaking on the deck, his jacket plastered against his skin. *What can I do with just a sword?*

"Finch," the captain called, "I am knowing you well in our short time together. I see your hunger. Take that rage and use it now to protect us. Any man who comes for Reed or Ridae, you are to cut them down."

"Aye, Captain!" yelled Finch.

What am I going to do?

"Reed!" the captain yelled. Reed turned to see him framed in lightning, holding his spear forward through the storm. *He looks like a madman. Or a hero in some story.* "Remember what I am telling you. Survive!"

But this wasn't some story. *How am I going to do that?*

"Aye, Captain," he mouthed. His voice wouldn't carry over the storm anyway.

A fist landed on his shoulder, and sudden terror ripped through him, only to find that Finch was somehow smiling at him. "With the way you just jumped, I'm starting to believe you're not behind this."

"We're lucky," said Tamn, looking to the aft.

"Tell me, which way do you think luck serves us?" Ridae asked, readying a long, slender bow. For the first time, their lantern was set aside, secured to a clasp on the wall. Reed noticed that Ridae never ventured beyond its light. "Is it that we're severely outnumbered, or that the storm might drown us before we can be overwhelmed?"

"Storm'll drown them, too," said Tamn. "Look aft. The currents are keeping them from pursuing us properly. That's our advantage. Just watch."

"Great, so we'll only be totally overwhelmed, not completely and utterly," Finch said. Despite her grim prediction, Reed could hear a strange joy in her voice.

"How can you be so happy?" Reed yelled over the storm.

"Because this is the only time the world is honest," she said, eyes shifting aft and forward. Her breath was picking up, fast and excited, as Tamn shoved them all to the deck.

"Arrows!" Tamn shouted. Reed could just make out through the rain a line of archers readying their bows.

The *Dragon's Breath* was a small ship, and worn, but it was custom, and over the years, her crew had learned her well. As Keresh twisted the ship along the current, Tamn used the wailing winds to help lift a fold of the heavy wood from the deck, bracing it as a shield between the crew and the hail of arrows. No steel broke through to the other side. Another volley came, their impact rumbling against the wood like a barrage of fists. Then another, and a fourth and fifth, drumming in a steady rhythm like the heavy rain. They were safe, but pinned in place.

Reed braced himself on the deck, rain puddling on the cold wooden planks beneath his hands. With his face to the floor, he spat saltwater and started praying to gods who had never listened that they might survive this night. His mutterings were answered by mad laughter, and he peered past Finch's crouched form up to see the captain standing alone and unarmored at the helm, howling like a monster in the storm. The captain wrenched the wheel all the way to one side, and the sails swung overhead, catching another twisting wind as the world rotated around them. Reed felt himself slipping from the cover of the wooden hatch. He wasn't the only one. Finch slid forward as the ship lilted, and he grabbed for her. When he wasn't enough to hold her steady, Tamn grabbed for him, and Ridae grabbed for them both, each of the crew helping to steady the other. The moment passed so quick that there was no time for fear, and Reed started to laugh without knowing why. He was in some strange dream. *How did I get here?*

Then the ship rose and fell, landing with a body-shuddering crash, and once the water washed out, the enemy vessel was floating at their starboard side, angry men readying weapons and rope to board the *Dragon's Breath*. When the rest of the crew rose to make their stand, Reed hesitated. He didn't know these people, despite what he'd told them. Maybe Keresh really had earned this punishment. There was every chance that Reed was standing on the wrong side of a fight that wasn't his. He'd set out on this journey thinking it would be like the adventures he'd dreamed of in childhood, when he and the other ship rats would play with driftwood sticks, but the dream was turning into a nightmare.

"Be coming, then!" the captain roared between crashes of thunder. "Come and claim your piece of flesh, if you can, and meet the man who burns the ocean itself!" Lightning flashed overhead, thunder rolled, the storm raged, and the waves rose and fell as the first of the enemy ships, *Ghostfire*, crashed against the *Dragon's Breath*.

The men were all dressed in uniform, worn yellow leathers with red trimming. Many looked similar to Keresh, with long ropes of hair and dark skin, some even had burn scars of their own, although none so extensive as his. A few leapt the gap between the ships before they drifted apart again, carrying lengths of rope with metal hooks. Only two made it on the first jump, the rest throwing their hooks over the railings of the *Dragon's Breath*, lashing the two ships together.

"By the light of the first fire, I walk and see this world for what it is," Ridae spoke softly. Their slender bow levied high, rapidly firing shots at the enemy bowmen. One of the men aboard tried to run for the lantern keeper. Reed went to draw his sword, only Finch cut him down first. "By lantern's light I pass through the shadow of doubt and ignite the great unknown." They loosed another arrow. "Let there be light." Another. "Let there be light." Another. "Let there be light!"

Beneath the roaring storm, the planks themselves started to rumble under Reed's feet. Tamn was running down the other boarder, arrows plinking harmlessly off her heavy plate. Her footsteps were near as heavy as the thunder overhead as she threw the man clear off the swaying ship, his screams drowned by the waves.

"Reed!" Finch yelled. He turned to see a man rushing him only steps away, swinging a great curved sword. Reed ducked and scrambled backward, fumbling at the leaf-hilt blade still in its scabbard as the man loomed over him.

He stood near as tall as Tamn and even broader than Keresh. "I'm sorry, boy," the man said in a thick accent, "but you are standing between me and my monster." He glanced up to Keresh, who was still battling the wheel. Then his eyes fell back to Reed, and the great curved sword sliced down.

Reed rolled to his side just as the deck heaved beneath him and found he couldn't stop, tumbling toward the side of the ship. He fumbled helplessly at the slick floorboards as everyone on deck reached out for anything they could to steady themselves.

The tall man held tight to the rigging as he watched Reed slip away. The railing came fast, punching the air from his stomach, and deliriously, Reed was thankful for it stopping him from going overboard. The ship swayed hard. Waves crashed and shot over the deck, and one of the boarders was still standing when he hit the rail a moment after, flipping head over heels and back again before disappearing beneath the water.

Reed wheezed. *Get up*, he thought. *Survive.* He coughed as he crawled on his hands and knees, riding out the righting of the ship, then lifted himself and leaned on the railing to catch his breath. The water between the ships was already staining red, too bright, as if the ships themselves were bleeding. *Ghostfire*, Reed thought, *Burning Waters.* Was this some kind of trap?

The *Ghostfire* men tethered the two ships, locking the *Dragon's Breath* into their duel. If one should go down, so would the other. Maybe this wasn't meant to be his fight, but Reed had chosen this ship, and it was clear that there was only one way out of it. It didn't matter what the crew of the *Dragon's Breath* had done in the past. They were *his* crew now, and they would live or die together. Steadier on his feet, breath returned, he finally managed to draw his steel, raising it overhead as he yelled. Nothing like the heroic battle cries he'd heard in stories as a child. All he managed to muster was a primal scream.

He ran for the tall man with the curved sword, needle-thin point aimed for his back, but the man spun around him. He even laughed the same as Keresh, yelling in a foreign, fluid tongue.

Reed tried another stab, then another, hitting empty air as the man stepped around his thrusts. On the fourth swing, he slashed down at Reed's hand, the leaf-hilt stopping the cut but not the impact. Pain cracked through Reed's hand up his arm, and he dropped the sword.

There was a clash of lightning, then came the sound of the captain's laughter.

Keresh Beldrick landed on the deck between Reed and the tall man, tucking into a roll before springing back up again.

"This is where the tides of vengeance take us," said the captain. His spearhead was soaked with red, sticking out from the other side of the tall man's stomach. The gleam was gone from the man's eyes, now wide with fear and hatred. His face twisted in fury as Keresh wrenched the spear free from his insides, and the man fell over dead.

"Captain, the helm!" Finch yelled. She stood beside Ridae, keeping the sunbursts from getting too close. When Reed looked over the gap between the two decks, he saw that all of the enemy archers had fallen.

"Let us be hoping their helmsman's hands are half so steady as mine," the captain said, stabbing his spear through the tethers between the two ships. "There is no sailing now, only survival. Let them steady us, or let us all drown."

Reed stood uneasily, staring at the violence around him, hand still throbbing with pain. The crew of the *Dragon's Breath* had held against the first wave of men, but more were coming, already climbing over the ropes. The sails of the second ship were closing in, battling through the shifting current, their prow swaying wildly through the rolling waves. If they managed to reach the port side of the *Dragon's Breath*, they'd be sandwiched.

But the captain had given Reed an idea.

"Finch!" Reed called, running over the deck. The ship heaved portside, and Reed rode the momentum, sliding to Finch and Ridae.

"May your souls return to ash and be embraced by the warmth that encompasses all, and your shadows fade to rest in eternal light," Ridae prayed as they fought, standing back-to-back with Finch, who held twin knives in a fist-fighting stance.

"Do you have to do that now?" she asked.

"Always."

"Finch!" Reed yelled again. She flicked her eyes his way, but kept her attention focused on the men crossing the ropes between the ships.

"What?" she asked as Ridae loosed an arrow, and the man leading the climb fell helplessly into the ocean.

"I need a knife," said Reed.

"Get your own," she said, looking more taken back at his request than anything. "Where's your sword?"

"I lost it. Give me a knife, now!"

Finch bit her lip, but she handed him the knife in her left hand. Before Reed could even properly grip it, she had grabbed another from her boot. "You lose that and you owe me half your share, yeah?" She grinned.

"Only if we live," said Reed, surprising himself by smiling back.

The battle raged on, the tethered ships heaving under the weight of the storm, lit only by brief flashes of lightning. A swell spouted up between the two ships with a sudden, terrible force, throwing men from the ropes against the railings and stairs where they landed with sickening crunches. Others fell screaming into the water, their last gasps swallowed by the spray. Reed's footing slipped as the two ships were torn from each other, decks tilting and dropping even more men into the water. Just as he started to fear they might capsize, the ships started to right themselves with equal force. Reed wrapped an arm around the railing, desperately trying to keep himself steady. His free hand pulled the rain-drenched hair from his eyes, stinging from the saltwater. When he could see, Reed was astonished at the sight of Keresh running hard for the starboard side. He threw himself over the crew's heads, crashing into two men on deck of the *Ghostfire,* and sent them flying into the waters below. Then he started running for the enemy helmsman.

"Another offering to the waves!" Reed heard him cry. "Sea and storm are favoring me!"

Reed was still clinging to the railing. With Finch's long knife, he started to hack at the ropes. They snapped free with a satisfying twang, whipping back toward the crew of the *Ghostfire*.

Reed ran to the next rope to do the same. Men were already climbing again between the ships. *They'd kill you if they could,* he told himself. Still, he was hesitant to actually take a life. He might not be killing them himself, but a fall into the water was as good as death.

The two men on the rope shouted up at him, first angrily, then fearfully. Their voices turned pleading. One hurried to reach the deck of the *Dragon's Breath*, and the other tried desperately to get back to the *Ghostfire*. Then the tether snapped, and they both fell screaming into the frothing red waters.

That's not blood, Reed realized with a start.

"Captain!" Reed yelled between the decks. Keresh was at the other helm, fighting men off with his spear. "There's something happening below the water!"

The pulsating light, whatever it was, now enveloped both ships. It was as if the sky and ocean had traded places, with sun drowning beneath the waves, staining them a bloody sunset red. Small shadows struggled and flailed and drowned, sinking to the depths. It was like something out of the worst story Reed had never heard. The ship swayed again, hulls creaking as he untethered them.

The captain was too busy to look. He held back two men with one spear, bobbing and swaying on his feet, looking almost lazy as he weaved between their swords. Still laughing, illuminated by the red light of the sea below, he looked like a horrible demon that had crawled out from the underworld.

Finch was doing her best to protect Ridae, who was still keeping the crew of the *Ghostfire* from taking up their bows. Reed cut the tethers alone until Tamn brought her greatsword down on the railing, cutting three ropes loose at once. The men making the climb screamed until they were silenced by the water.

"What the hell is that?" Reed screamed, pointing at the waters.

In the blood-red sea between the ships, red lightning arced through the water. Reed could see the silhouettes of drowning men squirming deep beneath the waves. Was this what Ridae was praying for?

The gods of sea and storm are real, Reed thought, terrified as a leviathan black mass appeared below the light. It was huge. Reed thought first it was some kind of fish, a whale or kraken or something elder, but the shape grew until both the *Dragon's Breath* and the *Ghostfire* looked like fleas on the back of some unfathomable beast. A shadowed limb stretched out from that vast darkness, long and lithe and lightning quick, lashing in an arc for the *Dragon's Breath*. Reed screamed as he braced for the impact that never came. Whatever was down there, it flinched when it touched the red light. Instead, it caught the underside of the *Ghostfire*, exploding the hull into splinters.

The fore and aft ends of the *Ghostfire* rose as its center sagged. Keresh Beldrick's cackle grew louder as he rode the chaos, taking a rope from the sagging mast and swinging between the ships, landing almost back at the helm of the *Dragon's Breath*.

"They're going down!" Finch yelled triumphantly.

"The storm is on our side!" Keresh yelled. "Come! Let us drive the last of these men into the sea!"

The crew rallied beside their captain. Finch and Tamn and Ridae—even Reed—ran in a wedge against the few men remaining on the deck of the *Dragon's Breath.* Tamn led, barreling forward with her sword raised, deflecting spear and arrow with her armor. Men screamed as they were cut down, or drowned in the waves, the howling wind loudest as lightning flashed and thunder rolled and the rain fell, until the air tasted of nothing but salt and blood and fear.

The *Ghostfire* was half in the water when the second vessel finally reached the battle, throwing hooks and rope into the water to save the few still remaining above the surface. Some of the men, Reed could see, were pointing at the waters around the *Dragon's Breath* and the terrible red glow and the leviathan beneath it.

Ghostfire and *Inferno's End*, the two were called. Each had come to claim the *Dragon's Breath*, and each had failed. The last few tethers snapped. Keresh Beldrick steered their ship away, forward through the storm.

"The battle of the sea continues!" he yelled. "Man the sails! Sea and storm might be with us, but we must earn our place above the waves!"

Tamn, Finch, and Ridae all went to their places to try to steady the ship, while Reed looked about helplessly for some way to contribute. He leaned dangerously close to the side of the deck again, clutching the railing for fear of falling as he peered into the waters in search of the dark leviathan. Somewhere beneath the white crests of rolling waves and the dimming sun beneath them, the long shadow that had torn the *Ghostfire* to pieces curled beneath their hull, not daring to breach the light.

The water swelled again, catching Reed and throwing him upward.

He never felt the landing.

13

LEAF

THE WOODS WITCH

The fire crackled softly, a lone beacon in the endless dark, while Leaf sat with Koomis.

"Did grandfather know his clan?" she asked.

"He did," Koomis said softly, "but they're gone now. And I cannot teach you their traditions."

"What happened to them?"

"The stonefolk came. The clan moved on. They're somewhere else now."

Those words had stayed with Leaf. It was the first spark that still burned every day inside her.

"Could I find them?" she asked, feet stamping anxiously in the dirt.

Her grandmother had explained in words softened for a child that the clan was long dead, and that she shouldn't go disturbing their ghosts, but something changed in the memory. Instead, her face tilted to the side, a little at first, and then too far, a stern expression without any of Koomis's warmth. Leaf could see a silhouette growing behind her, and the many limbs of the *something* wearing her grandmother's face.

Yes.

A long-haired girl stopped at a window a moment too long, her eyes drawn to the sun setting on the forbidden horizon. The robed men were always vigilant, quick to stamp out dissent or desire for home, and they fell on her quickly.

Leaf stepped out from the line of children and caught the robed man's hand with unfamiliar, scarred fingers. The rest of the robed men were on her at once. Two, three sets of hands grabbed at her—*him*—by the arms, wrenching him free of the robed man whose face lit in dark fury. They threw him on the ground, kicking him, pinning his hands tightly behind his back while the rest of the children were spirited out of the hall before they, too, got any ideas. The boy caught sight of the young girl still watching through the window; she'd been spared in the commotion.

As they beat him, something fell from his uniform they couldn't see. The window-gazer caught sight of it and discreetly recovered the spiderweb charm. Both the young boy and the young girl mouthed "thank you" in the familiar tongues of their people.

You have many questions, I'm sure, to brave such a place.

The young girl was sent to the smallest room on the tallest floor, a punishment for daring to dream of home. They never realized that this room was where she wanted to be. It was the only place where she could see the moon and stars, strained as they were through the forest. Mountains rose in the distance, the barest glimpse of the majesty of the Great Turtle. She held the spiderweb charm close to her heart.

Where are you? Talk to me.

Leaf's strength left her as the sorrowful man wrenched the knife from her chest. She stumbled forward, gasping for air as he frantically whispered meaningless apologies. He was too late. The dawn would come for this world too long lost in shadow.

Then she could see it, hanging low from her father's neck as he begged forgiveness, crying his final goodbyes. She took the charm in her pale hands and watched as they scorched black.

The king's tears turned to fear as she threw herself over the railing, grasping after her for the Ember. Even as the light burned, all she could feel was cold, and then she was falling, falling, falling into the depths of a dark lake.

Did you not understand?

Leaf was Leaf again, and she fell through the storm raging in the skies around her, lightning and rain and desperate fury, and then the clouds were behind her, and she was falling to the ocean. Somewhere far below, in the midst of endless black waters and shattered islands, she could see a turtle swimming. Beside it, the shadow of a serpent circled. Rearing from the water, it sank its horrible fangs into the back of the Great Turtle before coiling around it tightly.

Open your eyes.

Many voices swam together in Leaf's mind, singing and speaking as one until she was lost in a sea of noise so deep she thought she might just drown.

When Leaf finally woke, her mouth was dry.

"Koomis?" she moaned. Her arms felt weak as she tried to lift the heavy blanket off her. Someone must have forgotten to wake her. Slowly, and with great effort, she managed to turn her head toward a soft orange light flickering somewhere nearby. A fire? She could feel warmth, but where was she?

"Ash? Are you there?" The words barely escaped as a whisper.

The next time she woke, it was to the feel of cold-pressed dirt. Ash was kneeling at her side, feeding her from a waterskin. It fell on her like hard rain after a long dry summer, and she drank until the skin was empty.

"You're all right," said Ash. It was almost a question. Her voice was hoarse and her eyes were red, but her face was lit with relief. "You've been out for a while. I wasn't sure you were going to wake up."

"What happened?" Leaf asked, forcing herself to sit. Shadows had haunted her dreams, memories of the shattered lantern and silhouettes in the strange glow of the forest. She remembered walking through the Deepwood as creatures called in the distance. It had all been so beautiful, she thought, but somehow, walking had turned to dreaming, and now she was somewhere else entirely.

"We were attacked," said Ash. She was thumbing the edge of her axe. "A serpent bit you, but I…we killed it."

"We did?" said Leaf. Her skin itched with half-memories of something wrapped tightly around her.

"*We* did," said a voice from behind Ash. "I'm glad to see you're finally awake."

Leaf managed to twist painfully in the direction of a young woman, pale as Ash and heaped in layers of mismatched furs, standing at a small, circular door set into daub and wattle walls. Over her shoulder, she carried a fox.

"You wake at a fortunate time. You must be hungry, after being out for so long."

Leaf's stomach moaned painfully.

It took some time for Ash to explain everything that had happened, but Leaf sat and listened patiently. She could do little else. After the Deepwood serpent had attacked them, the strange woman named Rue had come to their aid, and she'd led Ash to a small cabin at the heart of a lake. Leaf was glad she'd been right to follow the water, but kept her smile small. They explained she had been sleeping for some time, but Rue had mixed the right leaves and herbs to stop the serpent's poison before it could do too much harm.

Ash wasn't sure how long they'd been in the Deepwood. It was hard to guess without the sun, and she hadn't slept while waiting for Leaf to wake. The exhaustion showed on her face.

Rue was a denizen of the Deepwood, and entirely unlike anyone Leaf had ever met. Her cabin was of meager means, with only a single large room fixed with a fireplace and a hanging bed set into the wall, which she had given to Leaf. Metal and glass trinkets glittered on shelves nearby, but Leaf's eyes were too weak to make them out. A set of antlers were mounted over the door, and the shape of a black cloak or some other clothing hung in the corner, hiding a bark-coated mask with eyes of shining stained glass in its folds.

Ash had waited with her alone while she slept as Rue roamed the Deepwood doing whatever she did out there, only coming back occasionally to check on them. Now that they were both awake, she set a small iron kettle over the fire, along with stripped fox meat to cook alongside it.

"Drink this," she said, handing Leaf a small metal cup that was almost too hot to touch.

"What is it?"

"Drink," Rue insisted.

Leaf looked at Ash, who nodded.

The drink was hot and sweet and thick, and its warmth spread quickly through her body. She could only manage small sips at a time, the taste almost overpowering, but Rue sat silently, waiting for her to finish. The strange woman seemed smaller up close, once you could see the figure beneath the furs. Her wrists were delicate branches that looked to snap from the weight of her clothing, and her brittle fingers reached like twigs for the empty cup. Her eyes were hollow at their edges, and pale white, looking like twin clouded moons.

"You've come a long way to speak with me," she said, and Leaf realized at once who she was. "I would know the reason."

Leaf looked again at Ash, who only nodded again. Had she not spoken with the Woods Witch while Leaf had been asleep? Maybe her mind was set on other things, or maybe she just didn't feel it was her place to ask about the Ember.

At the thought, Leaf jolted, fingers fumbling frantically through her shirt. Her heart settled once she felt its familiar glow at her chest.

"I needed to know something," Leaf said, her voice still sore. A hand at her back helped steady her as she struggled to stay upright. The cold Ember burned against her fingers, not with light or heat, but something more intense.

Ash continued for her. "Leaf likes to explore the old stonefolk ruins," she said. "The clans disapprove of it, so when she found something she couldn't explain, we had nowhere else to turn."

"You're an explorer, right?" Leaf asked, looking at the vague shapes of trophies and trinkets along the wall. They reminded her very much of the things Leaf kept in her bag. "You're not from the Turtle, are you?"

The Woods Witch watched impassively, with a face that betrayed nothing.

"So," Leaf continued uneasily. The stare from the woman's blank eyes made her feel uneasy. "I only found it this season, but I've been curious about the ruins my entire life. The Elders don't like to talk about them. We're supposed to be leaving the land to heal on its own, but the rest of my life might pass before that happens. I can't blind myself to the history living right beside us."

"And yet, curiosity can only drive us so far," said the Woods Witch. Her eyes were hazed and unfocused, but Leaf could feel them staring right through her all the same. "You've descended with purpose, and in doing so, set yourself against dangers greater than I think you even realize. There must have been a question burning brightly in your heart to brave such a place as this, so ask it of me, and I will tell you what I can."

Leaf took a breath, fingers still clutched tightly under her shirt. Hesitantly, she revealed the light of the Ember.

For just a moment, a glint seemed to catch in the Woods Witch's eye, but then it was gone, and Leaf was sure it had been a trick of the light. Shadow lingered along the edge of the firepit, reaching out with long fingers toward the strange stone.

If the Woods Witch was impressed, or confused, or surprised, if she felt any recognition or fear or anything at all, it didn't show on her face. *Maybe she doesn't use it anymore*, Leaf thought. *There's no one down here to see her.* Brittle hair swayed lightly to the side as she raised a withered palm up from her furs.

"Might I examine it?"

Leaf lifted the Ember delicately from around her neck, as if a sudden wind might steal it away into the dark forest. She placed it in the Woods Witch's palm, but held on tightly to the strap, and asked, "Have you ever seen anything like this before? Do you know what it is?"

"Seeing and knowing are different things, child, and one of those is beyond me now," the Woods Witch said, running her fingers over the Ember and feeling the grooves of the glowing stone. She pressed it tightly into her palm, muttering to herself, then hummed and sat in silence for a time.

Ash gave Leaf a wary look. Rue did not behave as the Elders of the clan did, nor like their storytellers, medicine women, or wise men. Her methods, if she was doing anything at all, were unknown to them.

Something scraped outside along the walls of the cabin. Leaf and Ash both started to rise, but the Woods Witch motioned for them to be still. A great crash continued through the brush, fading into the distance, and a low wind followed after it, rustling the leaves. Leaf could see Ash's hand gripping tightly on her axe. Looking around, she was greatly relieved her bow was still intact and lying beside her bag at the foot of the bed.

"Well," Leaf whispered, shifting restlessly, "do you know what it is?"

"It is a key," Rue said simply. "Or rather, the memory of one."

"A key?" Leaf asked. She furrowed her brow at the glowing stone. She had seen keys before, most of them were great iron things that unbarred the doors of old stonefolk ruins. There were even a few in her bag, if they hadn't fallen during the climb, that she kept as trinkets. Never, however, had she seen a key shaped like the Ember before, or any lock that might open by it.

"What does it unlock?" she asked.

"Something hidden and closed to the uninvited, as most keys do," said the Woods Witch. "As to what waits within that place, or even where it may be, I cannot say."

"But you have seen something like this before," Leaf pressed. Her mind was racing now. "You must have used one to know what it does. Do you know why it glows? Why its light doesn't touch anything else?"

"Perhaps it is shy," said the Woods Witch, shrugging. "Or too weak to face the world just yet. Might be that it's still gathering its strength."

"What does a key need strength for?" Ash asked. "You're talking like it's alive."

"I am."

Ash pushed herself back from the Woods Witch and the Ember, wide eyed as she looked uncertainly to Leaf.

"Have you seen something like it before?" Leaf repeated.

"You've been dreaming, haven't you?" the Woods Witch asked her. "Tell me what you've seen."

The question caught Leaf so off guard that she stopped to think. The quiet of the cabin was broken only by the softly crackling fire. She had been plagued lately by restless nights, but the things she had seen in her dreams were always hidden from her, glimpsed as if through the eyes of someone else, seen through a half-transparent curtain. It was confusing, a blurry dance of light and shadow, but she remembered one thing clearly.

"I've been dreaming of my grandmother," she said.

"And what have you been dreaming about her?" asked the Woods Witch.

"I think…I think I've dreamed about being her," said Leaf, trying to grab hold of the images flitting through her mind. "About her time in the stonefolk home as a kid. What she went through."

She had to stop and think again. The memories raced over the surface of her thoughts, distorting like a reflection in a rushing river. Leaf could only pull small details at a time. "And I dreamt of drowning."

"Where?"

"A river, I think?" Leaf didn't understand why the Woods Witch was asking about dreams, or what, if anything, they had to do with the Ember, but now, here, she had to know exactly what she had been dreaming of, because she had dreamt so often lately. "No, it was the ocean," she said. "But that was after I fell off a cliff, or a cave…there was someone with me, and something in the sky was watching me. I remember…"

The pale moon eyes of the Woods Witch watched her, waiting.

"I saw the Turtle swimming through the ocean," said Leaf. "And a serpent was swimming alongside it. And I thought I was talking to Koomis, but now, I think it was a spider wearing her face—"

"I'm sorry," Ash set a hand on Leaf's shoulder and turned to Rue, "but what does this have to do with what Leaf found?"

"The stone is a key," the Woods Witch said simply. "To what and where, I've explained I cannot say, but to you, I think…*yes*. The key knows its lock well, and it has been trying to tell you where it is."

"I'm confused," said Leaf. "How can a key, how can the Ember, tell me anything?

"It's been speaking to you through your dreams," said the Woods Witch. "Did you not understand?"

Did you not understand? She saw many faces reflected in the spider's eyes. *Did you not understand?* She could hear Koomis asking her again. *Did you not understand?* A storm greater than any she had ever seen was raging in the sky.

"The Drowned Palace," said Leaf. Just as the name of the Ember had come to her, so too had these words. When she spoke, she understood them.

"The what?" Ash said, raising a brow at her. The Woods Witch leaned closer but said nothing.

"The clans don't travel through the old kingdom anymore, but others from over the waters do," Leaf said, quiet at first, but her excitement was growing. "Some of them used to trade with the clans, I heard. Not just in what they found or brought from over the sea, but in stories, too. They said the castle and the city where the kings used to live was flooded, but that there were still treasures inside that no one could reach." Thoughts wove over thoughts like a charm forming in her mind, the way she used to weave with Koomis. "Whatever the Ember unlocks, it's waiting in the Drowned Palace!"

Leaf tried to sit up, tried to take the Ember back, but the Woods Witch clutched it tight in her hand.

"I would speak on your intentions first, before deciding what must be done next."

Leaf pulled harder at the Ember, but Rue's grip was surprisingly strong for such a frail-looking person. "What do you mean?" she asked.

"You seem intent on traveling to this Drowned Palace, as you called it. Why? What do you expect awaits you?" Pale eyes considered her carefully. "Have you even considered the dangers of this journey? What dangers the secrets whispered in your dreams might carry? Or did you simply feel the lure of curiosity and decide to chase it without a moment's thought?"

Leaf didn't like the question, or the tone behind it, and tried again to pull the Ember back. Ash's hand was still at her shoulder, her face writ with concern, as Leaf felt the weakness return to her limbs. She was still so tired. Slowly, and with a great deal of frustration, she laid back.

"We almost didn't make it this far," said Ash softly. She looked uneasily at the doorway. "Whatever the stone unlocks, whatever it's been trying to tell you, can it really be worth it?"

Yes, the answer came to her, obvious and clear, but Koomis's words echoed in her mind as well. *Slow down. Breathe. Take a moment to gather your thoughts and speak only once you're ready.*

"What if the Ember can tell us why the stonefolk disappeared?" she asked finally. It was a question at the heart of all the clans, and although many had offered answers of their own, no one could say for certain what the truth of it really was. "They vanished for a reason. Shouldn't we try to understand why? Maybe we can stop it from happening again."

"You want the stonefolk to come back?" Ash asked.

"No," said Leaf, "but I don't want us to disappear, too. If something could vanish the stonefolk away overnight, why can't it happen to us, too? If the Ember can really tell us what happened, shouldn't we do everything we can to understand it?"

"What if it's the other way around?" Ash argued, her voice strangely uneven. "What if the Ember is what made the stonefolk vanish in the first place? You go walking into their city, playing with something you know nothing about, you might disappear along with the rest of them. You might even take the clans with you."

"I know what I'm doing," said Leaf, knowing it wasn't true. "I'll be careful."

"No, you won't!" Ash was yelling now. "You almost died just getting *here*. If you go off into cursed lands, carrying a cursed stone you know nothing about just because you think it's talking to you in your dreams..."

Ash paced anxiously around the cabin, muttering as she tried to find her words, hand still tight on her axe. Finally, she halted on the other side of the fire. "Leaf, if you do this, I don't think you'll ever come back."

"Then don't come with me," said Leaf. She couldn't bring herself to look at Ash. Instead, she traced her fingers along the blanket, drawing circles into the fabric with her finger.

"Alone or not, it makes no difference," spoke the Woods Witch, her whisper like the rustling of autumn leaves. "If misusing your Ember could pose a danger to the people of this island, what makes you think I would let you leave with it at all?"

The fire burned dimly, and in its light, Leaf could see the Woods Witch had moved to the far corner of the room, milk-white eyes watching them from the shadows. Leaf forced herself to stand, frightened at her words. Ash rounded the fireplace to stand beside her.

Something grabbed them by the legs and quickly rooted them to the floor. Leaf fell limply forward when she tried to walk, suddenly aware that the Ember was no longer in her hands. When had it left?

"What are you doing?" Ash demanded.

"Let me go," said Leaf, struggling with a white root now wrapped tightly around her ankle. It wound its way up over her calves and around her knees. She tried to reach for her bag, tried to grab one of her arrows, but they were too far from reach.

Ash must have thought the same. Hacking through the roots with her axe, she pulled one leg free. Before she could cut through the second's bonds, another long root wormed through the cabin floor, snapping tightly around her hand and twisting the axe from her grip. Many more followed, around her legs and arm and neck, and they pulled her down to the earth. After only a moment, her face was buried beneath the writhing mass.

"Stop this!" Leaf yelled. The Woods Witch watched them impassively, her milk-white face lost in the shadows, and only a hint of fire reflected in her pale moon eyes. The Ember glowed brightly in her hand. "What are you doing?"

"I'm keeping you safe," said the Woods Witch in a voice that echoed beyond the cabin, deep into the dark forest. "You act without thought or reason, driven blindly by whims and with no one to tell you no. How could I, knowing this, willingly let you leave with the Ember? Were any harm to befall you, or the people of this island, the responsibility would fall at my feet. Do you not understand the calamity you've faced me with?"

But Leaf was still struggling, fighting to be free of the roots. "I'm not your responsibility!"

"You're wrong." The roots and vines all tightened. Ash was immobilized, perhaps even unconscious beneath the writhing mass. Her axe was somewhere out of sight, lost in root and shadow.

"Tell me what you see," said the Woods Witch, gesturing to a puddle on the floor. In all the struggle, the kettle had fallen from its place over the fire. The boiling water spilled through the dirt toward her face.

Leaf couldn't fight anymore. She was tired, and the roots held her too tightly. Her eyes fell to the floor. "I see a kettle," she said. "And a puddle of water."

"And you, girl. What do you see?"

The writhing mass of roots retreated slightly, just enough for Ash's head to emerge. She gasped for air. "What are you talking about?" Ash said, spitting dirt. "Let us go!"

"Tell me what you see."

The roots forced her face so close to the dirt that Leaf thought she might be burned.

"It looks like a cloud," Ash said, confused. "The drops are like little stars."

"You see the direct and the abstract, but can you see the meaning?" the Woods Witch said. "I see the grooves in the earth where the water travels, and in those, I see canyons carved by rivers over long eons. Strange, isn't it, how even a simple thing can seem so different to the many eyes that see it?"

Leaf didn't understand, but before she could protest, the Woods Witch spoke again.

"How much do you know of the stonefolk, truly?"

"I've heard stories," said Leaf.

"Stories grow in the telling, but search hard and you can find the truth at the heart of them. Tell me what you think you know, then, from the stories you remember."

Helpless in the dirt and too weak to fight any longer, Leaf couldn't see what other choice she had. Ash might be the stronger of the two, but she was held even more tightly by the roots.

"They came to the Great Turtle hundreds of years ago," Leaf said. "From some place far over the water. They said the land belonged to them now and built a kingdom on it. They went to war with the clans. A lot of us died. Some of the clans were wiped out forever."

"This is known to all," said the Woods Witch. "What else can you tell me? What else do you remember? Who built that kingdom?"

"The kings," said Leaf. In her mind, when she spoke the words, she saw not a man, but a mountain.

"How did he do it?"

"They say he could move the rock with sheer will."

"Yes. But how?"

"I don't know."

The Woods Witch sighed. "In so short a time, the truth of it is already lost." Her shadowed face continued to watch them from the far corner of the cabin, the Ember still glowing brightly in her hand. "But the first step on the path to knowledge is acknowledging just how little we really know," she said, with a queer mix of approval and pity. "It's a truth shockingly few can admit to, and so, in a way, I admire you."

The roots around Leaf loosened somewhat, allowing her freedom enough to sit. She wasn't free entirely, and certainly not enough to reach the Ember in the corner, but she was at least more comfortable.

"Her too," said Leaf, pointing to Ash, who was still held against the floor. After a moment, she was free to sit as well.

"The kings of old could move earth and stone through will alone," said the Woods Witch. "They wished the rock shaped, and it was done. A rare gift, and dangerous. One whose price they didn't realize until it came due."

Leaf had heard stories like that, she remembered, sometime long ago during her childhood. People always talked in ways that sounded true but weren't, and the others had laughed when she took the story of the kings at face value. "People can't actually move stone just by thinking it," the Elders explained to her. "It's just a fanciful way of saying they were skilled crafters."

But Leaf knew there had to be more to it, and now she could see it in the way the Woods Witch called root and vine through force of will. It wasn't a stretch at all to say the old kings had done the same with stone.

"You know how they did it," Leaf whispered.

"Yes," said the Woods Witch. "And no. I don't claim to understand everything, but I wait, and I listen, and I learn. In time, all things pass through the heart of the Turtle."

"So, what happens to us now?" asked Ash. Her voice was a low growl. Leaf could hear the wolf's edge in her words. "You steal from us and keep us trapped here? Take what Leaf's found for yourself?"

"I am not trapping you, I am educating you," said the Woods Witch. "Returning to the land above is something I will leave to you, but the possession of this stone is another matter entirely. You've stumbled onto something old and powerful and entirely beyond your understanding. I would not see it misused. I will take the stone far away from this place, and you shall not see it nor I again."

"You can't," said Leaf, reaching for the glow at the edge of the cabin. "It's mine. I found it. It called to me."

"I can and I will," said the Woods Witch gravely. "It was never yours to begin with."

"Maybe not, but *I* found it," Leaf said. The bitterness in her voice clear. "*Me*. No one else was willing to brave the ruins anymore, or face the truth of our past. I went in there alone, and the Ember called to me, not you! I found it in the fireplace, I dug it out of the spiderweb charm, and it spoke to me in my dreams. I left my home, and Koomis, and I climbed through the Deepwood because I thought you could help us, but I was wrong. I won't let you take everything from me!"

Her voice broke at that, and she slumped back onto the floor, determined not to let anyone see the tears forming in her eyes.

"Why does this stone mean so much to you?" the Woods Witch asked her. "I said before that there must be a reason for you to have braved such a place as this. A question was burning brightly in your heart. What is it that you wish to learn?"

"I want to know who I am," said Leaf, pulling at her bonds. "I want to know my history." She tried to stand. "And I want to know why it was taken from me."

The roots pulled her back to her knees. "My people were hurt," she said hollowly. She thought of Koomis and the children at the stonefolk home, the collage of memories she had seen woven through her dreamscape. They stood clear in her thoughts, those glimpses of a dark, forbidden past brought to light by the Ember, and she would face it, no matter how unpleasant the truth would be. "I don't know why they were hurt, or how it all came to an end, but I have to make sure it never happens again."

"You have no right to take that from her," said Ash. The wolf's head cloak fell low over her eyes, turning her into a beast in the darkness. "And I won't let you."

Ash slipped her wrist free from the roots and reached suddenly for the axe buried beneath. She must have felt it in the darkness. Before any more roots could bind her back to the floor, she hacked her leg free, and was rolling away. "Leaf!" she called, throwing her the bag from the end of the bed.

Leaf dug quickly for her arrows, but their points were too small to cut quickly through the roots. Ash was almost completely free but was too busy fending off the advance of more vine to help Leaf. Leaf dug deeper through her pack, hoping that not everything had been lost in the fall, and felt with great relief the shard of stained glass wrapped tightly in leather.

She was quick, but uncareful as she cut herself free. The Woods Witch's attention was on Ash, who was still fighting root and vine. She watched them, unmoving, with the light of the Ember still dangling from her fingers.

"Leaf," said Ash, grabbing her by the arm. They looked at each other and nodded, knife and axe in hand. "Together."

But all the plant life fell to the ground just as suddenly as it had risen. Outside, the birds were screaming, drowning out all other sounds of the forest. Leaf leapt forward and took the Ember from the hands of the Woods Witch, but the pale woman gave no reaction. She didn't put up a fight or even speak a word. Cautiously, Ash tapped her with the butt of her axe, and Rue's body fell limply to the floor.

"What happened?" Ash asked.

"Something's wrong," said Leaf.

They backed away cautiously from the body toward the door, feeling blindly for the handle. It wouldn't move. On the other side of the wood, they could hear the writhing roots trapping them inside. Ash tried hard to push through, and Leaf did her best to help, but the door held firm.

"You are free to leave my forest," the Woods Witch's words echoed through the walls of the cabin, "but not with that stone."

"Try to stop us," said Leaf. The door was blocked, the room windowless, but there was a small smoke hole in the roof. "Come on," she whispered to Ash, nudging her forward.

"It's probably blocked," Ash whispered back, but Leaf was already trying to gauge if they could squeeze through the opening. It would be tight, but she thought they could do it.

"It might be," said Leaf, "but I've never seen a vine last long against fire."

The flame had fallen almost to nothing in the commotion, but Leaf stoked it with the remaining herbs and oils from her bag. There was wood in the corner, and she wrapped it with scraps of blanket. It gave off a noxious smoke, so she raised her scarf over her face. Her limbs were weak, but the excitement coursing through her gave her strength. After taking a moment to breathe, she put on her stained-glass lenses.

"Come on. We're leaving."

With Ash's aid, Leaf shimmied into the chimney, torch raised in one hand. When she reached the top, a mass of vines quickly shrank away from the fire. Outside, she couldn't see a thing. All the light of the forest was gone, her torch and the Ember like two lone stars in an empty midnight sky, but she found her way down from the roof. Leaf took her broken lantern and spread the flame inside before handing Ash the torch. Now they would both have light, even if they were separated.

The cabin behind them was no longer visible, swallowed instead by a mound of thick vegetation that shrank from the fire's light. At the shadow's edge, they could see the surface of a dark lake, looking like a pool of bottomless ink lapping lazily at the shoreline.

They were on an island, Leaf realized, after following the edge of the water brought them round in a circle. There was nowhere for them to go.

"What do we do now?" Ash asked.

"Relinquish the stone, and I will allow you safe leave," echoed the voice of the Woods Witch, her voice rumbling the very earth.

Some of the roots rising through the water grew even larger than the trees, and they broke through the ink like islands and bridges. Leaf tapped Ash and nodded to one, then took off at a running jump. She slipped as the root tried to retreat beneath her, but its movement was slow, and her hands were quick. As its mass began to submerge into the water, she crawled along its length to a flat spot and picked herself back up. The strain of days lost in poisoned sleep was heavy in her limbs, but she pulled herself forward. Taking a breath, Leaf ran into another jump, Ash quickly behind her, as the root finally submerged. They ran over the surface of the water, Leaf and Ash, and beneath them a rainbow of fish started to gather, their dancing light following them like so many eyes.

They jumped root after root after root until the last was just ahead of them, sinking into the water as Leaf leapt through the air. She breathed deeply before plummeting into the water, her torch snuffed out by the sudden rush of cold. Leaf speared through the shadowed water until she found the edge of the shoreline. A moment later, Ash's gasp came behind her.

They were in the dark again. Leaves and root and vine rustled in the forest around them. Something came rushing forth, and a sudden crack split the air.

The light of the Ember was almost blinding.

A large tendril of a bone-white branch hung suspended in the air only a handsbreadth from the Ember itself, buffeted by the glow of warm sunlight.

The pale figure of the Woods Witch slowly came into view. She dangled limply in the air, suspended with thin silver strings that danced in the light. They pulled at her limbs and made her gesture as she spoke.

"You have chosen a dangerous course," came her voice, a vicious whisper like a howling wind. Alongside her, a chorus of ravens cried out.

"We're leaving," said Leaf, holding the Ember proudly forward. Its glow was touching her arm now, and she could feel the sunlight. "We're not your problem anymore."

But the *thing* that was the trees ignored her. "Your dreams will come for you again," it warned. "Your mind is opened now. Heed their warnings, Turtle, Spider, and Serpent all. Shadow grows as fire fades until all that's left is black. All that was will come again, if the wrong hand grasps the Embers. Be wary, but be brave as well. It seems I have done for you all I can."

Slowly, the bone-white branch pulled back from the Ember's light, and the roots in the forest around them opened, their tendrils slowly receding back into the dark. The sun continued to burn brightly in Leaf's hand as she and Ash walked uncertainly past the suspended body of the Woods Witch. Her pale moon eyes watched them sightlessly as they passed.

From then on, their only companions in the forest were the ravens singing feverishly in the trees above. Nothing else would come close to the sunlight in their hands, although sometimes they could hear movement in the distant wood.

Ash had protected her against the Deepwood serpent by marking it with glowing mushrooms. Leaf took the mushrooms she'd gathered in her bag to mark themselves. Curiously, all of them were now dark and plain, without a trace of the glow they once held.

They walked until the water led them to a far-off cliff wall, and they didn't stop climbing until they found a recess in its side deep enough for them both to sit. Ash would take the first watch, she said, and by the Ember's light, they found enough tinder to get a small fire going. After that, the light in the stone finally faded, as if it knew somehow that they were out of the reach of the Woods Witch.

"She said that thing is alive," said Ash, sitting as far from the Ember as she could. Her eyes jumped between it and the mouth of the crevasse without ever falling on Leaf.

"Yeah," said Leaf. She held the cold stone in her hand, admiring the light and warmth inside.

"If it's alive, then it wants something," said Ash, suspiciously. She drew a breath sharply through her nose. "How do we know that what it wants isn't something bad?"

"The Woods Witch also said it was a key," said Leaf, shaking her head. "And we wouldn't have escaped without its help." But that wasn't the whole story. If the Ember can share its glow, then why hadn't it done so before? Was it unable, or just unwilling?

The tense silence hung between her and Ash, the only sounds in their dark corner were the cries of distant creatures in the woods below, the crackling fire, and cawing ravens. Leaf couldn't bring herself to look at Ash, and from the way Ash focused on the dark beyond the fire, she suspected the feeling was mutual.

There was a time once, when Leaf was young, that she had asked Koomis about her parents. Her father was only a dim memory, and her mother not even that. Just a story implied by moments of silence. Leaf had sat on their packs and refused to budge as the sun fell. She wouldn't help gather tinder for the fire, or prepare food, or even let them unpack the tent and blankets. At first, Koomis was stern, but when Leaf didn't break, she tried instead to ignore her. To that, Leaf had screamed her questions over and over. As the sun set and her voice turned raw, Koomis sat silently by the fire she'd built herself. Leaf finally left her baggage and crawled beside her grandmother for warmth, only to find the old woman was asleep, tears still wet on her cheeks. When they woke the next morning, wrapped together in a blanket, they prepared for their day in silence, and Leaf never again asked her grandmother about her parents. Some things were doomed to lay unspoken from the fear of ripping open old wounds.

But Leaf had always believed that people should say what they mean. She stood, moving to the cliff's edge.

"I wouldn't have made it this far without you, either," she said, taking a seat beside Ash. "I'm sorry I put you in danger."

Ash's breath was slow and labored. With a long exhale, she straightened. "I came because I wanted to," she said from beneath her wolf's head. "I didn't want you to face this place alone."

The two of them sat in the silence, but it was warmer now, filled instead with quiet companionship.

"We found our way down here," Leaf said, "we'll find our way back up,"

"We will," Ash agreed, glancing at the Ember in Leaf's hand. "And then what? After everything that happened here, are you really willing to take this further?"

Leaf looked sadly at her friend. "I have to."

Ash only nodded and turned back to her watch without a word.

From here, Leaf wasn't sure exactly where they would go, but she knew the Ember would light the way. The twisting halls of the dark palace of stone grew in her mind from dream to vision to almost-memory, calling to her as its flooded halls whispered secrets waiting to be unlocked. She held the key. It had come to her, and no one else, and she was going to find out why.

Weariness weighed on her. She was exhausted, the poison lingering in her body, but between the Ember, the fire, and the watchful eyes of her only friend, she felt safe. They would leave the Deepwood the same way they'd come—together. And then they'd see what came next.

That night, she dreamt again of the crying king of stone, and the palace drowned beneath him.

EPILOGUE

REED

Reed woke to the gentle roar of the sea. His body felt heavy, head swimming through a haze of something like memory and dream and too-long sleep. There was a distant, gradual awareness of a bright light. All he could see was red.

"Augh," he moaned, trying to yell. His throat was parched. Every breath felt as if he were swallowing rocks. Harsh light stabbed at his eyes as he tried to pull himself up, reaching blindly for something, anything, to ground him. Where was he? What had happened? Was the battle won?

The red light.

Reed felt warm. Dry. The air was heavy with a noxious smell, thick and warm and somehow comforting. He fell backward. If he was dead, maybe death wasn't so bad.

"It seems you're still with us," said a familiar voice, light and airy. Reed tried to place it, but his thoughts were sluggish, as if they were still trying to catch up with his body. Finally, the blinding red subsided into something warm and orange, and he realized he was looking out a window toward the setting sun. Ridae stood over him, tending to a set of candles at a bedside table and the lantern overhead. "Do you know where you are?"

Reed shook his head. *The battle.* He must have been thrown by the ship, or the waves, or the storm. He could remember falling, catching sight of the red below the waves before darkness hit him. His throat still parched, he bit helplessly around words that wouldn't come.

Ridae stooped low and handed him a large cup. "Drink slow," the lantern keeper warned. "You've been out a night and a day now."

Reed took the water in as fast as he could, choked, coughed onto the bed, and drank some more. *I'm in a bed*, he realized. A real bed, not just the heaps of straw and sheets under the drippings of the Halfmug. A soft, heavy layer of blankets lay overtop him, weighing down and enveloping him in warmth.

"What happened?" he asked.

"There was a battle," said Ridae, simply. "You were injured. Do you remember?"

All Reed could manage was to lift his head, mouth again for words that wouldn't come, and fall back into his pillow. *Of course I remember*, he thought. In the haze of dreams, he could recall now how he had lived those moments over and over again in his sleep, watching the events from afar as if they had happened to someone else. Cold curtains of rain washing over the sea, hot tempers clashing on the deck, the heave of ships as they thrashed in the waves, and again, the strange red glow that stained the abyss below the water. There was the shadow of some terrible leviathan that had tried to take them. He remembered it all.

"Listen to me," said Ridae, leaning close. Their mask swirled and split in two, caught somewhere between shadows and light as Reed tried to keep his vision steady. "You need to focus. I'm going to tell the captain you've awakened, but I need to determine your state of mind. You've suffered a head injury. What we need is what you know, or else our journey overland will be far more difficult than we planned for."

Reed focused on the words, trying to keep the cabin in view, but it was like he was peering into two worlds at once. There were the candles and fire and distant sun setting over the waves, washing the cabin and his bed in red, and then there was the sea, dark and terrible, lit only by flashes of lightning that cracked the sky. Harsh rains lingered and left a ghostly cold in his bones. He jolted at the memory of the tall man with the curved sword who'd intended to separate his head from his body.

He didn't realize he'd raised his hands to protect himself until Ridae had pinned them back down.

"Reed," the lantern keeper said more firmly. "Listen to me. Do you know who you are?"

Keresh Beldrick had saved him from an unjust vengeance come long overdue. The sight of the captain, heroic and terrible, savior and monster, standing triumphantly at the helm of the enemy ship, lifted him from his fear. Reed had stood beside his crewmates, helping them to protect their ship.

His crewmates. *His* ship.

"I do," said Reed.

Ridae pat his shoulder comfortingly. "I'm going to speak with the captain. You'll be safe here. The captain will come see you as soon as he is able."

Reed meant to say something, but Ridae was gone, with only the gentle flickering of candles and the lantern to suggest they had ever been there at all. Reed turned his head and caught sight of the sun now half consumed by the waves. He might have fallen asleep then, but another thought sent him bolting upright.

Where was Torrin's journal?

He checked himself first. Hadn't he tucked it in his coat? No. Besides, he wasn't even wearing it. Someone must have stripped his wet clothes off after the battle. He could remember tucking the journal away somewhere for safekeeping before the battle, but where? Then he remembered. Panic pushed him through the pain and exhaustion as he sat up, ready to run for the closet he'd called his cabin to search through scraps of sail, but his hand fell on something cold and hard, tucked away beneath his pillow.

The journal.

Someone had found it. But who?

Finch came through the door before he had time to think. "Haven't lost your modesty, I see," she said, chuckling.

Reed slipped his hand from the journal and lifted the blanket quickly. His panic over the journal must have been seen as embarrassment because she laughed even louder.

"Relax, I'm just making fun," she said, taking a seat at the end of the bed. Reed shifted uncomfortably to make space. "Actually, I came down here 'cause I wanted to tell you something."

Reed swallowed a hard, dry lump in his throat. "Wait, let me guess," he said, lips peeling away from one another, slow and sticky. "You brought me more water."

"I'll get that for you soon," said Finch. Reed was surprised to hear softness in her voice. "I just wanted to tell you, you really stepped up for the crew. I wasn't sure about you, but you stood your ground for a fight that shouldn't have been yours. That means something."

Reed waited for her to roll her eyes, or for her smile to turn sarcastic. When neither happened, he took a chance. "Thank you."

Finch nodded, and the softness he'd seen was covered again by cocky swagger, and a look of irritation. "Yeah, well, don't go getting a big head about it. The real work's still ahead of us. Captain says we're maybe a week out from Turtle Rock. Plenty of time for you to get back into action."

"Are you sure about that?" said Reed, stretching his arms. He felt a sharp twinge in his shoulder. Now that his eyes could properly focus, he noticed the large bruise stretching from stomach to shoulder, and the half-dozen smaller ones dotting his body. "I've taken some beatings in my life, but nothing half as bad as this," he said, laughing bitterly.

"Yeah, the Flotilla was a real pit," said Finch, sharing his disdain. "I can only imagine what it was like, watching over your shoulder all the time, trying not to get robbed or beaten. Wondering who might be following you, looking to learn your secrets."

Or learn yours, Reed thought, gritting his teeth to push down the guilt gnawing in his stomach. There were plenty of rats in the underbellies of the Flotilla, and he'd been one of them. Sure, he'd stood beside the crew in battle, but he'd only gotten here on lies. The shadow of Turtle Rock loomed large in his mind, creatures and terrors and glories unknown, dangers in the wild that couldn't be quelled with a well-spun story. He'd bought himself a bed and comfort, a chance for a better life, but on a false promise.

Finch gave Reed a look that suggested she knew more than she was saying. It was something like understanding, he thought, but mixed with something else he couldn't place.

"You were right when you warned about people prying into our business," she said. "I should've listened to you then, brought my concerns to the captain. Maybe we could have avoided that whole mess with the *Ghostfire*."

Another lie. He'd only warned Finch because she'd found him hiding from Fox. "How did the battle end?" he asked, trying to change the subject.

"Their sister ship went in to save the drowning crew," Finch said with a shrug. "The captain took the helm, and we kept ourselves afloat. Somehow, we got out of there."

"What about the light?"

Finch gave him a look of confusion.

"The light beneath the water," said Reed. It had been everywhere beneath the waves, surely they had seen it. "The red light? And the creature below the water?"

"I think you need some more rest," Finch said quietly. "You did good, Reed. I won't forget that. The captain won't either. I'll go get you that water, but you should get yourself ready. We'll be at Turtle Rock soon enough, and we'll need to know what you know." She gave him a thoughtful nod, looking past him, her gaze lingering on his pillow before she left the room.

Reed waited until her footsteps faded down the hallway, then let out a loud, slow sigh. The bed was warm, the fire low, the sun setting. He could rest easy in all the comfort he'd ever dreamed of, but instead, he reached under his pillow for the journal. It was there. *Property of Torrin*. If the crew believed in him, then he had to believe in himself, too. Maybe a lie needn't always remain a lie. He opened the cover to the sight of Turtle Rock sketched across the pages, tall mountains scraping the clouds and covered with uncountable forests, and began to read.

ACKNOWLEDGMENTS

While this book was born from long walks in the woods and countless hours spent hunched over a keyboard, it wasn't created alone, and I'd like to give my thanks to some of the people who helped usher it into the world.

Thank you Mom, for teaching me to read almost as soon as I could walk. Your nightly readings of my favorite picture books instilled a love for storytelling in me that has never faded. Your enthusiasm in turn for my work has been a constant, and without you, I would never have known to submit to Second Story Press and the Indigenous Writing Content.

Thank you to the judges of the contest, Richard Van Camp, Sandra Samatte, and Jordan Ryder, for seeing the promise in my work and for giving me this chance.

Thank you to Phuong Truong, Emma Rodgers, Chloe Coome, Alayah Barton, Jordan Ryder, Laura Atherton, Michaela Stephen, and April Masongsong at Second Story Press for taking a chance on my work. Without you, this book would still be sitting in a folder on my computer, read only by friends and family. Thank you especially to Jordan for being a brilliant, encouraging editor, and my first fan. You have a real talent for saying in three words what I say in ten, and through your tireless work and development notes you've sharpened my meandering thoughts to a finely honed point.

A great thank-you to Brian Hoang, whose lovely artwork graces these pages. It was a real pleasure seeing my work brought to life through another's eyes.

There were others along the way, however, without whom I would never have made it this far.

Thank you to my grandmother and grandfather. While you're both long passed, you are not forgotten, and the lessons of your stories will, I hope, live on through me and my writing.

Thank you Dad. I'm sorry we didn't speak much in the years before your passing. I regret that I never took the chance to tell you about this book. Every time I introduce a moment of levity, or absurdity, or just a small bright spark in a moment of darkness, I remember you and what you taught me.

While my schooling years were far from pleasant, there are two who made a difference for me. Gabriela Rosilius and Al Wright, thank you for helping me to keep my fire alive at a time when I felt the world wanted nothing more than to snuff it out. Thank you not only for teaching me to recognize my strengths, but for challenging me to hone them further, and encouraging me to continue on.

Thank you to Anishnawbe Health Toronto for lifting me from a downward spiral I feared I might never pull out from. Thank you to everyone who attended group therapy and listened to me speak at a time when I thought no one cared what I had to say. And thank you to everyone at the writing therapy group, whose encouragement and enthusiasm reignited a love in myself that I had feared extinguished. Thank you Chris and Alex, for everything you did to pull me from my shell.

A journey of healing is never over. Thank you Nicola, for being there these last few years. You've always believed in me and saw the strength of my efforts when all I could see was the exhaustion.

Thank you as well Alisa, for being a continual source of enthusiasm on my behalf. You knew before I did that others would want to read this book. Thank you for believing in me.

Finally, but most importantly, I want to thank Eli. You have been my constant companion and partner through this journey, and for years long before. You've been there for every moment I was hunched over the keyboard in exhaustion, asleep in my chair, or just staring into space as I tried to collect my thoughts. When I devoted my days to writing this book, you not only made room for it in our lives, you encouraged it, doing everything you could to help me see this through. You are the kind ear to my ramblings, the encouraging hand on my shoulder, and the love of my life.

Thank you.

ABOUT THE AUTHOR

BEAR MEAWASIGE is the pen name for Kurt Wilson. Bear is an Ojibwe and Scottish writer and a member of Serpent River First Nation living in the Algoma District of Northern Ontario. He grew up in a small town on the border of his reserve, existing in the uneasy middle ground between the two cultures and his own ancestry. His interest in art and writing carried him through his tumultuous high school years, leading him eventually to study illustration and animation. His imagination and wonderings over his dual-natured ancestry ferment among his wild surroundings to become stories of worlds that might have been.